DON'T LOOK BACK
Hawaiian Myths Made New

Don't Look Back
Hawaiian Myths Made New

Edited by Christine Thomas

WATERMARK
PUBLISHING

ISBN: 978-1-9356901-4-6

Library of Congress Control Number: 2011940498

Cover illustration
Andrew J. Catanzariti

Design and production
Gonzalez Design Company

Watermark Publishing
1088 Bishop Street, Suite 310
Honolulu, Hawai‘i 96813
Telephone 1-808-587-7766
Toll-free 1-866-900-BOOK
sales@bookshawaii.net
www.bookshawaii.net

Printed in the United States

CONTENTS

Foreword

Dr. M. Puakea Nogelmeier

Lore from the past always becomes the seed of imagination and source of invention for the present. The stories in this collection sprout from myths and legends of old, and they flourish anew by tapping into the reservoir of experience that has shaped Hawaiian culture for centuries.

Legend and myth are foundations of every society, and Hawaiʻi has an expansive foundation of lore. Many Hawaiian myths are shared across the Pacific Ocean, part of the cultural cargo that sailed a four-thousand-year wave of expansion and interaction. Others developed here after the era of grand journeys ended five or more centuries ago, and are unique to these islands. All are Hawaiian, and many are still told today.

A repository of cultural knowledge, myths embody ancestral reference, documenting the heroes, deeds, and districts that frame social history. The thread of a single story can convey an amazing collection of data—the individual names of hundreds of winds; full sequences of chants for restoring life, or taking it; recitations of distant lands and archipelagos—encyclopedic knowledge in the vessel of legend.

A legacy from the past, classical stories were carefully entrusted from generation to generation, passed on intact, within the scope of oral tradition and regional lineages of tellers. Yet each carries the thumbprint of every generation that received it. Changes and embellishments are part of the storytelling process, connecting them to the ever-changing present, and making them relevant to persons, places, and events of the time. Thus do traditions continue and thrive.

During the 19th century, while Hawaiian literacy soared, many ancient tales were written down and published for the first time, mostly in the Hawaiian-language newspapers. They became standard fare in most papers as a new, national audience enjoyed the expansive range of Hawaiian myths and legends. Editors urged knowledgeable folk to share their stories so they would be safely recorded, for their own time and for the future. The reality of cultural and historical loss from depopulation and rapid change was apparent to all, and for scores of years many collaborated to put ancestral knowledge down in print.

While the literary legacy was first being publicly documented, completeness and accuracy were important, yet variations were embraced even in the oldest of stories. Corrections or additions were welcomed, and concerns about simple differences in narratives were laughingly dismissed with rejoinders like "What, do you think that was taught in only one school?" This inclusive embrace allowed a great body of traditional stories to be recorded, in their varying forms, for posterity.

The perpetuity of myth and legend is, and has always been, paralleled by a lively tradition of distilling, retelling, and recasting the epics and grand tales in completely new, often abbreviated, contemporary forms. These recast stories are themselves brand-new and sometimes spontaneous productions. With themes and dynamics drawn from the classics, the characters are often contemporary and may barely reflect the original heroes and gods, the settings are intentionally familiar, and the issues and actions are intentionally current. The myths, in their "classical" forms, connect the common roots of human society from times ancient to today, while the recastings make the longevity of those attitudes, principles, and ethics immediately relevant.

Heroes and champions, voyagers, tricksters, demons, and guardian spirits exist in every generation, and certainly here in Hawaiʻi. Such characters are understood through the cultural norms that frame societal values like respect, tolerance, responsibility, and generosity. Those norms change over time, and new tales offer new understandings that reflect, or may contrast with, more classical forms. For example, navigators who once charted unknown seas may be presented as navigating swells of an urban landscape, but the themes and the actions mirror, in a very contemporary way, the deeds of a modern Māui.

Human interface with the extraordinary world around us makes up an ancient genealogy of experience—one that extends right up to what surrounds us today. The narratives of a society are carefully crafted expressions that document and chart the flow of that experience, from primal to present. Just as the refrains of Greek mythology hum through Shakespeare and Hollywood, so do the ancient songs of Hawaiʻi echo in these now-told stories that are sprouting from venerable seeds. The contemporary tales in this collection are presented as chants of celebration, arias of advice, and revelatory refrains, composed in resonance with the tempos and scales of stories long known and legends long told.

INTRODUCTION
Christine Thomas

IN THE BEGINNING

ONE STEREOTYPICALLY RAINY EVENING IN LONDON, I SAT AT A BRITISH LIBRARY CUBICLE READING THROUGH BOOKS ABOUT HAWAIIAN MELE AND MYTH—RESEARCH FOR A NOVEL I HAD BEGUN WRITING during my master's course in creative writing at England's University of East Anglia. At that point, my research didn't have firm direction, but when I began reading "The Legend of Halemano" in Samuel Elbert's *Selections from Fornander's Hawaiian Antiquities and Folk-lore* (UH Press, 1959), I was struck by its eerie echoes of the story I had been writing.

This somewhat peripheral legend and my novel, in general strokes, are both set in part on Oʻahu, involve a man and woman from opposite circumstances who have fallen in love, and spotlight the man's close relative who tries to help him, yet I had never before heard of "The Legend of Halemano," nor considered bouncing off or retelling a myth in my own fiction. Soon, though, this legend became a subtle blueprint in the back of my mind as I wrote the novel's first draft and provided the first spark of my continued fascination with myths and their retellings.

About four years later, in 2005, I had already moved back to Hawaiʻi when I learned of British book publisher Canongate's launch of its now well-regarded myth series, offering book-length, contemporary myth retellings by modern storytellers, or—as it calls them—"mythmakers." By way of contextual introduction, Canongate explains on the series Web site that "Myths are universal and timeless stories that reflect and shape our lives—they explore our desires, our fears, our longings, and provide narratives that remind us what it means to be human." These words continue to resonate, and I believe these qualities help myths endure and maintain our appetite for narrative. And I am not alone—to date, fourteen writers have participated in Canongate's delicious experiment, including Margaret Atwood, who retold *The Odyssey* from Penelope's point of view in *The Penelopiad*, and Ali Smith, who recast one of Ovid's Metamorphoses in *Girl Meets Boy*.

When I first learned of the Canongate series, I thought: *Wouldn't it be great if someone gathered modern retellings of Hawaiian myths?* The idea captivated me, and I eventually decided that instead of waiting for someone else to do it, I'd take up my own challenge. Beyond writing my own retelling, I became determined to entice today's storytellers to retell a Hawaiian myth that intrigued and excited them, and thus develop a collection of dynamic voices and themed stories that continue to percolate through modern island society. The resulting, often meandering, journey of conceptualizing, organizing, and completing this collection of mythical retellings has finally culminated in its publishing. This journey has provided a stimulating outlet for my interest in lasting stories. It has been my delight to meet and get to know many of today's storytellers throughout nearly two decades working as a professional writer, book critic, author profiler, and fiction writer.

Every time I read through this collection, I'm impressed anew by the uninhibited creativity and unexpected, often laugh-out-loud, and even meditative invention in these old-meets-new stories. I swell with gratitude for these talented storytellers who have contributed such heartfelt tales revealing deep love for people gone, here, and coming, and for this place we call home, and without whose distinct and potent perspectives this collection could never have taken such effervescent shape. I will be forever thankful for their stories—stories that enrich my life and will, I hope, enrich yours. Because I now put these echoes of past, present, and future in your hands.

EXPECT THE UNEXPECTED

Why is Pele in therapy? What 21st-century form does Kamapua'a the Pig God take? Which events caused Menehune to leave their Mānoa enclave? And why should—or shouldn't—one look back? Intriguing and provocative answers to these mythical quandaries and more wait inside this pulsing collection of ancient Hawaiian mo'olelo that have been recast, reimagined, and vibrantly retold by modern writers.

Some of the myths in *Don't Look Back* will be immediately recognizable as ones that continue to course through contemporary Hawai'i; others are more esoteric and may even have been temporarily forgotten by some. Yet there are tangible reasons why each has survived into the 21st century, and reading them here reveals new waves of significance. Each new voice that retells them injects these legends with today's meaning and context, revealing their essence—the parts that transcend occasion, trappings, and location. At the same time, they provide palpable and relevant lessons for modern lives, whether in recognizing true love, gathering strength to abandon a route headed for destruction, garnering self-confidence, or avoiding and escaping domestic violence.

These and all myths ultimately serve to instruct and inspire. They educate; they counsel. And they put into evocative and entertaining form the values important to our society and culture, inspiring greatness and binding readers together despite differences. Ultimately, all the stories we tell, here and across the globe, reveal and inform the world we create. Continuing to tell and reshape our most basic and trusted narratives helps secure and illuminate the path forward.

Each of these authors has included a short summary of the original myth before his or her story begins, and the stories are arranged by theme, such as *Heroes and Villains* or *Love and Family*. Readers, then, can head to a myth which holds particular fascination, choose an archetype that intrigues them, locate a favorite author, or just start at the top and work through each tale, marveling at the range of approaches, styles, and plots, and experiencing the prowess of present and future literary stars.

Our country's seventeenth Poet Laureate, Maui resident W.S. Merwin, spins an inimitable, lyrical version of "The Bird Man of Wainiha." Science fiction writer and East Oʻahu dweller A. A. Attanasio employs a deft and humorous touch while conjuring the lustful tale of "Kamapuaʻa and the Wandering Vagina." Playwright and mystery author Victoria Nalani Kneubuhl unearths the underworld, retaining the ancient setting but transforming the story's previous loser into the heroine. The late Ian MacMillan, observer of social interaction and cultural tension, takes "Paʻu o Hiʻiaka" to the world of Oʻahu teens with pitch-perfect dialogue, while writer and educator Gary Pak gently meditates on modern-day moʻo as ʻaumākua.

Some writers chose to explore more personal territory. Marion Lyman-Mersereau immersed herself in the naupaka myth, which has enchanted her since childhood. Maui writer Wayne Moniz conjures the origins of a home legend about the white lady of ʻĪao Valley. Oʻahu resident J. Arthur Rath III takes up the truth about his ancestor's purported role in the departure of Menehune from Mānoa, while Robert Barclay soars through humanity's continued mythmaking, his story derived from current events and personal relationships. I have included an excerpt of the novel that was the first seed of this collection—tackling dreams, love, and sorcery—while one-time Hawaiʻi resident Maxine Hong Kingston tenderly resurrects her family's time living among island ghosts.

There are, of course, more myths to discover, as well as crossovers, connections, and retellings within retellings. Pele, Hina, and Māui make repeat appearances in different tales. Alan Brennert, bestselling author of *Honolulu* and *Molokaʻi*, and writer and educator Timothy Dyke both actively retell a myth in a fictional setting. Bestselling author and Big Island resident Darien Gee (who also writes under the name Mia King) touches on lava rocks and ti leaves along with Christopher Kelsey, who probes the superstition invented by a non-Hawaiian park ranger to prevent vandalism and erosion. Ai Kanaka takes two very different forms in Kuʻualoha Hoʻomanawanui's heartfelt story about the moon goddess and in J. Freen's delightful romp about Oʻahu's cannibal king.

Through all of these discrete tales, a glimmering whole subtly and delicately emerges. Whichever way you engage with these inescapably powerful cultural stories, they will each reveal why they retain a profound and thriving grasp on the people of Hawaiʻi now—and, I trust, for years to come.

FIERCE BATTLES
AND CLOSE ENCOUNTERS

SPF 50
Ian MacMillan

Inspired by the Legend of Pa'u o Hi'iaka

"The Skirt of Hi'iaka" is the story of 'Ohai, a shrub, and her shy friend, a vine that has no name, who live on the sand dunes of Mānā on Kaua'i. Pele is looking for a place to live in a new land and beaches her magnificent canoe where they live. She asks the two to babysit her little sister Hi'iaka and leaves her with them. As the sun advances, they both fear that the little girl will be burned, so the nameless vine grows quickly to cover her, remaining there all day. Pele returns and is grateful for their help, and asks if she can give them something in return. 'Ohai says, "Yes, you can give my friend the vine a name." The grateful Pele replies, "Your name shall be Pā'u o Hi'iaka, skirt of Hi'iaka, the beloved of Pele's heart." So the shy vine has a name. This comes from Frederick B. Wichman's *Pele Mā*.

I like the tale of Pele and the giving of the name Pā'u o Hi'iaka—easy to translate into a modern story. It isn't dramatic on the surface, but lots can be done with it.

✿ ✿ ✿

Trina held up a handful of sand and let it drop in a line, like fine sugar, between her feet. "So you're too timid even to try another name? A real stage name?"

Mary rested her forehead on her knees. It was hot already. Steve and Bob had dropped them here on the little beach on the bigger of the two Mokulua Islands a mile off Lanikai, and had apparently forgotten them. Too much excitement in Lanikai, she guessed. She couldn't really blame them. Word was that Tahiti Griffith was on a boat somewhere, cruising the shoreline looking for a house to buy. Steve had an inside track because he did maintenance for one of the real estate companies listing one of the houses Tahiti Griffith was to visit. She'd arrived the day before, in the wake of tabloid news of a house fire in the Hollywood Hills. CNN repeated the chopper footage of the huge house burning, about fifty times. So as soon as they dropped Trina and Mary here, the guys jumped on the kayaks and headed back toward the line of houses on Lanikai Beach.

"Do you think they'll have a warrant for her arrest?" Mary asked. "On TV her sister was, like, super pissed." She squinted. Something was out there. A boat and little dashes of color, kayaks, materialized on the water.

"I asked you about your name."

"I don't have a name. If I changed it my dad would kill me." She picked up the little red sarong she wore over her bathing suit, shook it out, and folded it.

"You're all 'if I changed blah blah blah.' You have no guts."

"I'm too scared anyway. I didn't even want to win the audition."

Trina picked up another handful of sand. "You don't, like, 'win' an audition, okay? You do well enough to get the part, okay? Pick a name already." She flung the sand out toward the water and sighed. "So we're, like, marooned here."

"Oops," Mary said. She shaded her eyes from the morning sun. Some kind of rubber boat was heading straight for them and kayaks followed far behind. "Oh," she said. "Mygod."

"Hey," Trina said. "Do you think she'd…"

The strange boat advanced upon them, coming in at a speed that seemed reckless, leaving a fan of glittering water arcing behind it, and ran right up on the beach, the skipper a woman in a green bikini, her hair so red that there was no question. Mary stumbled back, and Trina stood at a kind of stunned attention, then turned and said, "Come on up here. Don't hide."

The woman jumped off the rubber boat into the sand. Mary backed away while Trina stood waiting. When the woman saw Mary moving backward up the beach, she smiled and then waved back to her.

Oh. Mygod. She had to. She walked back down the incline toward her. She was taller than the tabloids showed, nearly six feet, Mary thought, and so perfectly built that Mary felt ugly in her presence. Her red hair was nearly unnatural in its redness. Her skin was like caramel, perfect, her breasts high and formidable inside the green bikini top. If anything, that old story about how stars appear more beautiful than they really are on screen was opposite here—on screen she was beautiful, and in reality she was beyond that, almost frightening.

"Can I talk to you girls?" she asked. The voice was so warm, silky, that Mary was startled.

"Uh, yeah," Trina said. Mary moved up and stood beside Trina, trying to act normal. The woman turned and jumped into her boat, then came back with a baby, who also had red hair.

"Oh," Trina said, "she's so pretty. How old is she?"

"We call her Red," Tahiti Griffith said. "She's thirteen months. Her name is Puakai, which means a kind of red. She's my sister." She bounced the baby in the crook of her arm. The little girl also had beautiful, tan skin, and wore a tiny red bathing suit bottom. Red. Another Griffith sibling. There were twelve of them, half of them boys, Mary understood; Moana was the oldest, the screen goddess, and as Mary understood it, The Bitch. You could forget the Baldwins, the Bottomses, and all those other screen families. This family blew them all away. This family was Hollywood royalty.

"Are you Trina and Mary?"

"Yeah," Trina said.

"Couple guys back in Lanikai said you'd probably be willing to watch her while I jerk around with this circus."

"Couple guys? Oh," Trina said. "Steve and Bob, yeah."

"They said you got into a play in L.A."

"Yeah—*Left-Handed Riddles*. Liam McMurtry's play."

"Cool."

Tahiti Griffith turned. Out on the water, an armada of different-colored kayaks advanced awkwardly over the water toward them. "Hah," she said. "I can dodge those idiots. All I'm trying to do is, like, look at a couple of houses."

"Who are they?" Mary asked.

"Pardon?" Tahiti Griffith said.

Mary cleared her throat. Her voice had been mousy and weak, and she flushed with embarrassment. "Who are they?" Still weak.

"Paparazzi," she said. "Next time they'll rent motorboats. So, what are your full names? I'll be in L.A. in the spring."

"Trina Grace," Trina said.

"Mary Holie," Mary said. She sighed. She saw her name on the marquee, saw people standing in line joking about it.

"Listen," Tahiti Griffith said, "that story about me burning my sister's house is—" She paused, staring into the middle distance. "I'm doing a movie, set in the 19th century, *The Five Lives of Count Mephisto*, okay? That fire story is balderdash."

"Balderdash?" Trina said.

"I like that word," Tahiti Griffith said. "There are a lot of other neat ones too: obstreperous, iniquitous, scapegrace, indeed. Stuff like that. The movie is, like, up to here with words like that. How do you spell your name? Is it like, holy cow, or—"

Mary spelled it for her.

Tahiti Griffith thought about this for a moment, then bounced Red in the crook of her arm again. "Da?" Red said.

"I know, honey. They're almost here." She looked at Trina and Mary. "So, if you could watch her here for a while, I'll be back." She stepped back to the boat and drew out a Ziploc bag of what looked like Cheerios. "She ate, but if she has nothing to do, give her these, okay?"

"Sure," Trina said. Tahiti Griffith handed the baby and the Cheerios to Mary—why her, Mary didn't know, but there she was standing with Red in the crook of her arm while Tahiti Griffith ran down to her boat, started it, backed up, and then did a quick turn that sent a fan of spray at them, and roared off toward the kayaks, that red hair floating out behind her head.

"Bah!" Red said, waving. The rubber boat raced out and right through the armada, the wake tipping two of the kayaks over while the other kayaks worked at turning to follow her.

Mary was now aware that Red was staring intently at her, from about three inches away, one hand gripping the side of her neck. She turned slightly to look at Red's eyes, and they stayed locked on hers, as if Red were carefully studying Mary's features. "Huhh," Red said.

"Can you believe this?" Trina said, her face crossed with an awed wonder. "We're watching Tahiti Griffith's sister. We could write an article for a tabloid."

"Yeah," Mary said, bouncing Red in her arm. "Like the one that said 'Pyro Flees Hollywood.' What was 'Suicide Watch'? I saw that from a distance at Safeway."

"Gahh?" Red said, and then leaned away from Mary.

"Omigod," she said. "What is she doing?"

"Maybe she wants down," Trina said.

Mary let Red down into the sand, and she began a weird four-point walk toward the water. "Why doesn't she just crawl?" Mary asked.

"That's a kind of crab-walk," Trina said. When Red got to the wet sand, she sat in it and began slapping the sand. Mary went and sat beside her. She looked up at the mountain over Lanikai, and at all the multimillion-dollar houses. On the water near the shore she saw tiny dashes of color, kayaks moving.

"Anyway, the suicide watch one claimed that their mother, who's only like forty-four or something like that, was suicidal because the sisters were at each other's throats," Trina said. "But that's—that's balderdash."

"Totally," Mary said. "I heard that their mother still wants more kids."

Red got a strange look on her face. Her cheeks and neck swelled a little, and she stared intently at nothing. Then the skin on her face began to flush.

"Something's wrong," Mary said. The baby sat, her fists clenched, and stared at nothing, her face seeming to bloat, her skin reddening.

"Uh-oh," Trina said, "she's pooping."

"What do we do?"

"Dip her in the water."

Red sat there, making sounds as if she were trying to lift something, her fists clenched, that intensely focused look on her face. Then she relaxed, and slapped the sand, picked up a handful, and started to eat it. Mary grabbed her hand. "Oops," she said. "Yucky."

"Da?" Red said, and then went into a sustained Bronx cheer, her lips fluttering. Mary peeked down and saw that her tiny bathing suit was full, actually beginning to seep with it, so she picked the baby up and walked into the water, up to her knees. Holding the baby against her knee, she pulled the bathing suit bottom off and let the poop loose in the water, then repeatedly dipped the suit in the water. "Catch!" she called to Trina, and then threw the balled-up suit bottom to her. She dipped Red in the water several times, cleaned her off, and then, with Red on her hip, walked back up on the sand. Just as she got there, she felt something hot, nearly scalding, running down her hip and leg. "Okay," she said, "she's peeing on me now."

"Huhh, gah?" Red said.

Mary walked back into the water, carrying Red, and dipped down to rinse it off. She took Red back up the beach, thinking that it was Trina's turn to hold her now, but when she held Red out, Red began to cry and squirm as if scared of Trina. "Okay," Mary said, "no problem." She got the suit bottom and worked it over Red's legs up into place.

Now, in the distance, the armada had moved east, toward the point and the last group of houses. Mary sat down just above the wet sand, so that the little waves raced up and tickled the baby's feet. Trina sat down a few feet away.

"Gah."

"Yes," Mary said. Then she looked at Trina. "Meryl Streep lives over there somewhere. Michelle Pfeiffer too." Something occurred to her. "You know, Meryl Streep doesn't seem to mind being named Meryl Streep. Why is that?"

"Yeah, it's a little weird," Trina said. "But it's just a name." She threw sand at the water. "Where are those guys?" she asked. "I mean, is it that important to chase her all over the place?"

"Mary Holie," Mary said. "Mary holy cow. Mary holy shit. Oops." Red didn't seem to take offense. She was piling sand. The day was getting hotter now, and she looked around at the small bag she brought out. She needed sunblock and a sip of water. "Hey," she said. "What about Red? She didn't give us any real food or water. All she's got is Cheerios."

"Got water. She'll be back soon anyway," Trina said.

"Can we put SPF 50 on Red?"

"I don't think so," Trina said. "Gotta be toxic somehow, right?"

"Yeah, but there's no shade here. What do we do?"

"She'll be back."

"Dadadadadada," Red said. Then she looked up at Mary and smiled. "Gudelikunk?"

"Oh, yes, you little cutie," Mary said, and when the little wave receded, ran to get her water bottle. She took the cap off and held the bottle up to Red's mouth, and Red drank, water running down her chin. Then she went back to piling sand. Mary studied the child, the outsized head and the little, lean body underneath, the toes with toenails so tiny you could barely see them. But she was worried that she would burn, now that the sun was way up.

"We have a problem," she said. "We—"

"We have a problem all right. Those idiots forgot us is our problem, like, big time now."

"Gidaloitagunkle?" Red asked, a query made seemingly in reference to the problem.

"Yup, that's me, Mary holy mackerel, left off to the side watching. Mary Gidaloitagunkle."

"If you'd stop doing that, you'd like your name more, you know. I mean, like, you do it more than anybody else."

Mary helped Red pile sand. She looked at the water, expecting to see the rubber boat, but it refused to show. She supposed that if they were stuck here, it wasn't bad to be stuck in one of the most beautiful places anywhere. Clear day, sumptuous clouds over the mountains, the water perfect. While Trina baked in the sand, Mary looked around for shade, but there was none. The only thing she had was the little red sarong. They didn't even have mats or towels.

In a little while it became clear that no boat, no paparazzi, nothing, was coming their way. Trina put SPF 50 on herself and on Mary's back. Mary would have considered using it on Red, but the little tube was flat. There was no other option. She sat with Red between her knees, and then draped the sarong over her knees. Red was inside a little red cave now, piling sand, after which she leaned back against Mary's stomach and, in what seemed like two seconds, fell asleep.

A little later, while Trina walked on the beach fuming, muttering to herself, Mary looked up and saw the rubber boat, about halfway in, cross at a high speed, leaving the water and then slamming down onto it, the sound coming across the water like an unsynchronized drumbeat.

"That was her," Trina called. Then she threw sand at the water and yelled, "Balderdash!"

"Indeed," Mary said.

Red slept on, her body sweaty and hot against Mary's stomach. Even the red curls on her forehead were pasted there by sweat, but the tiny girl seemed comfortable nevertheless. Mary sighed, feeling the sun blast at her back. Here she was, scared half to death about going to L.A. to act in a play, trying to figure out what to do with her name, and a baby was lying against her, sweating up a storm, covered by a little red sarong. A philosopher might say all this meant nothing. He might say just grit your teeth and do it, because nothing really meant anything anyway, and in sixty or so years we'll all be dead. But she cringed at the idea. The imagined philosopher wasn't helping at all.

How, she wondered, did Tahiti Griffith, or even Trina, do it?

Faintly, in the distance, she heard a siren. Trina made her way to her. "Hey," she whispered. "Hear that? Do you suppose…"

Mary laughed softly. "How could she start a fire while she's in a boat?"

"One tabloid said she can project fire."

"Balderdash."

"Yeah. That was the one that also said something about having sex with Elvis's ghost at Graceland."

"If Tahiti Griffith picked a guy, who do you think she would pick?"

"She's Polynesian. Maybe The Rock."

"Keanu Reeves?"

"Nah, not tall enough."

They could no longer hear the siren. Now, between them and the houses dotting the flank of the mountain above Lanikai, there was nothing. Red slept on, oblivious of the heat, sweating away, and Mary's back began to ache because of how she had to hold her legs out to create the little red tent. She was tempted to be angry with Tahiti Griffith, but then decided against it—after all, she was out there looking for a house and dodging paparazzi.

For a while there was no shadow, and then the beginning of her shadow appeared on the sand to her left. So, it was probably afternoon now, and Trina, giving up even on being pissed off, sat and piled sand. A yellow kayak moved across the water, only two hundred yards out, a man in street clothes apparently trying to paddle and fiddle with a camera at the same time. Then they heard the sound of cursing, not the words themselves but the inflections, and the man put the camera down and paddled toward the shore.

"Bummer day for him," Trina said.

"Soggy wallet," Mary said.

Trina sighed. "Okay," she said. "I'm going to swim in."

"Okay."

"Uh, like, no, I'm not. If I do, that boat'll pass by."

They waited. Red stirred, then sat up and looked with a goggle-eyed fascination at the red ceiling of her little tent, and said, "Oh-h, da."

"Well, hello there," Mary said.

Red picked up a fistful of sand and tried to eat it. Mary got her tiny fist just in time. "Hey Trina, could you give me those Cheerios?"

Trina went and got the Cheerios bag and brought it to her. "Man, I could use some of those too," she said.

"Gotta be after two, right?" Mary said. She opened the bag, cleaned the sand off her hand, picked out a few, and held them in her open hand. Red picked one up, and put it in her mouth and chewed, her mouth puckered, her face held in an expression of studious concentration. "Huh-uh," she said. Mary gave her another.

The feeding of the Cheerios, along with sips from the water bottle, went on for a half an hour. Red tried, from time to time, to pick all the Cheerios up, but Mary fed them one by one in order to stretch the process out.

A little later Trina went for a swim, and Mary asked her to watch Red so she could, but Red balked. "Oh well," Trina said. "It looks like you're the mom."

She was stuck. Keeping Red inside the little red tent, she piled sand, dug holes, fed occasional Cheerios, and kept Red busy. She took a break to stand in the water and pee, Red sitting in the crook of her arm and watching her. The frustration of being out here on this beautiful little island while everything was happening somewhere else made her want to cry, but she couldn't do that in Red's presence. Maybe she was destined from the beginning to be a world-class babysitter. Maybe that was the Mary Holie she didn't know existed until now. Maybe she should pass on L.A. The temptation of that, for some reason, picked up her spirits. Proof, she thought, of who she was.

The shadow pointing toward the east was now getting longer. Baked as she was on her left side, from the morning sun, she now felt it baking her right side. Trina had given up and divided her time between being in the water and walking on the sand.

She was feeding Red more Cheerios when the child looked out at the water, pointed, and said, "Gah! Gah!"

The rubber boat raced toward them, the spray behind it high, the little dashes of kayaks turning into dots. The rubber boat advanced, came over the shallower water, and because of the tide, beached higher up on the sand than it had in the morning.

Tahiti Griffith jumped out onto the sand. "I'm so-o sorry," she said.

"That's okay," Trina called.

"No problem," Mary said, not loud enough for anyone to hear. She picked Red up and held her in the crook of her arm, then stood up, sore and stiff.

Tahiti Griffith turned and looked out over the water. "Fifteen minutes at least," she said. "Then on the way out I'll dump some more of them." She turned back. "Really, I'm sorry. Listen, is there anything I can do?"

"Well," Mary said, and looked at Trina, who shrugged. "Oh, that's all right." She handed Red to Tahiti Griffith, who kissed her. Red threw her arms around her neck and pointed back at Mary.

"The guys are on their way out," Tahiti Griffith said. "I made them promise. I'd take you, but—"

"Oh, that's all right," Mary said.

"I saw you with her under that sarong. I forgot sunblock. I mean, I wish I could do something."

"Well," Trina said, "there is one thing."

"What?"

"Mary. She needs a stage name. She thinks Mary Holie won't cut it, and she thinks her dad'll be really mad if she changes it."

Mary flushed. She wished Trina hadn't done that.

Tahiti Griffith studied Mary, and it made her uncomfortable.

"There's nothing wrong with that name except that it's syllabically static. It's syllable-locked."

"Uh, I don't understand," Mary said.

"Okay, so we do some syllable theory here, okay?" Tahiti Griffith said. "It's two syllables followed by two syllables. Syllable theory goes like this: you want either a jump or a sigh."

Trina looked at Mary. "A jump or a sigh," she said.

"That's it. If you need a new name, you do it. Your dad'll understand."

"Okay."

"A jump is one followed by two, or two by three. Take Jean Harlow. That's a jump, one followed by two. You," and she pointed at Trina, "are a sigh. Trina Grace. Two followed by one. It needs to be either a jump or a sigh. Marilyn Monroe is a sigh."

"I'm a sigh, then—"

"Yes, for the sake of argument, Mary should be a jump. Indeed, she needs another syllable." She gazed upward and laughed. "And look, I don't want to offend the syllable-locked people. Some overcome it: Harry Truman, James Dean, Martha Stewart, Michael Jackson. And there are variations, like a four-to-one sigh: Maximilian Schell. Or syllable locks that work. Listen to this, because it's poetry: Richard Rogers and Robert Russell Bennett. Locked big time, but poetry."

"Ohmygod," Trina said. "Now I know why Meryl Streep works. She's a sigh."

"You got it," Tahiti Griffith said. "I'm a sigh, too. Now, Mary needs a jump."

"I'll say she does," Trina said, and giggled.

"Shut up," Mary whispered.

Tahiti Griffith paused, looking at Red, who seemed enthralled watching her as she spoke. "You need a name, huh? Let's see." She thought a moment. "You know," she said, "my mother wants Red to be a politician and not an actress. That's why she's got two followed by two, Puakai Griffith. You could argue that Pua is one syllable or two, so she left that little door open."

"I'd rather have a jump name than a sigh name," Mary said.

"It'll look way better on the playbill to have sigh and jump," Tahiti Griffith said. She looked carefully at Mary, until Mary again felt uncomfortable, almost as if she wanted to run away from those eyes. "Keep Mary," she said. "Sarong. Blanket. No," and she looked at Red, pushing red curls up on her forehead. She thought, focusing on the sarong lying in the sand. Her eyes narrowed, shifting to some contemplative middle distance. "Mary Redmantle," she said.

"Mary what?" Mary asked.

"How old are you?" Tahiti Griffith asked.

"Twenty-two," she said.

"Whew," Tahiti Griffith said. "I'm twenty-three. So can I talk to you the way my mother talks to me? It wouldn't be proper if you were like, twenty-four."

"Sure," Mary said.

"Then say your name. It's Mary Redmantle."

"Mary Redmantle."

"No, speak up."

"Mary Redmantle."

"Trina," Tahiti Griffith said, "read the top of the playbill."

"Trina Grace and Mary Redmantle."

"Perfect—a sigh and a jump." She turned back to Mary. "I'm the mom, okay?"

"Okay."

"Stand up straight, square your shoulders, stick your tits out."

"Well…" But she tried it anyway.

"Say your name."

"Mary Redmantle."

"Stick them out, now. Keep your shoulders square. Look the world in the eye, and say your name like you mean it."

"Mary Redmantle. That's me. I'm an actress and my name is Mary Redmantle."

"Louder."

"Uh oh," Trina said. "The kayaks."

Tahiti Griffith turned. Red pointed. "Ah, presently they approach," she said. "The obstreperous nincompoops." She turned back to Mary and Trina. "I must be off. So," and she shifted Red in her arm, nodded, and said, "you are going to L.A. Why?"

"To be in a play?" Mary said.

"No. You are going to L.A. for the purpose of kicking some major ass."

"Yes," Mary said. "I will, like, kick major ass."

"You know what? I'll be there, how's that? Opening night."

"That would be so cool," Trina said.

And within five seconds, she was churning backward off the sand, white water boiling around the black rubber pontoons. When the boat was out far enough, it turned, tipping to a forty-five-degree angle, and raced out toward the kayaks, which began to divide in a garish rendition of the parting of the Red Sea.

"My God," Trina said. "One, two, no—four. Four kayaks over."

But Mary was only half-listening. She was whispering her name to herself. It was strange—the more she whispered it the better it sounded to her. The more she whispered, "I am Mary Redmantle and I am going to kick some major ass," the better she felt. She was not a babysitter. She was an actress. She walked into the water up to her knees, cupped some up and onto her head, and feeling it trickle over her face and back, she squared her shoulders. ✹

Māui the Superhero Fights the Eight-Eyed Bat!

Alan Brennert

Inspired by the Legend of Māui and the Eight-Eyed Bat

Māui has been fishing off the coast of O'ahu and is enjoying his catch when he happens to look inland and see his wife, Kumulama, being abducted by the evil Pe'ape'amakawalu, "the eight-eyed bat." Unable to overtake the airborne Pe'ape'a, Māui seeks his grandfather Kuolokele's counsel. (In some versions, Kuolokele is not Māui's grandfather but a wise, humpbacked man whose hump Māui helpfully knocks off with the toss of a stone.) Kuolokele shows Māui how to fashion a kite-like ship from bird feathers, ti leaves, and 'ie'ie vines. Māui uses the ship to fly to the island of Moanaliha, where Pe'ape'a rules, but he is captured by the bat's followers, imprisoned in a kapu box, and taken to the bat's house. Pe'ape'a rejoices in his foe's helplessness, but that night, Māui waits patiently until the last of the bat's eight eyes have closed, then decapitates Pe'ape'a and drains his eyes to make a cup of 'awa. He rescues his wife, and the two of them fly in the bird-ship back to their home on O'ahu.

In my novel, *Moloka'i*, the old Hawaiian legends are told to Rachel by her adopted aunty, Haleola, in the way these tales had traditionally been handed down in Hawaiian culture—orally, or "talking story." Rachel, in her turn, passes them on to her daughter and to children like the ones evacuated from Honolulu after Pearl Harbor. I took a special pleasure in writing this section, in which the exploits of a legendary Hawaiian champion are juxtaposed with the new four-color mythology that had just burst onto the American pop-culture scene.

It illustrates, I hope, the common roots of so many heroic myths, even as Rachel uses the analogy to comic book superheroes to interest her listeners in Hawaiian legends. And by likening the evil Pe'ape'a to then-current enemies like Hitler and Hirohito (as well as Captain America's arch-nemesis, the Red Skull), Rachel was doing what humanity has done down through the centuries: keeping its most cherished stories and champions alive and fresh by reinventing them, contemporizing them, for each new generation.

Pearl Harbor brought an unexpected joy to Kalaupapa. In recent years, the number of children at the settlement had steadily declined as the Board of Hospitals and Settlement chose to keep more young leprosy patients at the hospital in Kalihi, closer to friends and family.

But now, fearing further attacks on Honolulu, the Board decided the children might be safer at Kalaupapa—and in March of 1942, twelve girls and twenty boys shipped out at the furtive hour of four in the morning aboard the *S.S. Hawaii*, bound for Moloka'i.

When the children arrived they found themselves the puzzled recipients of more love and attention than they had ever dreamed of. Kalaupapans, delighted to hear the laughter of keiki again, spoiled them mercilessly—buying them candy and ice cream, treats and toys. There were birthday parties and lū'au and trips to the beach; the children went fishing, explored sea caves, played softball and volleyball, learned to ride horses.

Rachel found herself spending more time helping Sister Catherine—at seventy the eldest sister at the convent—at Bishop Home. Given her infirmities Rachel couldn't do much manual labor; but she had no lack of energy or strength to play croquet with the girls on the convent lawn, or to read aloud from L. Frank Baum and Jack London. At one such reading—which took place on the beach with children from both Bishop and McVeigh Homes—a ten-year-old boy named Freddie asked Rachel hopefully, "Do you have any comic books?"

Rachel blinked. "'Comic books?' What are they?"

"They're like the funny pages in the Sunday paper," another boy explained, "except in a magazine."

"I can show you!" Freddie announced, racing back to McVeigh Home and returning a few minutes later with an impressive stack of magazines under his arm, which he handed to Rachel. Every title was an exclamation promising adventure and excitement: *Whiz Comics, Thrilling Comics, Smash Comics, More Fun Comics, Amazing Mystery Funnies, Crackajack Funnies, Slam-Bang Comics, Wow Comics, Sensation Comics, Pep* and *Prize* and *Jackpot* and *Top-Notch*. The glossy covers were populated by a wondrous cast of characters: hawk-winged birdmen flying through the air, strongmen lifting cars, men made of fire, men made of rubber, spectral figures cowled in green, turbaned swamis with magic wands. In gaudy costumes they squared off against leering gargoyles, evil doctors, murderous cavemen, Grim Reapers, rampaging mummies, fiery rockets, even Nazi tanks and Japanese Zeros.

"Ah," Rachel said, "I see. Heroes and magic. I know some stories like that." She asked the children, "Have you ever heard of a hero named Māui?"

A boy objected, "Māui's an island, not a hero!"

"Oh? Where do you think they got the *name* for the island?"

"Māui was a real person?" a girl asked.

"He was more than a person. He was the son of a goddess, Hina, and a mortal man, so he was half-human and half something more than human."

"Like the Sub-Mariner," Freddie observed sagely.

"Māui was what they call a 'trickster' because he used his wits as well as his mana, his power. And because he was a little mischievous. Like the time he turned his brother into a dog."

"My brother's already a dog," a girl said, and everyone laughed.

"According to legend, when the world was new the sky and the clouds rested on top of the earth. They pressed down so heavily that when the first plants began to grow, their leaves were flat."

A boy nodded soberly. "That makes sense."

"When trees started to grow they pushed the sky up farther—enough that the human race could now walk upright. But the skies were still much lower than they are now. One of Māui's first great deeds was to lift up the sky—he braced himself against the top of the clouds and *pushed*, pushed the heavens up to where they are today.

"Also back then, the nights were longer than the days; the sun moved too quickly through the skies. There was hardly time to dry kapa cloth—it had to be taken up at night and put out the next day again. So Māui fashioned ropes of green flax and used them to snare the sun, forcing it to move more slowly across the sky."

A girl looked skeptical. "Why didn't the ropes burn?"

"The greener a plant, the harder it is to burn." The girl seemed placated by this cunning use of science.

"Did Māui ever fight anybody like Hitler?" Freddie asked, impatient to get to the action. "Or the Red Skull?"

"Oh, he had many great battles," Rachel assured him. "For instance against Pe'ape'a, the Eight-Eyed Bat." This quickly captured their attention. "Māui had been fishing along the shore of O'ahu when he looked up and saw his wife Kumulama in the grip of a horrible creature—a huge bat with eight terrible eyes, which had seized his wife in teeth like razors and carried her aloft. Māui dove into the sea after it, but the creature was too fast and Māui had to turn back, weeping, as the Eight-Eyed Bat carried Kumulama to a distant island.

"Heartsick, Māui went to a wise old kahuna, who told him to gather tree limbs, thick vines, and the feathers of many birds. Māui did this, and from the tree limbs the kahuna fashioned the hollow skeleton of a giant bird, then covered it in feathers. The vines were attached to the bird's wings, and when Māui climbed inside and pulled on the vines, the wings flapped—and with Māui's great strength as a motor, the bird took flight!

"Māui piloted the flying machine—the first in the whole world!—to the island of the bat. It was a beautiful island, but Pe'ape'a was its ruler—its dictator, like Hirohito—" The keiki booed and hissed. "—and when Māui landed he was captured by the bat's people. They imprisoned him in a cage and took him to their ruler, who rejoiced that he had captured such a mighty warrior.

"Māui waited until the bat had fallen asleep—watching as first one eye, then another, and another, closed in sleep. When the eighth eye drooped shut, Māui quietly freed himself from the box and, wielding a huge blade, he cut off the bat's head with one swipe!" Rachel swung her hand in a wide arc and made a whooshing sound. Her listeners cheered, but the best was yet to come:

"Now very angry at what was done to his wife, Māui gouged out the bat's eight eyes and had its people make them into 'awa—a kind of bathtub gin usually made from kava root. And do you know how 'awa used to be made?" They all shook their heads. "People used to chew the kava root, then spit it out and strain it. So Pe'ape'a's people *chewed his eyes and spit them out*, and then Māui *drank* the 'awa made from the bat's eight eyes!"

This was greeted by a chorus of cheers, gasps, *Wows*, and *Yeahs*, from boys and girls alike.

"And then," Rachel finished triumphantly, "Māui flew back to O'ahu with his wife at his side." She turned to the boy who'd expressed doubt about the trickster hero. "And *that's* why they named the island of Maui after him."

There was silence a long moment; then:

"Tell us again about the eyes," someone said, and so she did. ✹

Sex, Love and the Mighty Fine Structure Constant

A. A. Attanasio

Inspired by the Legend of Kamapuaʻa and the Wandering Vagina

This myth describes the creation of Koko Crater, which, from the viewpoint of Honolulu to the west, looks like a typical promontory. Seen from Kalama Valley in the southeast corner of Oʻahu, the cinder cone exposes two coalesced craters; early island settlers named them *Kohelepelepe*, which I understand to mean "inner lips of the vagina." The Hawaiian story of Koko Crater actually begins 150 miles away on the Big Island; there, the lusty Pig God, Kamapuaʻa, assaulted Pele, the Goddess of Fire.

The frenzied Pig God would have ravished his victim if not for the intervention of Pele's sister, the sorceress Kapo, who distracted Kamapuaʻa from his lewd advances by detaching her vagina and tossing it from the Big Island to Oʻahu. The Pig God chased after it. The flying vagina slammed into the earth. And Kamapuaʻa, unable to stop quickly enough, crash-landed, gouging out Kalama Valley, now a suburban community—but, until 1975, a valley of pig farms! Kapo retrieved her portable genitals, leaving behind this impression in the land—the tuff ring of Koko Crater.

I live in Kalama Valley, and the surreal account of Koko Crater's origin occupies my daily landscape. So, of course, it's the first myth to come to mind when asked to retell an ancient Hawaiian tale. Is there a 21st-century way to relate to gods and goddesses? That's the challenge I set myself with this retelling. We are not a mythic people, we who invented the printing press and the hydrogen bomb. Who—or what—are the gods to us? This short story is a contemporary answer to that question.

My sister has problems. She's a real bitch—and I mean that literally. But you're not going to believe a word of what I have to say without some heartfelt explanation. So, let me get this over with right up front: I'm a god. Well, I'm a goddess; however, given the exacting scruples at this feast of tact we call the postmodern age, where actresses pass as actors, I guess I'm a god. I know that sounds alarming. Just hear me out, and what I have to say will piece together all the arbitrary plastic of this world's broken heart.

My name is *Kapo-ʻula-kina-ʻu*, which means "the sacred night streaked scarlet," or "red eel woman," depending on whom you ask. I picked up those aliases among the islanders, I suppose because I like the night and I hang out a lot with my sister, Pele, the bitch I mentioned whose name means "lava flow." Night above incandescent volcanic badlands is one of my favorite forms. Many times, I have been eelish streaks of scarlet light in the night. I've also been birds, deep-sea fish, a variety of butterflies, and distinctive boulders. The akua—the gods—can take many forms.

Right now, I'm an astrophysicist, and I work on Mauna Kea at the University of Hawai'i's 0.6-meter telescope training undergraduates and experimenting with focal pane arrays for various low bandgap infrared photo-detectors. But enough about me. "I" is a bird that tugs the reins of the wind. "I" is a fish without a thought in her head. "I" is a butterfly heavy in the air. "I" is a boulder feeling for some inner truth. "I" is an astrophysicist with a shoehorn smile. "I" is mythology.

Let me tell you, instead, about the bitch, my sister. She's a white bull terrier—the "gladiator of the dog world." When she's a bitch, she's always white. *Le rouge et le noir* of lava wear thin after a few centuries, and she prefers white when she's a bitch. This thing she has about dogs, I've never understood. She says it smells good. What's good about it for me is that when I'm at work, I never have to walk her because she adores romping around the observatory where the landscape is so grim it is beautiful.

Unfortunately, the tainted dog food from China that made headlines a while ago began a cavalcade of problems for me. Pele got sick. That was the real cause of the strongest earthquakes in twenty years that rocked the Big Island on October 15, 2006. The temblors broke safety bolts at most of the observatories, including mine, and bollixed my scope's alt-azimuth drive. That kept me plenty busy, and I wasn't as attentive to my sister as I usually am, which led to Pele drifting again into her obsession with the opposite sex. And that's always been trouble, because she has this monumental penchant for other women's men.

But before I get into that, a necessary and salient aside about akua. I just said that the "real" cause of the earthquakes was my sister's sickness. I should explain, because it is probably news to you that in the manufactured world gods are real. We are things, as you are—only different. For over a hundred years, science has closed in on a definitive understanding of who we are, and physicists even have their own name for us: Boltzmann Brains.

Oh, you were expecting something more poetic? "Long ago on the path of stars, midmost between the worlds, there strode the gods of Old. In the bleak middle of the worlds, They sat and the worlds went round and round, like dead leaves in the wind at Autumn's end… And the centuries went where the centuries go, toward the End of Things, and with Them went the sighs of all the gods as They longed for what might not be."[1] That's from another writer, Lord Dunsany, a lantern-bearer for the gods, who wrote fantasies around the time science first began to speculate about Boltzmann Brains—so long ago that now his words are in the public domain and I can bandy them about to make my point: the gods recline in tinted fields above the morning, their bodies swirling up and down the world with other dust, all in the center of life's hopes, rejoicings, and laments.

Do we really recline on clouds? Nah, it's not like that. The gods are random vibrations in the fabric of spacetime, a.k.a. vacuum quantum fluctuations that attain the status of actual observers who are, in the parlance of legal scholars, "not erroneous." That's me. And Pele and all akua.

I don't want to lose you in the *je ne sais quoi* of technicalities. It all makes sense once you get a handle on the 21st-century realization that the universe is a vast membrane hovering among lots of other membranes in a higher dimension … sort of like Dunsany's dead leaves in the wind, where each leaf is a universe and the wind is the fifth dimension. On any given leaf, including this one we call our cosmos, there may be things like you, Ordinary Observers (OOs), who have evolved over billions of years to a physical complexity capable of making elegant observations about the universe. But you should know that OOs are not the only kind of entities capable of making observations about the universe that are not erroneous. Sometimes—very, very rarely (but then "rare" has a special significance in the fifth dimension where "time" is infinite)—observers simply appear who are not ordinary, not biological, but made up of manifold properties of spacetime itself, so that we can be anything anywhere anytime and fully conscious.

Weird, huh? For an OO, you bet. Bear in mind, though, the truth is democratic. The truth plays the lottery with skull-bones and Boltzmann Brains alike. In this universe, on this planet called Earth, humans and gods happen to have both won the cosmic lottery simultaneously. Now, the gods have made a harp out of the heartstrings of all humanity, and we play upon that harp the song of scorn and mercy, of love and homicide. And every note is a life caught up among the many notes and lives entangled with flesh, that plaything of the gods. And although in the prison houses of all the skulls on Earth all memories must die, the gods forget nothing. Boltzmann Brains capture everything, every memory of every life, weaving together the filaments of memory into a melody that passes between the gods, sad at heart for memories that are not. Be very quiet, Ordinary Observer, and you shall hear that melody, where the things that might not be have at last become. Be but very quiet, man and woman, and hear what voices cry from the harp of heartstrings, for the things that might not be.

Such is the busyness and business of the gods, iridescent as flies swarm-

---

[1] *Time and the Gods*, Lord Dunsany (John W. Luce & Co.), 1905

ing among the organic mess of human life. Hence, when my sister got sick as a dog and her convulsions shook the whole island, leaving me busy fixing the equipment in my observatory that she had knocked loose, she was done being a dog. Fraught with charisma, wearing volcanic mist like a negligee, Pele took off to fool around with OOs.

Pele can be cruel. The oblique joy of sadism is not unknown to her, and she gets a kick out of dancing nude in front of tourists and luring the intrepid close enough to coil a brimstone wind around them tight as a sphincter, dropping them dead. On March 2, 1983 she got the crimson thought to enter Royal Gardens, an OO community under development, and burned down the first house on Queen Avenue. *Who is the Queen?* Her vengeful lava spoke louder than words. Four years almost to the day, she poured into a capacious, water-filled fissure at Punalu'u known as Queen's Bath and filled it to the brim. *Who is the Queen?* Twenty-two OOs who didn't answer that question right have died in the quarter century since Pele started strutting around naked again.

She was up to her usual mischief after the bad dog food, not just with the OOs by burning down rare protected rain forest near Kāne Nui o Hamo, but causing trouble with our older sister as well. Namaka is one headache of a Boltzmann Brain. As our elder, she is so big with entitlement she tucks the sun in her back pocket at the end of the day, smokes twilight, and exhales the Milky Way. At least, that's what she thinks of herself. She's haughty, and you'd never catch her representing as mere bird, fish, or rock. She does everything large: the whole coral reef is her recliner, the coastline her shawl, sea cliffs stupendous bling, and the moon her dance partner. When Pele seduced Namaka's husband, Aukelenuiaiku, king of the ancient homeland, a cosmic brawl ensued that continues to this day down in Kamokuna where lava and sea meet and recreate prehistory.

The thing to remember about Boltzmann Brains is that they are not made up of atoms and molecules but the fabric of spacetime itself; so, our demeanor—what you call myth—repeats endlessly. Our natures don't really change: each god is a freeze-frame of behavior. And you … well; you are nothing but change, all jittery atoms and tangling molecules. That is the real matter of the human soul, isn't it? Behind the dirty windows of sense and the door with your name on it, in the house of self sits the mutable "I."

I don't want to frighten you. Yet, consider the Laughing Greek,[2] who observed that "atoms and the void" are all there is for your ilk; whereas, for us

---

[2] Democritus, circa 460–370 B.C.E., pre-Socratic philosopher who postulated that matter is composed of assorted indivisible units, which he called *atoma* (sing. *atomon*), that comprise all sensations: "By convention sweet, by convention bitter, by convention hot, by convention cold, by convention color: but in reality atoms and the void." The Flemish master Hendrick ter Brugghen, in 1628, painted his masterpiece "Democritus Laughing."

akua the void quivers like a drum and atoms dance to our tune. Our actions are excursions to infinity. Our lives become proverbs among Ordinary Observers. And so Namaka, with all her waves about her, seizes hold of red-hot, adulterous Pele, and they grapple furiously till the centuries make them hard but no more wise—and not all the marvels of the future shall atone to them for those old memories that burn sharper every year as they recede into the ages that akua have gathered. And always dreaming of her sister's bitterness and the forsaken husband and lover of an olden time, Namaka and Pele both shall fail to see the grandeur to which a hurrying people attain in this fabricated age.

Soon, they shall perceive OOs changing in a way that they shall not comprehend, knowing what they cannot know, till they discover that these are Ordinary Observers no more, and a new race holds dominion over the earth whose forebears were their worshippers. These shall speak to the akua no more as they hurry upon a quest that the gods find surprising, and the gods shall know that they can no longer take part in shaping destinies, but—in a world of luminous cities crystallized from cyberealities run by nanotech phantasmagoria of Planck-length sylphs and djinni, holographic artificial intelligences, genomic miracles and monstrosities—only pine for the time when flesh was the gods' plaything. Then, even this shall end with the shapes of the akua in the darkness gathering all lives and memories, when the hills of Earth shall fling up the planet's long-stored heat back to the heavens again, when this rock shall be old and cold, with nothing alive upon it but numb atoms and the void.

But, hey, I'm getting way ahead of myself. That's my luckless propensity. As a goddess of sorcery and an astrophysicist, I already hear the deep gong at the end of the world. This universe is flying apart ever faster, accelerating to nowhere. Dark energy, science dubs it, having no idea what "it" is except that "it" is the opposite of gravity, is pushing apart atoms in the void faster and faster the farther apart they get. Inside our own telling, there is this sweet moment of "now," of "I," and of "being" someplace in the order of nothingness.

That's why I like it when my sister is a dog. As a white bull terrier, she yaps and darts, craps and farts. We play. It's fun to watch her scampering around the observatory, up and down slopes of gray scree in full sunshine above the clouds. At this altitude, snow sits in the saddles of hillsides: Poliʻahu, the snow goddess, lives here, and the wind frequently lashes us with ice crystals on our walks or, during my undergrads' 'scope time, fouling our sunspot observations with surreal swirls of snow gleam. These are spiteful reminders that Pele once stole a lover from Poliʻahu. In her original fury, the snow goddess smothered this volcano with thick blizzards, dousing the fire pits and forcing out my lascivious sister. Now, Mauna Kea is an extinct cinder cone, which is good for astronomers—though troublesome for me when the ice wind freezes the sponges of blood in my bones and I get to thinking about sex and love and their impossible deadlock.

No, that doesn't ring true in the acoustics of skull hall. Poliʻahu's ice-cold shoulder on these dead gray elevations makes me realize sex and love are a *lifelock*—like the sphinx, serene and terrible, inventing a primal spirituality out of bestial depths. Desire riddles organic life, because DNA single-mindedly climbs its spiral ladder up from the slime to the stars (I think of the Hubble photographs that DNA has taken of remote, monumental, and majestic star-birthing clouds, the mass of which relative to the mass of an Ordinary Observer is greater than 10^{40}—an astonishing and overpowering relationship between minuscule organic sentience and cosmic immensity). But the gods? For we who tread the void, blood and its emotive compulsions mean nothing. We have no DNA. There is Something Else coupling the akua, an obscure power of penetrating desire. I didn't fathom It until I became human and an astrophysicist.

What makes the gods couple is what physicists refer to as—surprise!—the coupling constant. Delirious about names as Adam, science also identifies this Something Else as the fine structure constant, the symbol "alpha," the ratio 1/137, and the decimal 0.007297351 +/- 0.000000006. No matter what you call It, this constant is the sex life of matter and energy. It measures the promiscuity of atoms and light—how readily they couple (*pronto fortissimo!*) and how often (a lot!). It doesn't have to be that way. There are darker universes where the fine structure constant is so large that matter and energy rarely hook up. In others, they copulate so vigorously that molecules can't form and space is a radioactive glare of busted-open atoms forsaken of form. Ours is an uncommon cosmos. The fine structure constant is fine-tuned to precisely the balance that marries here and now and births you and me and the glistening dew.

Most akua have sex frequently, and with many partners, because space-time has that propensity. The coupling constant makes sure that Pele is not constant to any one partner any more than is Aphrodite or so many of the gods. The pact with death works the same for you. Trade up or even sideways, because you only go around once. And though the gods keep going around, we're not original or inventive with our differences. That's how I knew exactly what mischief Pele would get into when she got sick of being a dog.

At 14,000 feet, repair work on precision optics is tedious, and—despite the fact I was aware that my sister walked fire sidelong to the sea leaving lost paradise in her wake—I didn't focus on her until I heard her unsayable cry for help. The contrapuntal echoes of telepathy and our mythic past pierced my human dream. With lightning-flash prescience, I knew what was happening before the hugeness of memory closed in like a thunderclap: the divine swine, the hog-god Kamapuaʻa, had determined to rut with Pele.

Pig God and Lava Flow share a long, aggressive history. The love-hate relationship of these two akua is the story of Hawaiʻi. And it begins long before Pele and I showed up in these islands. We are haoles, meaning foreigners. We come from another island of underground fire, the faraway magma plume of Lýðveldið Island,[3] where the tortured feud with Namaka began when Pele scored with Aukelenuiaiku (Storkjøre-svømmer-soldatsønn, as he was known on that island: "Great traveling swimmer, son of the officer"). After one too many of Pele's flagrant adulteries with the overeager husbands of troll queens and ice giantesses, we fled and got as far away as we could. Only spiteful Namaka followed, and we thought we might make a clean start (still young and ignorant of the eversame malady and compulsion of myth).

One of the first akua we met was Kamapua'a—"Pig-Child." His father had named his handsome son that in a blind fury at the boy's mistaken illegitimacy. That warped the kid, and he stalked the mountains like thunder, harrying his father's people, raiding their lands. Named a hog, Kamapua'a maliciously acted like one. He turned goth, shaved his head to a bristly Mohawk, and tattooed his body black. After he killed the old man, he went on living his father's curse. Then, he met Pele.

My sister is a looker. Not as lean, lovely, and fragile as Poli'ahu, who as a snow goddess has that "hollow of cheek as though she drank the wind"[4] look, Pele carries a more robust beauty, a fierce grace, and a challenging smile that plays with fire. Her proud, tough glamour radiates psychosexual rawness, an argument with reality. Kamapua'a recognized a match for his tantrum passion in that outlaw tita and fell for her hard as the meteor that killed the dinosaurs.

Now, if the big guy had been married… Ah, well, that was his misfortune because my fiery sister only wants lovers she can't have. She rebuked him for his ugliness, thwacking him with goblin laughter, which you can hear to this day in the percussive noise the wind makes in 'ōhi'a lehua boughs, that red-flowered tree sacred to Pele. Her flailing guffaw enraged the Hog God, and he tried to force himself on her. When akua brawl, spacetime groans, cantankerous as bulls getting castrated, sunspots flourish like acne, tides shove the wrong way, clouds twist into the faces of dental patients, and lightning slices rocks like a cheese cutter. Kamapua'a doused Pele in a hurricane torrent, and she threw it back as acid rain. Howling through his smoking bristles, he rooted the ground under her, and she shot to her feet again as a fiery geyser. That seared him to a snarl of pork jerky, and he unraveled those fire-hardened sinews to tie back her arms with tourniquet knots and lash her legs wide open. Then, he shoved his purple-nozzled pizzle full strength at the scarlet target.

At that point, I showed up, appalled as the falsetto sea captain in James Cook's unwritten opera *Tahitian Fire Dancers in the Gunpowder Room*. What

---

[3] Iceland
[4] W. B. Yeats, describing his lover Maud Gonne in "Among School Children"

was I to do? I fell back on my specialty—sorcery. For those who don't already
know, sorcery weaves God's baby blue breath and Heidegger's "*Dasein*,"[5] and
from the resultant array of spirit and matter unfolds an entire chess set of
powers. (This works for akua. If you are an Ordinary Observer, there is only
Dasein. Sorry.) I quickly deployed an *en passant* maneuver of higher dimen-
sions that refracted me into cubist segments. My vagina detached like the
passenger seat in a James Bond movie and shot between my sister and her
tumescent assailant. The rocketing pudendum trailed a comet-streak of sex
chloroform. When Kamapuaʻa's inflamed nostrils inhaled those payload
pheromones, his eyeballs clicked like dice rolling snake eyes, and he pulled
back from Pele, spellbound in a maze of amazed dreams wherein the sorrows
of this world are lost.

Kamapuaʻa hurried after my flying yoni, and not all the magic of his
porcine powers nor yet any foreseeing, nor perceiving of his divine swine mind
could equal the might of my vagina's flight. To an island far to the northwest my
genitals arced, and the Pig God followed aloft and beheld the sea and long koa
ships of the olden mariners and star navigators since dead, and went down at
trajectory's end into the earth on the southeast point of Oʻahu with the whistling sky behind him and plowed into the ground, chiseling out Kalama Valley.
He lay there some while, covered over with weeds and green with the damp of
years, as ever to the soul of his lewd desire my bewitchment added a more ardent
fire. While time slogged by, the rampant glory of his ferocious past sang into
song and all the clattering news of today grew old, far down, forgotten beneath
his snoring snout.

That was then. Since that distant day, there have been numerous mythic
repetitions. You can read about them in the lore of sacred geography, such as
the rugged coast in Puna called Lua-o-Pele, where the struggle I just described
ripped up the earth. At this place, my sister's hallowed lehua trees flourish all
the way to the water's edge, alone in all the islands.

Visit Koko Crater, the terrestrial imprint left by the impact of my genitals, known in former times as Kohelepelepele, "the inner lips of the vagina."
There's a botanical garden there now, and you can conduct a gynecological tour
of the flora adorning a goddess's vulva.

While on Maui, notice the cleft between Wailua and Wailua-iki and the
steep trail still traversed by letter carriers to the valley. Kamapuaʻa tore open
that gap taking a tumble during a similar assault. If you look carefully, you'll
find my vaginal impression in the adjacent cliff.

At another Maui cliff, Puaʻahoʻokuʻi, you can examine stone formations
created when Kamapuaʻa lost his whiskers chasing Pele at Huluhulu-nui ("many

[5] German: *Da* = there/here; *Sein* = being; *Dasein* = existence

bristles") before he slammed her into the ground on the hillside called Kaiwi-o-
Pele ("the bones of Pele").

But this time, it's different. I'm in human guise. I could change out of
my mortal semblance, of course, but my dissertation took forever—and I like
being an astrophysicist. This is the wildest sorcery I've worked in ages. The
light we take in with telescopes cuts loose our shadows, and even Ordinary
Observers can forget briefly their failed freedom and see how beauty cooper-
ates with truth. So, what am I to do? I leave a grad assistant to reprogram the
'scope's guide drive and head south in the school's Land Rover. A couple hours
later, shortly after noon, I'm at the former site of Kaimu, a small town that
Pele smothered beneath fifty feet of lava in 1990. On that black cinderland,
green feathers plume the cracked lava: these young coconut sprouts planted
by residents reclaim the land and defy the sublime otherness of the barren,
uncanny terrain.

I cross the burned tract toward the sea, the fresh-minted and secluded
black sand beach in New Kaimu Bay. Here, Namaka and Pele clashed. Plates
of rock jut out at the sea's edge, ribbed like gigantic butterfly wings, marking
the jumping-off point where fire and water took to the air, striding through
steam along the road that leads across the world. Behind me, beyond acres of
primordial rock, rises Kilauea Volcano where my sister thrashes, convulsing
two hundred small earthquakes in one weekend alone. This tantrum is what
brought me here.

But where is Kamapua'a? Wearing my human form, sitting here so
quietly in skull hall, I have trouble seeing the akua as anything but the familiar
spirits of rock, wind, sea… There is nothing to know behind these eyes other
than flying spume and salty aerosol, this din of crashing waves, this powerful
argument of sea and land under a still, blue space where all that the gods have
left for us is the holiness of sunset. That's hours away. The brilliance of noon
reveals desolate rock and the ocean's horizon carrying a toy-size cargo ship
bound for O'ahu with building supplies for the construction boom there. Ah!
There is Kamapua'a! He's a big, fat freighter! In my Ordinary Observer brain,
the gods are like passengers snoozing in the backseat who would be astonished
to wake and gawk around at the world as people see it.

Look! My sorcery from mythic times is still working: the divine swine
follows his lust to O'ahu. His pig heart glides across the dazzling face of the
waters. He will dig up the islands with his greedy snout as he has always done
in story. He will root for the root of his carnal desires, burrowing with his
snoot and his backhoes, tearing up the earth to wrench out hope from the
dim future, building one crowded residential development after another. And
when he wakes, he will have nothing. He will have lost the beauty he tried to
take by force.

And Pele? My sister has problems. But telling you this helps. I had to become human to really grasp the complex and consummate interdependence of life in all life's surprising mutabilities. From Ordinary Observers to Boltzmann Brains, we are transparent to Eros, the coupling constant—the depth of love. What a wonder to find this truth in words, to make something like beauty from truth, and know that what I've written here is not disembodied like my sorcery, or simply hungering for a body like the Hog God's insatiable lechery, but present through pages of text as you. My sister has problems, and among the fading and forgetting, the ever dying and the musing sorrow, I have you.

Writing is the most wondrous sorcery I've ever known. And I must tell Pele about it. But for now she's sulking. She wants to tear the white clouds out of the sky. She shakes the earth and seriously considers kicking a whole mountainside into the sea with a cancerous shriek, shoving a colossal tsunami over the Pig God's heaps of houses. She stamps and fumes. And if she could, she would char the whole earth black.

She was so much happier as a dog. ✸

Pele in Therapy

Darien Gee

Inspired by the Legend of Pele's Exile

There are variations to the story of how Pele, the Hawaiian goddess of volcanoes, came to Hawai'i, but a common one holds that she was exiled from Tahiti by her parents, who were concerned about Pele's ongoing battles with her older sister, the water goddess Namaka o Kaha'i, whose husband Pele had seduced. Pele fled in a canoe with some of her siblings, including her little sister Hi'iaka, whom she carried in her armpit in egg form. They were pursued relentlessly by Namaka o Kaha'i, and on the island of Maui, Pele's body was torn apart. Her spirit flew to the island of Hawai'i where she took up residence at the summit of Kīlauea, in the Halema'uma'u Crater. Contemporary folklore talks of Pele's ability to change her form, and sightings of Pele as a beautiful young woman, an old hag, or a white dog abound, usually before a lava flow and as a test of people's goodness and values.

Even today, Pele is a goddess who is alive and well. She's not a bedtime story of the past, but very much in our present. Every day on the island of Hawai'i, we see evidence of her and her ability to transform the land on which we walk. "Pele in Therapy" is a loose translation of Pele's exile to Hawai'i and her own awakening that occurs as a result. I entwined several Pele myths, both classical and contemporary, to create a modern view of the goddess. While I am loath to say that any deity would be in need of therapy, it is not inconceivable that the opportunity to "vent" might be welcome, especially when you consider that this particular goddess reigns over an active volcano.

MY TEN O'CLOCK APPOINTMENT IS LATE. I'M SITTING IN THE LIVING ROOM OF THE SMALL CONDO I'M RENTING, WAITING FOR A CLIENT WHO PROBABLY WON'T SHOW. I KNOW THIS BECAUSE IT'S ALMOST two o'clock.

But still I'm dressed and waiting, a fresh pad of paper and two glasses of water in front of me. I'm dressed and waiting because I have nothing else to do, and because I am pathetically desperate. I have been on this island for three months and have managed to burn through what little savings I have. I'll take any client I can get.

I glance at the calendar and realize that three months ago to this day I was sitting in a suite at a hotel on the Kohala coast with my husband, David.

We were on a second honeymoon because we didn't really have a first—no time, no money—and before we knew it twenty-five years had passed. David surprised me with a trip to Hawai'i, but that wasn't all. On the night we were scheduled to catch the red-eye back to Seattle, he told me he was having an affair with his secretary and would be leaving me once we got home.

That was certainly a night to remember.

David flew home and I barricaded myself in the hotel room with my suitcases. The bellhop thought I'd gone insane. Once I was alone, I opened everything I had so carefully and laboriously packed, upending everything. I swam among bags of Kona coffee and vacuum-packed macadamia nuts; I buried myself in tie-dyed sarongs. I scooped white honey out of the jar. Dashboard hula girls and dolphin key chains littered the floor. The pīkake-scented soap set I'd bought for David's secretary was hurled off the balcony.

I stayed in the hotel four more days until David cancelled the credit card. Then I packed everything and came up the hill to Waimea.

The pounding on my front door startles me. It occurs to me that I should have developed a way of screening people before they show up for an appointment—I imagine myself cut into small pieces with no identifying body parts. Nobody will know who I am or what has happened to me. I haven't made a single friend since I moved here; I realize now how alone I really am. The pounding continues and all I can feel is dread.

When I open the door, I see that it's my landlady, Mrs. Fukumoto. She's Hawaiian but her fifth husband was Japanese-Hawaiian. She looks about eighty, a bit crusty and with an annoyed, disapproving look on her face. A lit cigarette dangles from the side of her mouth. Next to her is a little white dog, an annoying yapper that starts barking the minute it sees me.

"You're behind on rent." Mrs. Fukumoto jabs a gnarly finger into my chest, poking me so hard it actually hurts. Ash falls from her cigarette onto the carpet.

"I know. I'm sorry, I should have the money soon." I have to look at my feet when I say this.

Mrs. Fukumoto cranes her head to look inside my condo. She lives in the adjoining unit and constantly boasts about how much property she owns on the island.

She glares at me. "What are all those boxes?"

My cramped, 900-square-foot living area is overrun with boxes stacked up to the ceiling. David shipped all of my things to me via slow boat, which means that after two months at sea they finally arrived just the other day. That was the one blessing about not having children—it made the division of assets much easier. The only thing left is the house, which my lawyer says will be split right down the middle when and if it ever sells. We'll fight for alimony, too, but until we go to court, I'm on my own. I can't afford a storage unit, so here we are.

"They're just some old things," I say. I can't even begin to think of what's inside. I haven't opened any of them, my name scrawled across each box like an afterthought.

"You should just take them all to the dump," Mrs. Fukumoto says with a smirk. Her dog yaps in agreement. The cigarette has completely burned out, but it seems to be permanently stuck to her bottom lip.

The idea of hauling everything to the transfer station and adding it to the island's growing landfill holds little appeal for me. What's left of my life is in those boxes, I want to say, but instead I keep my mouth shut.

I see an odd-looking man hovering tentatively by my sign. Mrs. Fukumoto frowns. "Too many visitors," she snaps. By the way the man is squinting at me, I have a sinking feeling that he's my ten o'clock, four and a half hours late. Not a good sign.

"Mrs. Fukumoto, I told you: I'm a trained therapist. I see clients in my home." I do my best to sound like the professional I'm clearly not. That's the problem with starting a career mid-life: I'm clueless. I don't have the business background or life experience necessary to build a successful practice—I just have a license to see patients and dispense advice and not much more. It's one thing to study psychology in college and grad school and another thing entirely to attempt practicing it twenty years later.

"I don't want any crazies around here," Mrs. Fukumoto says loudly. The man looks understandably nervous, his eyes flickering between the two of us. "You know what you need? Better marketing. You need a hook, get good customers in. Forget these nut jobs." She thumbs my client's direction and throws him a surly look.

As desperate as I am, I am not about to take marketing advice from my landlady.

"Um…"

"That reminds me," she says abruptly. "Can you watch my dog?"

"What?" I look down at the mangy white dog at my feet, baring its teeth.

"I have to go out of town tomorrow for a few days. And I'm almost out of dog food so you'll have to get some from the store. Take it out of what you owe me."

"Mrs. Fukumoto…"

Her eyes narrow and I find myself saying, "Fine. All right." I just want her to leave before I lose this client.

"Keep a dish filled with the water in the bottle on the counter. It's special."

"Yes, yes."

"Food four times a day. Small meals."

"Four times a day. Small meals. Got it." I clench my teeth, willing her to go.

Mrs. Fukumoto nods, apparently satisfied, and heads back to her place. Her dog follows her and glances back at me with a look that says he'd eat me if he were big enough.

I beckon the client into my home. He stares at the boxes in horror and then at the stuffing coming out from the couch, the mildew on the wallpaper. It takes me less than a minute to see he has OCD—obsessive-compulsive disorder. He's a neat freak. I don't expect our session to last long.

It doesn't.

The next day I decide Mrs. Fukumoto is right. I do need a hook—a catchphrase that will draw people in. And, while I'm at it, I'd like to find a way to get the men to self-select out. I've already had two ask me out, which is inappropriate and a little creepy. I get the feeling that they're less interested in self-improvement and more concerned with having someone to go barhopping with in Kona on Saturday nights.

At Ace Ben Franklin, I wander the aisles. I spend the last of my savings and buy two folding screens, some needle and thread, and a container of Clorox wipes. I add a packet of red adhesive letters. On the way home I stop by the gas station and pick up a spam musubi for lunch and some dog food.

Mrs. Fukumoto was gone this morning, her rusty Toyota no longer in the carport. I filled the dog food bowl and poured water from the gin bottle on the counter but the dog was nowhere to be seen. It's my secret wish that she took the dog with her and forgot to tell me.

Now, as I step inside her place once more, I see that both the food bowl and the water bowl are empty. I replenish them, whistling for the dog, hoping it doesn't come. It doesn't. I can only hope we continue to avoid each other until Mrs. Fukumoto comes home.

Once inside my condo I push the boxes to one side and hide them behind the folding screens. I take the needle and thread and fix the couch as best I can. I wipe down the walls. Then I go outside and stare at my sign.

KATHERINE O'DELL, MFT. WALK-INS WELCOME.

After a moment's hesitation, I use the adhesive letters to add: "Discover the Goddess Within!"

I know, I know. But since I've lived here I've noticed that people tend to be into this New Age sort of thing. And it turns out that this town is already full of psychotherapists, not to mention real estate agents, so unless I want to call David and demand that he advance me some money, I need to find a way to differentiate myself.

Already, drivers and passersby are starting to turn their heads to read the sign. I feel my cheeks redden as I hurry back into the condo, near tears that I've had to sink this low. I'm forty-six and from their assisted-living facility in Boca Raton my parents cajole me to reconcile with David, a thought that enters my consciousness when I'm at the lowest of lows.

So he cheated. Is that really a deal breaker? I can overlook this unfortunate incident in exchange for a lifestyle of companionship and security. Independence is overrated. Besides, the affair has only been going on for two years, a little less if you take out the days we were in Hawai'i and the other time we visited my parents for Easter. I never really asked David to take me back but maybe I should? Maybe it's time to face reality.

There's a knock on the door.

I seriously consider escaping through the kitchen window. That's what I want to do—run. Hide. But to where? I'm already on an island in the middle of the Pacific. Where else could I possibly go? This thought fills me with despair.

When I open the door, there's a striking young woman on my doorstep, her dark hair pulled away from her face. She's wearing a sundress, but you can see the outline of her body through the thin fabric. Her figure is so perfect that I can't stop staring. I have a weakness for dessert, for chocolate in particular, and I know I've let my body go. Normally I wouldn't care, but being in Hawai'i has made me envy youths with their flat stomachs and perfect breasts. And their butts—they have no cellulite. I can't even remember life before cellulite.

The woman is muttering under her breath, twisting a loose strand of hair around a slender finger. I want to say she's in her twenties but I can't quite place her age.

"Can I help you?" I ask.

"I don't have an appointment." Her face is dark.

"That's fine. I happen to have an opening…"

"I'm having a bad day," she continues, forlorn. "I saw your sign outside. Find your inner goddess or something?"

"You mean 'Discover the Goddess Within'?"

"Close enough." She steps into the condo before I have a chance to invite her in.

I offer her water or tea but she shakes her head. We settle in the living room, which is more spacious and comfortable with the small changes I've made. The woman's forehead is puckered in a frown.

"My love life," she says. "It's on the rocks."

"I see." I nod and clear my throat. "I should mention that there's a ten percent discount if you pay for your session in cash…"

She ignores me. "I think he's in love with someone else." She lets out a heavy sigh and the whole room seems to sigh with her. "He saw me in a moment when I didn't look like this…" She gestures to her body, her perfectly made-up self. "…And he fled."

She now has my full attention. Men!, I want to spit out, but instead I nod sympathetically. "I understand." I can't imagine how difficult it must be to always look so beautiful. People start to expect it, and the minute you have a bad hair day, their illusions are shattered. I pick up my notebook in an attempt to look like I'm doing something. I write the day's date, the time, and realize I don't even know her name.

"I'm Katherine," I say. "And you are…?"

"I am sick and tired of everyone assuming that I don't want love!" The look on her face is explosive. She stands up, begins pacing, her red dress swirling around her. "I don't have time to be frivolous like everyone else. I have my own life, my own responsibilities. I do more than all of them!"

"Them? Who's them?"

"My sisters. Their responsibilities are nothing like mine. I have to do so much more." She tosses her head in defiance.

I nod in what I hope is a reassuring manner. "How many sisters do you have?" I ask. It's important to get the family history; it's elemental to who we are. At the end of the day, that's where most of our issues lie.

"Seven. Seven sisters and seven brothers."

I can already see where this is going. The young woman in front of me is fiercely competitive and independent. Definitely not a firstborn or the oldest girl—this one's always had to fight for her place.

I write down "Big Family" on my notepad. Then I ask, "Are you originally from Hawai'i?"

She flops back down on the couch. "No. I came here some years ago. I didn't plan on being here exactly." She looks away and I can tell she doesn't want to talk about it yet.

"A lot of people seem to have that experience," I say. Myself included.

"I'm not everyone else!" she retorts.

"No, of course not," I reassure her hastily. I add "Middle Child" to my notes followed by a question mark. "Why don't you tell me more about what's happening in your love life? You said it's on the rocks?"

"I've never been great with relationships," she admits. She tucks her legs underneath her. "It's one reason my older sister and I don't get along. She was very angry at me for seducing her husband." She rolls her eyes derisively.

I try to hide my shock but she notices my discomfort immediately.

"What?" She arches a perfectly plucked eyebrow. "It's not as if we can control whom we love. Or desire." Here she gives a slight smile but it completely rubs me the wrong way. It reminds me of David. He said the same thing to me that night when he told me about Janine, his secretary.

It takes all my willpower to remember that I am here to help, not judge her. She's my client—there's no room for my personal opinion even if I find myself siding somewhat with her sister. "So, have you ever been married?"

She nods indifferently. "It didn't work out."

I write "Commitment Issues" and tap my pen, thinking. "Did you try marriage counseling?"

At this she bursts out laughing and her face lights up. Even I can't help but chuckle. David wasn't interested in having couples therapy with his therapist wife. The question even sounds asinine coming from my mouth.

"Have you ever been to the volcano?" she asks me suddenly. "Kīlauea?"

I nod. "Once. But it was pouring rain and foggy. I didn't see a thing."

She nods, not surprised.

I shrug. "I'm more of a beach person anyway."

At this her eyes harden. "Beach?" she spits out. "Kīlauea is alive. Flowing! The most active volcano in the world!"

"Well, it's not like I didn't try to see it. My husband and I…" I stumble here, unsure if I should say ex-husband, since our divorce is far from final but our marriage is clearly over. "We were hoping to see the lava flow. Maybe catch a glimpse of Pele in the lava." The concierge at the hotel had told us that people sometimes saw the image of Pele, the Hawaiian goddess of the volcano.

Now her eyes seem to flash. "That's ridiculous!"

"What? Why?"

"Why would the goddess reveal herself to anyone?" she snorts. "She would have nothing to gain from that!"

"More tourists, maybe?" I venture.

The woman shakes her head in disgust. "Just because a child sees an animal in the clouds does not mean that animal is actually there," she says. "People see what they want to see."

I can see her point. "A goddess would probably have more important things to do with her time," I concede.

At this the woman grins. "Exactly." She reaches up behind her head and pulls out the bone clip holding her hair in place. Long, gorgeous locks tumble down her back, dark as lava rock. "I mean, if she needed to vent, for any reason, that would be different. But to pose for a photo-op? I don't think so."

I remember something else I heard. "Then again, there is Pele's curse."

"Which one?"

"I didn't know there was more than one," I say, surprised. "I just know about the one with the lava rocks. If you take a rock from the volcano as a souvenir, you'll have bad luck."

I can tell that she doesn't think much of this because she doesn't say anything, just casts her eyes around my condo, bored.

"I hear that every year the park rangers are flooded with several thousand pounds of rocks that are being returned to them," I continue. "People write letters explaining how they've had a run of bad luck and ask that the rocks be returned to their home. People sometimes make offerings of these rocks back to the goddess."

"Returning pōhaku that have been inappropriately taken in the first place is just putting something back," she retorts. "It's hardly an offering."

"You seem to know a lot about this," I say.

"I know about a lot of things," she says.

I glance at my watch. It's time for me to feed Mrs. Fukumoto's dog again, but I don't want to end our session. "Can you excuse me for a moment? I'll be right back."

Inside Mrs. Fukumoto's condo, the dog bowls are empty again but thankfully the dog is nowhere to be seen. I refill them quickly.

When I return to my living room, I find the woman trying to set fire to my two plants. Since one of them is plastic, she's got a good chance of succeeding.

"Don't do that!" I say, already imagining the conversation I'm going to have with Mrs. Fukumoto and the fire department. I don't have a fire extinguisher, much less property insurance. I try not to panic as I hold out an ashtray.

She tosses me an annoyed look before blowing into her palm. The flame flickers, then disappears. I place the empty ashtray on the side table and take a deep breath as I settle back into my chair. I jot "Pyromaniac" into my notebook. She's glaring at me but I don't care. I add "Destructive to Other People's Property" and "Unremorseful."

It's time to get this session back on track. I pull out a questionnaire I've printed from the Internet that helps pinpoint the specific goddess a person most closely resembles. I hand her the questionnaire and she skims it, guffawing along the way.

"It should only take you a few minutes," I say. "Just choose the answer that most closely matches you."

She ignores me. "Demeter, Aphrodite, Diana." Her voice is filled with disinterest. She perks up when she comes across the one Hawaiian goddess, the one we have already been talking about. "Pele as Creator," she reads, and starts giggling.

"And Destroyer," I append.

"It's the same thing," she tells me blithely. "It's all relative." Her hair fans out over her shoulders. "Well, I think I'm done." She stands and I'm struck by how tall she is. I didn't notice before but maybe that's because I'm still sitting down.

I get up and follow her to the door. "Are you sure?" She's in better spirits, but I don't feel like I've done much of anything.

She turns and gives me a serene look. "Oh, and I don't have any money to pay you. I'm afraid I don't really have much to do with that sort of thing."

Great. My first real client and she can't pay. "Barter?" I venture. I had one person pay me in bananas. It's better than nothing.

She laughs, her eyes crinkling in amusement. She rests her hand on the doorknob and thinks about this. "I don't barter," she finally says. "But I'll send you referrals. People who can pay."

I'm skeptical that she'll send anybody my way but you never know. It's my own fault for not discussing my fee up front—I'm going to have to work on that. "Well, okay. I appreciate that."

The woman smiles and leaves. As I close the door behind her, I jerk my hand away when it touches the metal knob. It's so hot it seems to be glowing.

Over the next few months my practice takes off. Women from all over the island are vying for any available time slot. I watch my bank account, and my confidence, grow. I start to lose weight. Not eating on a budget lets me make better choices and I start eating organic salads, fresh fruit, and sprouted bread from the health food store and farmers markets.

Mrs. Fukumoto does little more than grunt when she sees me, now that she's getting her rent money on time. She still disappears on random jaunts leaving me to care for her dog, which thankfully makes itself scarce the minute I step into her condo.

I am not entirely surprised to see David waiting by my door one evening. It's coming up on one year; our divorce is almost final. We haven't talked in a long time, everything going through our lawyers. I can hardly remember what transpired in the past—it all seems so long ago. I've been meaning to call him but somehow I never get around to it. And yet here he is.

"Hey." He steps forward gingerly and gives me a hug. He smells just like I remember, and I want to melt in his arms.

"Hi."

"Wow, you look great." His eyes wander up and down my body appraisingly. Then, embarrassed, he gestures to a stack of boxes in Mrs. Fukumoto's doorway. "I wasn't sure which place was yours. I brought over the last of your boxes. They were in the attic."

"Thanks." I'm flattered that he noticed me and I feel a blush warm my cheeks. "Would you like to come in?"

"Sure."

Inside, he tries not to look shocked at the boxes still stacked high behind the folding screens.

"I'll get to it eventually," I say with a shrug. "I've been busy with work." I casually open a bottle of wine, suddenly hoping that maybe we will have cause to celebrate. In some ways this couldn't be more perfect—I had to get away from David to find out who I am. Now, I can come to him not needing anything, just wanting what feels right, right now. I light a candle and blow out the match, a smile tugging on the corners of my mouth.

He accepts the wineglass easily. "It's great that you're doing so well," he says. He downs his wine in one gulp.

I'm having the strangest feeling of déjà vu. "You didn't come all this way just to give me my boxes, did you?" I ask.

Guilty, he shakes his head. I refill his glass and perch on the edge of the sofa, crossing my legs. They're tanned and nicely shaped from hours of Pilates. I see David's eyes linger on them hungrily.

"Let me guess: you have something to tell me."

He downs his second glass. He looks tormented and miserable, and I can't tell if I'm enjoying this or feeling a bit sorry for him. Both, I conclude. "I'm getting married. I mean, remarried," he corrects himself. "Once the divorce is final. Janine is pregnant."

I'm certain David was expecting a repeat performance of my dramatics last year. Even I'm surprised by how calm I am.

"Twins," he gulps, and I see that he's stunned by this development. David is a few years older than me, which means that he'll still be changing diapers when he's fifty. He'll be well into his sixties when his kids go off to college. Any hopes of an early retirement have just gone out the window. And I see that he knows this, too.

"Oh, Katherine," he says, and I open my arms and take him in.

The condo is on fire. David is sound asleep—he's always been a hard sleeper. I wrap a robe around me and cover my nose and mouth. I nudge him until he wakes up, his eyes quickly filling with alarm.

"Go!" I say, and point to the window. He stumbles out, half asleep, a sheet wrapped around his naked body.

In the living room, my boxes are on fire, flames licking the ceiling. The furniture, the folding screens, the plants. Everything is being consumed.

I glance around frantically, knowing that I can save one, maybe two boxes. There are my client notes, too. My identifying documents. I try to gather them quickly, the smoke already filling my lungs.

I hear David call my name, the siren of a fire truck. Then the unmistakable sound of a dog barking.

The fire is dancing on the curtains, the carpet. I touch the door and it's hot—the fire is in the hallway we share but it's the closest way into Mrs.

Fukumoto's condo. I drop to the ground, then throw open the door. The heat of the fire pushes me back and the dog is louder now, hysterically yapping.

It is so hot that my body feels aflame. I crawl across the hall, my robe catching fire. It falls off my body like ash and I am naked, my skin on fire. I fling open the front door of Mrs. Fukumoto's unit. The dog races out and into my arms, and we tumble down the stairway. I feel a lick on my face, a tickle of fur. The last thing I see is someone standing over me before I black out.

—————

My ten o'clock appointment is late. I find this extremely inconvenient as I'm seeing very few patients under the circumstances. I could have easily filled this slot with another client.

The fire started in my living room and in Mrs. Fukumoto's bedroom. A fallen candle, a burning cigarette. Together we started the fire that burned down the place in which we lived and everything inside. I wish I could say that I escaped with the clothes on my back but even that would not be true. I escaped with nothing.

When I awoke I was in the ambulance. When I asked about the dog, they told me there was none. I fell to the bottom of the stairs with nothing in my arms. Mrs. Fukumoto, too, it appears, is missing.

Burns cover fifteen percent of my body but they are second-degree burns. Almost all are expected to heal. The scabs will fall off as the new skin comes in.

David stayed with me for a couple of days before I told him to go back to Seattle. It's true, I realize: we can't control whom we love. I love him, pure and simple, but I no longer want him in my life.

After I was discharged from the hospital, I came straight to the hotel. I ended up in the same suite I shared with David a year ago, but instead of looking at the ocean, I find myself casting my eyes toward the mountains instead. I'll stay here for a couple of weeks, a gift to myself, before I start looking for a new home in Waimea.

There is a knock on the door.

"I don't have an appointment," she says, unapologetic.

I smile and step aside, and let her in. ❀

Luahinepiʻi: Ka Wahine Piʻina

Wayne Moniz

Inspired by the Legend of the White Lady of ʻĪao Valley

ʻĪao Valley has figured in both myth and history as one of Maui's sacred spots. The mystical locale seems right for dealing with death and spirits that live on. Moderns call them ghosts. And it was here that the mention of a White Lady originated. Who was this White Lady haunting ʻĪao Valley? It would be hard to find an established Mauian who knows more than the fact that there is a white lady. The thought looms in one's imagination if, like me, you've roamed the valley on a moonless night. Shadows, rustling leaves, splashes of the stream, whistling of the wind down the canyon, and its history of burial and death all rouse paranormal images.

I decided to develop the myth because it only existed as a one-liner: "There's a white lady that haunts the valley." I wanted to know who this white lady was and if she was merely a silly prefabrication. If there was a white lady, where did she live, how did she die, what caused her presence, and why does she haunt? I returned to all the sources I've used over the years and, finally, I came across one paragraph in *Sterling's Sites of Maui* (an out-of-print treasure trove of Maui culture and history). These few sentences dealt with a woman called Luahinepiʻi, her suicide, and—a first—a somewhat cryptic chant about calling out one's name while having sex. With nothing other than that, I had to connect all the dots. It was my calling to put the whole story together. The result was this, my version of the white lady story.

It was all part of the ritual among the boys. They had been at it for years. The object was simple: scare the hell out of the girls! Suspension of disbelief is essential to horror fantasies, and the boys knew that the girls were as good as acting frightened as the boys were in playing evil maniacs who could jump out of bushes and chase the fair maidens for yards.

The guys had honed in on their paranormal mischief from their weekly Sunday attendance at the King Theater that featured cheesy B horror movies from American International in black and white. Of course, the girls were victims of psychotic maniacs so often that they would have felt disappointed if they hadn't been targets of an elaborate hoax the next week.

The *modus operandi* to scare the girls was, for the boys, to alternate the responsibilities of "Monster of the Week" to keep the girls thinking. The object was also to rotate the locations of the encounters. At this time, in the early '60s, Maui was still quite rural. There were so many spooky sites to perform these mini-productions—valleys, beaches, and forests still untouched by coming developments.

Tonight was Leslie's chance. First, there was the alibi as to why he wouldn't make it to the big St. Anthony–Baldwin High game: his grandmother was sick. Agnes and Bill were out of town and Leslie had to take care of his ailing Nana. The girls were already suspicious of his excuse, made earlier that day, as they waved their pompoms on what would again be a lopsided victory. For one thing, Leslie's Nana had died twenty-five years earlier. Second, Aggie and Bill had been seen by one of the girls buying poke at Nagasako Fish Market that very morning.

The White Lady story had been passed down from earlier generations. She was said to have appeared in ʻĪao and Waiheʻe Valleys as well as along the road to Hāna. No one could pinpoint the rationale behind her appearances. Was she Pele? But Pele wore red and did not appear in the folklore of these Maui locations.

Even Old Man Costa, who had lived in ʻĪao Valley when it was a series of taro patches, claims to have talked to The White Lady. He professed to have seen her in the midst of the kukui forest drying her gossamer-like dresses. He said that she was not Hawaiian, but, true to her moniker, white! His wife claimed that he had been heavily drinking ʻōkolehao during that period and that the mystery woman was probably a pre-hippy who was living off the fertile land above Wailuku.

Tonight, Leslie would be part of the White Lady performance. He had snatched from the school's moldy costume room a stringy white wig that had been used by the witch in a past Spring Festival production of *Hansel and Gretel*. Even Leslie's sister, Blanche, had got in on the act by sewing a flowing lavalava and kīhei to fit his boyish body.

Luckily, he had kept a stash of greases and paints from past Halloweens. He would apply them to his entire body to make sure there was no doubt that this was, indeed, The White Lady. The homecoming game would probably be out by nine. The gang would first head over to Shirley's for some burgers and cokes. Then, one of the boys, as credibly as he could, would suggest, "Hey, let's go up ʻĪao Valley tonight."

One of the girls protested that there was no moon and that it would be dangerous running through the valley on the darkest of nights. After all, some-one could get hurt. After a few clucking sounds by the boys attributed to her lack of guts, the play-along girls reinitiated their bravado and agreed to the great adventure. In their minds, however, was the demand, "This better be a damn good show!"

At about halftime, Leslie packed his Valiant with his wardrobe, makeup, and the plywood ax he'd made in Cub Scouts and headed up the valley. He would change and apply the makeup and eventually find a good hiding place down by the stream, where he knew the girls would be taken. He would let the "victims" pass him and then "terrorize" them. With no outlet, they would run off the beaten path deeper into the inky forest.

The valley was quiet as death when Leslie arrived. He parked his car down in Kepaniwai Park, hidden so the girls wouldn't see it. The guest monster then walked up the winding road toward the Needle, a 1,200-foot phalanx that protruded from the now extinct volcano. Leslie knew that the Needle and caldera were more than geographical phenomena. They were steeped in legend in the stories of the Valley Isle. The Needle was Puʻuokamoa, the merman, who fell in love with ʻĪao, daughter of Māui and Hina, when they lived in the sacred place.

ʻĪao had been forbidden by her father to continue her love affair with the man who lived in the stream that cut through land. She ignored her father, and when he caught her he asked if she wanted to see Puʻuokamoa forever. She agreed, and her father transformed Puʻuokamoa into rock, the Needle that ʻĪao, sadly, had agreed to see forever.

He also knew that this was the valley Hiʻiaka had visited on her way to fetch Lohiaʻu for her sister, Pele. The aliʻi nui of the valley was an insensitive ogre who refused to meet with Hiʻiaka, much less share aloha with food and lodging. In retaliation, she flung the king's body all the way to Waiheʻe, his bones imbedded into the cliffsides of that valley.

But Leslie doubted the White Lady story. He presumed it had been concocted by fathers and grandfathers and kept alive for years, perhaps to keep truant boys from late-night adventures. Still, as Leslie squatted in the bushes, uneasiness came over him. Perhaps it was the dead silence. Perhaps it was the wind that occasionally rattled the leaves. Perhaps it was the sudden, arrhythmic splash in the stream. He thought he heard chanting in the distance from Camp Dole, burned down by some anti-Hawaiians after Liliʻuokalani had visited there.

He looked in that direction. His mind stopped the chanting. All he could see in the distance were the lights of Wailuku peeking through the gap in the valley. Then in back of him he heard a voice—a voice that sounded like it came from a cracked record played at the wrong speed. He couldn't believe what he saw. A woman in white made her way up the path—perhaps a joke by one of the other boys? Leslie wondered. Months later, remembering a few key words, he'd find out from his old Hawaiian uncle the meaning of what she kept repeating: *Ua lohe ʻia ka leo kapu e ke ipo i moealoha.*

His heart beat like a pounding pahu. She was headed his way. Like any normal human being, he ran like hell up the steep embankment, looking back every few steps to notice that he was not shaking her away.

A protruding guava branch snagged Leslie's silly witch wig, and he ran hairless into the night. The lavalava started to slip, exposing his BVDs. The malo dropped to his ankles. He lost his balance up the incline and tripped. He rolled downhill onto some large boulders that bordered the stream just under the long bridge that traversed it. He passed out.

Water dripped onto his face. Leslie could hear the placid stream again. He was relieved that he was among the living. Or, so he thought. He looked straight ahead and felt secure that he had survived that silly fall caused by his over-imagination about a white lady and all that jazz…

"You made fun of me."

He turned suddenly to find that his nightmare was not over. There, seated on a boulder, was The White Lady. She repeated the complaint: "You made fun of me."

"I'm sorry," Leslie replied, confused. "I … I thought you were just made up."

She responded with her gravel voice.

"Just because you don't know history doesn't mean I never existed. Those who are alive foolishly believe that things only exist within their short passage through this life."

Although he was repulsed by her atrocious voice, he finally noticed, with the clearing of his head, that she was extremely beautiful, not like the old-hag ghosts from the movies. Curious, he asked her for a name.

"My name is Luahinepi'i."

His knowledge of Hawaiian, limited to short phrases and foods, was of no help.

"What does it mean?

"It means 'old woman.'"

He was confused. She was young and beautiful. Perhaps it had to do with her harsh voice.

"To dispel your ignorance, I will share with you what very few know—my story."

As she said this, Leslie became more aware of the sounds of the stream that split the valley at the point where the rickety wooden bridge spanned it. The sounds began to lull him and, like a liquid mantra, cast him into a hypnotic state. He leaned his head against a boulder and fell into a coma.

A sound of a baby crying woke him. He was no longer in 'Īao. He was in a pili-grass hut. A woman reposed on layers of leaf and kapa holding the crying baby at her breast. A male hovered over her, concerned.

"Where am I?" asked Leslie.

No one responded, perhaps busy with the concern of birth at hand. He tried the question again. They acted as if he wasn't there. He moved to the puka and looked out. He recognized it as Paukūkalo; his Aunty Mary had a house makai of the road. But there were no wooden houses, just a series of grass huts. He had gone back in time.

The baby cried again, the voice agitated, like ʻiliʻili rolling at the ocean's edge. The parents gave looks of concern. "Waʻu, waʻu!" they repeated over and over again. Although he was not fluent in Hawaiian, he understood every word. "Grating, grating!" It was said of something being scraped. Leslie moved in closer to the child, now aware that, despite his closeness to the couple, they were oblivious to their visitor from the future. He looked at the child—a beautiful girl.

The parents wrapped the child in kapa and headed for the heiau for her blessing. As Leslie left the hut to follow them, he noticed something strange. The clouds zipped by, the sun and moon alternating in the heavens like a movie scene where time passes.

A young girl in her teens raced toward the hut. Leslie recognized her eyes as those of the crying baby. Her eyes were still filled with tears. Behind her followed girls of her age taunting her with epithets: "Coconut-shredding ʻopihi! Lava scraper! Clawing boar!"

Her father, hearing the slurs, rushed to the hale puka and yelled at them, "Hele ma kahi ʻē!" The teens scattered. Luahinepiʻi rushed into her father's arms. From their conversation, Leslie found out that this was not the first time cruelty had been hurled at his daughter. Her father assured her that she was beautiful and the girls were simply jealous so they had to make fun of her voice.

He only wished that her mother were still alive to give her the comfort that only a mother can give. He emphasized that her voice was akua-given and that she should accept the fate the gods had given her. But her father's consolation could not erase the hurt she felt. Her depression was somewhat relieved by long walks up from the mouth of the stream deep into the forests of ʻĪao Valley.

Leslie followed her on some of these walks. No one doubted the therapeutic benefits of such hikes on most human beings. The tranquility of the ʻāina would have soothed the souls of the normally troubled. But Luahinepiʻi's sojourns seemed to aggravate her hurt. The valley, as all natives knew, was more often cloudy than sunny, so the sable clouds further scarred her state of sadness.

Suddenly, Luahinepiʻi's life took a change for the better. Someone new moved into Paukūkalo. His name was Manaʻolaula, a Hilo boy whose mother had returned to her home village by the sea after his father had drowned on a fishing trip. She had noticed him at a hukilau one night, surrounded by young girls who were drawn to his charm and looks. Now she noticed his rippling muscles as he tugged at the net. He glanced at her with his ebony eyes but she shook it off. He might be initially interested in her but all would end when he heard her voice.

A week passed. One day, Luahinepiʻi went mountainside to pick lauaʻe. As she passed a pond, she noticed a naked body dash from the water to a nearby clump of mountain apple trees. A malo was grabbed from a branch of the kamani tree that shaded the pool; ebony eyes peeked from behind the grove, laughing.

"Sorry. I didn't know anyone else was around."

It was Manaʻolaula. Luahinepiʻi was pleasantly surprised at the chance visit. She giggled shyly.

"And you are Luahinepiʻi," he pronounced.

"How do you know my name?"

"Paukūkalo village is as small as Hilo."

"I must go."

She gathered up the lauaʻe and turned.

"Don't go!"

"I have to. I must prepare tonight's meal," she insisted.

"The sun has only a short time ago passed toward afternoon. There is plenty time to prepare for only two of you."

"How do…?" She halted mid-sentence, aware of the intimacy of a village.

"Come sit on these rocks while I continue my interrupted swim. Or, are you up for a swim, too?"

"Single men usually don't swim with women," she insisted.

"When no one is around, there is no one to accuse," he retorted. And in one movement, Manaʻolaula tore off the malo and dove into the placid pool.

"Come on, Luahinepiʻi. I'll turn the other way."

His twelve-hand-spanned frame turned away, the young woman paying attention to the detail of running droplets of water glistening as they flowed down his back. Leslie felt uncomfortable watching, but became immediately aware of the blossoming love of the two.

Luahinepiʻi slid into the pond.

Days went by; meetings were discreet. But Manaʻolaula never spoke of the raspy voice of Luahinepiʻi. She became more and more puzzled about it. Other boys her age had been as insensitive as the jealousies of the gossipy girls. Attracted first by her beauty, they coiled repulsively at her first pronouncement. She waited for a day to bring up the question. He invited her to walk along the sand dunes of lower Waiehu. Leslie followed the couple and listened in.

The trades were blowing softly and Haleakalā stood clear in the distance. She had brought along some kūlolo to nibble at and found a flat area above the dunes for sitting. After some talk of the beauty of the area, Luahinepiʻi asked the big question.

"Manaʻolaula?"

"Yes?"

"I'm curious. You haven't mentioned anything about my voice. I was wondering why?"

"I had a very wise father."

"I'm sorry. I heard that he died while fishing."

"A rogue wave suddenly came out of nowhere and overturned the canoe. The outrigger hit his head and he began to sink. When his fishing friend pulled him up, it was already too late. His breath had left him."

"I'm sorry."

"We cannot undo what has been done. That's one important thing I learned from his advice and his death. Now you know why I have not reacted to your voice. Oh, I'm not crazy; I hear the same voice as others hear. But the gods, not you or your father or your mother, caused this. The only thing we can do about our flaws is to accept them."

"I understand. I wish others would."

"Lack of understanding is their flaw. They will just have to face it in the future. But there's more than that flaw, Luahinepiʻi. The rest of you is so full of love and kindness. And your beauty... You're fairer than the lokelani. What more is there?"

Luahinepiʻi blushed naturally. She almost couldn't believe what she heard. Everything said about her voice had been negative. Even if it were true, doubts haunted her. It would be hard just to forget all the negativity in one day while perched on a bluff watching the rain clouds skip over Pāʻia.

Unfortunately, Manaʻolaula's tutu wahine, aged ninety-five, was coming to the end of her life. Her husband and sons were long gone and so the responsibility fell to the eldest grandson. Manaʻolaula set sail to Hilo to take care of her in her final days.

When he told Luahinepiʻi, she immediately fell into a gloom. Without him, she felt vulnerable and subject to the taunting of vicious girls. Days passed and Manaʻolaula's grandmother continued to hold on physically. Her days in the loʻi had made her strong in body despite her increasing confusion. The wicked gossips of Paukūkalo took advantage of the situation to begin rumors that Manaʻolaula had not only returned to Hilo but to his former lover as well.

Luahinepiʻi, separated from her lover by the ocean, conjured up images of betrayal in spite of the fact that she knew they were fabrications of jealous women. Leslie felt her hurt. From that day on, Luahinepiʻi would only wear white as a sign of waiting for her lover to return.

Two full moons came and went. Luahinepiʻi fell into a darker time. She didn't know whom to believe. One of the destroyers of reputation, Hoʻolapa, returned from Hilo. A fellow member of Luahinepiʻiʻs hula troupe, she felt wickedly obliged to set Luahinepiʻi straight.

Leslie watched from the window.

"Luahinepiʻi!" Hoʻolapa called from outside the sad one's hale.

Luahinepiʻi came to the puka. Noting Hoʻolapa as one of the village's uncontrolled tongues, she snapped back, "What do you want?"

"I've just returned from Hilo with news of Manaʻolaula."

"It can't be good news, coming from your mouth," she muttered.

"I just wanted you to know so you wouldn't be hurt."

Luahinepiʻi ground her teeth at the statement. "Ignorant of all the previous hurt," she said to herself, "you crab." Then out loud, "Well, let's get straight to the point. What did you see him do?"

"It's not only what I saw; it's also what I heard."

"Heard?"

"He's been seen around Hilo with a woman of his age. Some say she is as beautiful as the rainbows above the Wailuku River. I didn't want to leap to a conclusion. After all, she could be a cousin. But one night, a few of us girls were returning from a day at the beach. The moon was already up and we were in an especially good mood, having met a man with some strong ʻōkolehau. As we approached Manaʻolaulaʻs compound, we heard sounds of lovemaking coming from the hale. How he could do that there—with his tutu wahine fading away in another area—disturbed us."

Luahinepiʻi kept repeating in her mind over and over as the story unfolded, "Liar, liar. Manaʻolaula loves me!"

"But that's not all," Hoʻolapa continued. Luahinepiʻiʻs heart sank.

"He accidentally called out your name in the act of love."

The gossip then started to leave, but turned. "I thought it best that you know that he is not a true lover. It's best to know before you get hurt." She turned and walked away.

"Before you get hurt? What about getting hurt now?" the young girl cried out.

Hopelessness shadowed her mind. Unstoppable tears flowed. Luahinepiʻi raced from the hale and up along the path into ʻĪao Valley. She ran and collapsed on the dirt trail. The girl with the gravelly voice picked herself up and continued on, talking to herself, letting the sordid scene play over and over again. She spiraled downward in her misery. Clouds initially dropped small tears from the heavens to commiserate with her. Then, blackened billows began to gather up beyond Puʻuokamoa.

Now it was pouring heavily, but the depressed woman was oblivious. She pressed on, slipping occasionally into puddles that were forming. Small streams spilled off the cliffsides onto the path. Finally, Luahinepiʻi spotted the place that would end her misery. It was a steep climb up to the ledge that would take her out of suffering.

Lightning flashed in the distance. In her mind, the gods were telling her this was the right decision. She clawed her way higher and higher, slipping occasionally, slamming her knees against the cruel rocks. She groped at lava shards that sliced her palms, blood commingling with rainwater that poured from the precipices above. She was oblivious to these pains; they were minor compared to the larger dolor that ripped at her heart.

When Luahinepi'i reached the top of the ledge, everything stopped. She gazed up and down the weeping valley. Exhausted, she faced the thought that she would soon be home. She would be with her mother and ancestors. As the rain resumed, Luahinepi'i raised her arms to the heavens and leaped; her body hurtled several hundred feet down onto a canopy of quivering kukui leaves and then onto the boulders alongside the 'Iao Stream.

A trickle of water flowed down Leslie's face.

"Leslie?" The teen opened his eyes to the woman standing over him. "Are you good? I know that not everyone gets to relive another's life. But, perhaps, you will understand more than others." She retreated back down toward the stream from which she came.

"Luahinepi'i?" he called out after her.

"Yes?"

"Like ghosts, you have to tell me why you continue to be here."

"Ghost? I am not a ghost. I do not haunt. I do not scare. I am just a sad woman who waits for her lover to come back from Hilo. When Mana'olaula returns, he will tell me the truth; then we will live happily together." ✸

LESSONS LEARNED

IF YOU GOOGLEEARTH 1118 BISHOP STREET
J. Freen

**INSPIRED BY THE LEGEND OF OʻAHU NUI, THE CANNIBAL KING,
AND HIS COMEUPPANCE**

OʻAhu Nui was a Hawaiian aliʻi who lived a long time ago in central OʻAhu. A bunch of newly arrived Tahitians, known as Lō ʻAi Kanaka, move into OʻAhu Nui's neighborhood after being thrown out of nearby Waialua due to their cannibalistic habits. The ʻAi Kanaka, hoping to get on OʻAhu Nui's good side, invite him to dinner and serve him up some human fare. Over the space of a few months, OʻAhu Nui develops a taste for people. The problem is that OʻAhu Nui's subjects are not dumb—they notice when Uncle goes out to collect hīhīwai in the stream and never comes back. Everybody knows the ʻAi Kanaka M.O. by now, and OʻAhu Nui's priests put pressure on him to cease visiting the cannibals, stop eating humans, and generally behave himself.

OʻAhu Nui tries, but the lure of human flesh is too great. He decides to eat his sister Kilikili's two young sons. He sends Kilikili's husband on a fake errand, has his retainers kill the two kids, and eats them for dinner. Kilikili's husband returns, sees what happened, and kills OʻAhu Nui and Kilikili, who, along with anyone else who aided in the killing and consuming of the two boys, are turned to stone by the angry gods. The unusual-looking rocks are still there, of course, in an all but forgotten location near Wahiawā.

Who could resist writing a story about cannibals?

❀ ❀ ❀

TRY GOOGLEEARTH 1118 BISHOP STREET, HONOLULU, HAWAIʻI. TAKE OFF FROM ABOVE THE MAINLAND, CROSS THE PACIFIC IN A SECOND OR TWO—MAKES YOU KIND OF DIZZY THE FIRST TIME. BEFORE YOU know it you're above the harbor, coming in, coming in, mouse in hand—hold it—hovering above the office tower on the corner of Beretania and Bishop, at the gateway to the city's financial and legal district. Lots of stuff goes on here, interesting stuff, but to find out you need to climb out of your computer screen, put on some clothes, some shoes, and hit the street for real.

It's a toasty January morning in the city. You feel the sun on your face. You are standing on the corner, looking up at the steel and glass tower. In front of you is a short, dark-haired fellow dressed in a bland aloha shirt and neatly pressed slacks—the uniform of the local businessman. His name is Case Izumi. Follow him. He won't notice you because, actually, you're still back home, staring at the screen, dressed only in your underpants. I was just kidding about making you do anything realworld today.

His finger is on the button for floor number 21 and up we go. Suite 2110 is to his right, the door with the tasteful sign that reads: Alvin Alakawa, Attorney at Law. Push the door open, and the warm and pleasing face of the receptionist greets the visitor.

Her name is Kilikili, which means "fine misty rain" in Hawaiian. The kind of rain that often fills Nuʻuanu, the big valley behind downtown, in the morning and evening of a day like today. Kilikili's last name is Pulena, a famous name in Hawaiʻi, the family name of a long line of kings and nobles. She is proud of this but more proud, truth be told, of her two sons, Kai and Kawika, aged six and seven—kids she has raised as a single mom ever since their dad took off and left her to fend for herself, which she did, landing a job with big-time attorney and politician Al Alakawa. For six long years now she has been Al's factotum, a fancy Latin word that means slave treated like dirt.

She smiles at the visitor, who she takes for yet another local Japanese businessman here to beg her boss for something because her boss is not just a lawyer, but a Senator, too. In a small state like this one, with a legislature that's in session for just three months, politicians wear several hats, rain or shine.

Kili's smile is so genuine that the visitor is taken aback, accustomed to almost everything being faked. Plus, he knows that Al Alakawa is one of the biggest assholes in this small pond.

"He's been expecting you," the charming Kili says, opening the inner door to the boss's immaculate office.

"Great," he says, catching a whiff of perfume as he passes. How does such a prick keep such a terrific employee, he wonders, taking hold of Alakawa's sweaty brown paw. Earth to Izumi, Earth to Izumi: employee has two kids and rent to pay, you jerk!

"Mister, uh, Izumi, right? Have a seat, have a seat."

"Thanks for finding the time, Senator. I know how busy you folks are right now."

"Yeah, got a vote on the floor at ten."

"Good thing you work just walking distance from the Capitol."

"Walk? That's for haoles and fags."

"Uh…"

"Joke, joke! Here, have a cigar."

"Uh, thanks."

"Now, what can I do for you, in, like, seventeen minutes?"

"Senator, I represent an organization that maybe you've heard of, but maybe not. We like to keep a low profile. We find we can be much more effective that way."

"And does your organization have a name?"

Al Alakawa is blowing smoke all over his office, obscuring the spectacular green view of Nu'uanu Valley out his floor-to-ceiling windows. Case Izumi, who doesn't smoke, is feeling a bit nauseated. Al is never nauseated—has, indeed, never thrown up in his entire life; however, he has no problem making other people sick to their stomachs.

"'Ai Kanaka." Izumi says, letting his voice lower into the cigar cloud.

"Oh. Oh yeah. I hearda you guys. You got that big old mansion up in the valley. You're in my district," he says, nodding toward the mountains. "Used to be an embassy or something."

"The former Korean Consulate."

"Whatever. I hearda you, although I thought you'd look a little different, you know, because of your organization's name. Everybody's gotta be Hawaiian these days, yeah?" Al pauses for some kind of effect, lost on his guest. "Somebody told me you guys have, what, a clubhouse up there? Whattaya do? Sit around and yell banzai a lot, sing Misora Hibari songs late at night…?" Case Izumi must be looking at him sharply, because Al grins and quickly says, "Hey, no offense. I'm a quarter Japanee myself. I just look like a friggin' moke."

"None taken, Senator," Izumi says, returning the display of teeth. "And you're not that far off the mark. We are a kind of club—of local investors."

"Your name—shit, my Hawaiian sucks. I know 'kanaka' is, uh, 'man'…"

Izumi is nodding his head the way people do when they've been asked a familiar question and can't wait to get to the prepared answer.

"Very good, Senator. See, we—well, our leader actually—wanted a name that really described us as a group, and as individuals, who share certain values."

"You're gonna tell me what 'Ai Kanaka means eventually, right?"

"Senator, you're familiar with the expression 'dog eat dog'?" Izumi asks without asking, taking Al's impatient nod and running alongside it. "Well, as you know, that is merely a figure of speech, isn't it? What we're really talking about is the world of men, going *mano a mano*, survival of the fittest. Who cares about a couple of dogs mixing it up?"

Al is looking at him with an expression he reserves for people who waste his time. Hell, when you hit fifty you realize life is short and then you die. Izumi, who looks about forty, hasn't tumbled to this yet.

"That's why our leader decided not to beat around the bush with our name. Why not tell it like it is? You're right—kanaka does mean 'man.' Man, or human. And 'ai means 'to eat.' Get it?"

"Man, eat…" Al has always hated puzzles of any kind. He finds them … puzzling, which really pisses him off. "Eat, man… Man-eater?"

Izumi is smiling triumphantly while thinking: boy, is this guy frigging slow, or what?

"That's us. Somebody gets in our way, tries to beat us in a deal, take away our business, whatever—they get eaten, simple as that. We're the cream of the local business community, Senator. Our careers are littered with the carcasses of guys who went head to head with us and lost. We take no prisoners. 'Ai Kanaka!'"

"'Ai Kanaka to you, too."

There is a pause while the two men look at each other. Al is thinking how it's amazing, the amount of bullshit that comes out of such a short Buddhahead like Izumi. Izumi is thinking this guy is so dumb, I wonder how much of that he got and should I go over it again or what?

"And you know, Senator, you were right about another thing. We do have get-togethers—we're a sociable bunch. In fact, we'd like to invite you to a dinner we're throwing tomorrow night. No strings, no commitments. We just want to get to know you better, and vice versa. You know, we heard you like to eat. We have in our employ the finest chef in the greater Pacific Rim. Can we set a place for you at the table, Senator?"

Al spends some additional seconds staring at the visitor through the haze of smoke.

"Sure. Why not?" he finally says.

"Say, eight o'clock?"

"Ate o'clock. Ha! Joke, joke."

In busy lives, time moves along at satellite speed, with the earth whipping by below. For Kili Pulena it seems like she is just putting her little ones to bed that night when suddenly the alarm clock rings and she's awake, drinking coffee, opening up the office, having lunch, then picking up the boys at school, then sitting here again, in the same chair, telling them another recycled go-to-sleep story. For her it's always Thursday. The scariest movie she ever saw was *Groundhog Day*, starring Bill Murray as Kili Pulena. Despite the fact that there is nothing inherently funny about her life, she passes through it with a smile, with a hundred or so smiles reflected back at her on a typical day.

For Al Alakawa it's the same twenty-four hours, passed in the same mid-Pacific city, but that's where the similarity to Kili's experience ends. And this fact can be driven home visually by use of a hidden camera mounted on Al's forehead. If sharks can be said to smile, then so does Al. Examine closely the faces that, through no fault of their own, encounter the Alakawa smile this day. What do you see? On the face of the little old Chinese man—who owns the herb shop on Maunakea, whom a client of Al's is suing for everything he has because the client says he slipped on a wet ginger root left lying on the floor of the shop and now he'll never work again, even though, point of fact, he never has worked—you see unalloyed hatred. On the face of a fellow Senator—the possessor of a vote that Al needs in order to pass a piece of regulatory legislation that will mean an immediate payment of $125,000 in Al's account in the Bank of Aruba, and to whom Al has just reported what a little bird has told him about the fellow Senator's girlfriend not really being a girl—you see frozen fear.

Ah, let's turn off the camera, shall we? Before we get sick and really make Al's day.

So, the point might be, time doesn't give a rat's ass—it races blindly along for busy people, nice ones and assholes alike. So saying, to Al it doesn't really seem like an entire day has jumped past as he wheels his Hummer through the ornate gate, up the curving coral drive, and under the *porte cochère* of the finely restored Victorian, once the house of a rich and powerful Jap-hating white guy, now the playhouse of a bunch of money-grabbing local Asians. He flips the keys to the Hawaiian-looking valet and strides up the wide stairs and into the big main room, complete with a gargantuan, ugly-as-sin chandelier that must have cost a bundle.

Everyone is glad to see him. He recognizes several men—there are no women present, at least not yet. Case Izumi parades him around the room, introducing him to everybody like he's royalty come down to Earth—the correct approach, as far as Al is concerned. After drinks on a lanai the size of a basketball court, overlooking a lawn that could play as a par five, they retire to the dining room.

The drinks flow, the food comes in waves, indescribably delicious dish after dish after dish after dish. The room gets loud; it fills with smoke. At one point Case Izumi drunkenly pokes him in the ribs and says, "This next one is the best. The *coup d'état*."

"The coo de wha'?"

"The chef calls it 'Ai Kanaka pork. It's sorta like, you know, kālua pig— but there's something about it, something extra. The chef's signature creation. Pairs it with this understated little Pinot from the Central Coast."

Al doesn't know a Pinot from El Niño, but when the dish arrives he chugs the wine and digs in. Hard to say, in words—or sign language, or grunts and groans for that matter—what this dish does to Al, but it is a journey where his stomach takes him by the hand on a guided tour of Pleasureville, with stops at Ecstasyland and Ambrosiaburg thrown in. Smothered in mysterious spices— broiled but no, perhaps baked, maybe steamed—it is pork loin, filet mignon, rack of lamb rolled into one. Al, who never met a slab of meat he didn't like, falls in love. No time for the knife—no need! He stabs big pieces of tender, quivering flesh and rips it off in huge mouthfuls, barely stopping to chew.

"Guess you liked it, huh?" Case Izumi says, looking down on the swiped-clean plate.

"I gotta … meet … the … chef," Al manages to say, at last coming up for air.

Izumi blanches a little, hesitates a lot. "That, uh, could be difficult."

"Difficult?" Al belches. "What's difficult about it? He walks out here in one of those little gay hats, I compliment him on the best goddamn food I've ever eaten in my whole fucking life, he says thank you, sir, and goes back in there to whip up the dessert. Done deal."

Not quite, Case Izumi is thinking, not by a long shot, in fact. "Thing is, the chef is ... a little shy. A little temperamental. Doesn't, uh, take to people real well."

But Al is looking at him and smiling, the smile saying: look, I know you want something from me—everybody does. So why not get the little shithead of a chef out here right now so that you at least have a prayer of me listening to your pitch when the time comes.

And Izumi, who is in actuality formulating that very pitch in his head at this very moment, receives the smile loud and clear. He catches one of the waiters by the sleeve as he is passing, tells him something (hard for Al to hear over the din of male voices), which the kid registers with a surprised and maybe fearful reaction, and in a few minutes a diminutive figure under a very large floppy hat can be seen making its way through the smoky room.

Al turns and anticipates the meeting, imagining some Iron Chef kind of pak-e sort of dude under the hat. A little crusty—doesn't suffer fools, et cetera—but an artist, a pro. And in this he and Al will be simpatico, Al being the artist of the deal, a professional shark with the biggest damn dorsal fin in the room.

When the chef flips back the folds of the stupid hat to expose his face, Al does a double, then a triple take. For one thing, it isn't, maybe, a dude at all, but, maybe, a really strange-looking female, four feet tall max. Her height is one thing—a dwarf chef—but the main weird and unsettling thing is her/his face, which is brick red in color. Okay, that's weird, but weirder still are her eyes, which are big, buggy, and white-white, with tiny coal-black pupils. They look like the eyeballs on those reconstructed Easter Island statues Al once saw on the Discovery Channel. Not only that, the little gnome reminds Al of his grandmother on the Hawaiian side of his family. She has that same evil look in her eye. Yikes.

"Uh, glad to meet the person who cooked up such a, such a, such a..."

"Delicious?" Case Izumi says, ever helpful, totally nerve-wracked.

"Yeah yeah yeah, delicious. Delicious, delicious, delicious." Al is extending his hand, not knowing what else to do. The chef backs up half a step, safe from any chance of ever touching any part of Al.

After staring at Al for way longer than Al (or anyone else) would like, the chef opens her mouth to speak. Strange to say, but it seems to Al that everyone in the room stops talking at once, on cue, and time itself holds its breath for the few seconds it takes the midget to say her piece. Her voice is deep, and scary as shit. It's like what's-her-name, Linda something, in that movie where her head does a three-sixty.

"You love to eat, don't you, fat one? You love food because food is helpless, powerless. But half the time you don't know what you are eating, do you? And one day the food, long-suffering, will have its revenge. *Bon appétit.*"

So saying, the chef—she's a guy, Al decides—leaves them there, retracing his steps across the room, the conversation filling in behind him, until everything is back to normal. For everybody except Al, that is. For although the evening is just getting started, with plenty of food and booze and strippers to come, Al is unusually quiet, unusually thoughtful, for the rest of the night.

And when he finally makes it home, he sleeps poorly, a certain red face with white pop-eyes peering around the corners of his dreams; it's still there, right beside him in the mirror as he shaves on Friday morning.

At the office, he walks right past his secretary Kili without the usual bark of orders and insults, catching her on guard—needlessly, for a change. Maybe the boss is sick, though thinking back, she's never seen him sick—more likely planning something big. Count your blessings, girl, she tells herself. And she does.

At his desk, Al is fidgeting with his electric pencil sharpener, a gift from a constituent. After sharpening several pencils, he looks at the clock on the wall—almost nine. He knows he's been sitting here waiting for something, but it's taken him this long to realize what it is. He dials the newest number in his book. Case Izumi answers, his voice a little ragged from last night. Al has only one question for Izumi: does 'Ai Kanaka do lunch? It does, and Senator Alakawa is more than welcome to join him at high noon up in Nu'uanu.

It's another bright, crisp Hawaiian winter day outside the temperature-controlled interior of the Hummer, and normally Al does take note of the weather, by cursing delays caused by rain or the annoying glare of the sun, but today is different. Everything he sees or touches or thinks about somehow or another turns into a plate of the chef's signature dish, and the only thing he sees himself doing is shoveling forkfuls of the stuff into his mouth, letting the flavor infuse his tongue with that taste, that taste, that taste.

It gets so bad that he's only halfway to the 'Ai Kanaka mansion before he finds himself stopped at a light, licking the Hummer's leather-wrapped steering wheel, lovingly, while a bus full of school kids out on a field trip point and laugh like the little hyenas Al knows they are.

Up at the mansion, he brushes Izumi aside and shoulders his way into the dining room. There are far fewer guys here at lunch than last night; it's much quieter and reserved—none of which Al notices. While he waits for his order, he half-listens to Izumi's pitch. It's the typical shit: their organization has purchased a large piece of ag-zoned land from one of the big trusts, land that has been leased to small farmers since way back in the last century. The 'Ai Kanaka guys plan to throw the farmers off the land—that's a no-brainer, their leases are up soon—but there's no real point unless they're guaranteed a zoning change up front, one that would allow commercial development.

"What kind of commercial development?" Al asks, not really giving a shit.

"Now this," Izumi says, getting excited, "is the really cool part. We are partnering with a mainland company—well respected, long track record in the industry—to build Hawai'i's first world-class theme park."

"Theme park? You mean like Disney World?"

Izumi hesitates, looks quickly around the room, lowers his voice. "Funny you should mention that."

Al waits. He's heard nothing remotely funny so far.

"You've been?"

"To Disney World? Yeah."

"Did you by any chance visit, uh, France while you were there?"

"No way. I went to Germany. Oktoberfest. Beer, chicken dance, girls in those low-cut fuck-me dresses. Outstanding."

"Ever been to the real Germany?"

"Hell no. Why bother?"

"Exactly. Exactly, Senator. Our sentiments exactly."

There's a pause—this guy Izumi loves pauses. Okay, he'll bite, what the hell.

"So, you guys are planning to put…"

"Senator," Izumi pounces, "if the Disney World thing works for you, okay, fine. But we're talking something bigger. Appealing to the locals, but also to an international consumer."

"Bigger than *Disney World*? You ever *seen* that sucker?"

"Bigger concept, bigger idea. I wish I could let you in on the particulars, Senator, but I think you understand, if word got out… Our investors…"

This gets Al's attention. "Investors. Would I be, uh, a potential investor, by any chance?"

"You are at the absolute top of our list. We're ready to offer a two percent…"

"Five percent."

"Five percent share," Izumi says, nodding, smiling, sweating, "in our operation, uh, the, uh, moment that the final paperwork is approved on the zone change."

At which point the food arrives and Al instantly forgets everything they've been talking about.

But of course the 'Ai Kanaka people, in the form of Case Izumi, keep reminding him. Through lunches and dinners (even a breakfast or two), Al returns again and again to the culinary fairyland created by the little chef. His car seems drawn, as though on autopilot, through the shady streets of Nu'uanu; by the time he roars between the iron posts of the front gate Al is salivating, already tasting that first bite.

In a couple of weeks, he's consumed the chef's trademark dish twenty times, each plateful more satisfying than the last. And all the while Izumi keeps up the pressure, keeps coming back to the idea that: gee, we really need this to happen soon. A lot of money is at stake. The big mainland investors won't wait on promises—promises about our influence, politically, to get the job done—they want results. Now, Senator.

———————

To say that Al Alakawa is, after a week or so of this, a changed man does not really describe what happens to him. Kili notices it that very first morning, and every morning and every Monday through Friday after that. Overall, she is happy with the new Al since he's too distracted or something to be the shit that he normally is.

As for Al, his brain gives up its authority bit by bit until he is almost completely taken over by his stomach. Under the rule of Stomach, all Al can think or care about is the chef's specialty, available piping hot in only one location: the 'Ai Kanaka dining room. The remnants of his original shark brain realize that the 'Ai Kanaka people aren't feeding him because they like him, but he cannot seem to remember, from minute to minute much less day to day, what it is they want from him. So, Stomach orders him to return there, over and over again, and he does nothing else.

Doing nothing is not that unusual in a politician, and no one important notices anything odd about Al. He probably would just continue this way indefinitely if it weren't for Case Izumi and his ever more hysterical phone calls. Here's the last one Al receives, on the second Friday morning of his new life.

"Senator."

"Case, howareya?"

"Been better, Senator."

"Oh yeah? Maybe we can talk about it over lunch?"

"I'm sorry, Al. There won't be any more lunches."

First time Izumi's ever called him Al. Not a good sign.

"Oh. What about dinner, then?"

"No more dinners, either."

"Something wrong with your chef? She, he, uh, sick or something?"

"Or something. Look, we've been straight up with you. I don't know if you can read, but it's been in the papers—we threw those dumb-fuck farmers off their land already. I mean, it's not like we didn't warn them months ago, so what's their problem, right?"

"Uh, right."

"Point is, we took some flak in the press for that—even had an investigative reporter come snooping around. Not that he'll be a problem, anymore, but now we gotta lay low for a while—as per orders from the top. Another point: we only cleared out the land of people and their lame crops to get it ready for the big plan. And we have it from reliable sources that you, Al, have done nothing to move things forward on your end. NOTHING!"

Al holds the phone back from his ear. Why is this guy yelling at *him?* Wait a minute—did he say no more lunches, no more dinners? Does this mean breakfast is out, too?

"Listen, Al, you might think you're the only corrupt, lazy, fat-ass politician in this town, but I'm here to tell you…"

Al hangs up. He doesn't have to listen to the next part. He knows when he's being dropped, passed over. As soon as his hand lets go of the phone, though, he immediately regrets it. He forgot to ask about the possibility of a breakfast meeting.

We need to leave Al there, brow furrowed, because there's a whole other side to this story that needs to be told, in order for the ending to hopefully make sense. We could open another window in Windows, over-top the story; go a-Googling again, utilize a high-priced piece of steel spinning a hundred miles above the streets and byways of this island to move us around, zoom up, out and over Al's office, race up Nu'uanu, over the Pali, where the windward side opens up with its greenery and '70s-style suburbs. Zero in on an orderly pattern of vegetation, recognizable the world over as farmland. But really, we don't need high tech to do this. This is fiction. We can just start a new paragraph.

He's standing in light rain, hands gripping a hastily erected chain-link fence. A tall man, dark and lean with a wild head of curly hair just beginning to frost gray. On the other side of the fence, a big yellow bulldozer is merrily destroying a stand of banana trees, slicing through acres of green like, well, a D-9 through a bunch of defenseless banana trees. The man is dressed simply in worn shorts and a stained undershirt. He could be from any decade—pick one—stretching back the last five or six. His cell phone rings in his pocket, narrowing the time frame.

"Where are you?"

"Where do you think?"

"Go home. There's nothing you can do."

"What? Done deal. Game over. Pau."

"Go home. The boys need you at home, not in jail."

Pause. His sister knows how to work him.

"I will. Later. Some stuff … I gotta do. Don't wait up."

"You're going to do something stupid, aren't you?"

"Probably," he says, ending the call and turning away from the sight of the big machine chewing up his past, present, and future.

At the office, Kili is still holding the phone to her ear, redialing, praying it was just a dropped call, knowing it wasn't. After trying three times she stops, when she hears more crashing sounds behind Al's closed door. It's been going on all afternoon. Several times she has knocked on the door. No answer.

When four-thirty comes she turns off her computer, locks up her desk, and leaves to pick up the boys from Aikido class. She's worried sick about her brother, Lee, but has no idea where he's gone or what dumb thing he has planned. She continues to worry into the evening, cooking dinner, setting a place for Lee. She is not surprised when he doesn't show.

All day long Al's stomach and what remains of his free will have been in a battle royal, a fight to the finish that never seems to end. The crashing sounds Kili Pulena has been hearing from the front office are the noise a big body makes when it is thrown against a wall or has its head beaten on a desktop. "Take that!" says Stomach, tossing Al to the floor and strangling him with Al's left hand while Al's right hand pries the fingers loose one by one. "No way, José!" screams Freewill.

It's total war. Prisoners are invited to surrender, laughed at, liquidated. In the end (is it really over, Al wonders, sweated through, drooling on the office couch), Stomach's relentless offensive exhausts Freewill's subtle but ultimately irrelevant jujitsu, until Stomach is master of all it sees, doing crazy little end-zone dances, pounding Freewill into unconsciousness.

In his first executive action as dictator, Stomach orders Al up to Nuʻuanu that night. But they won't let me in, argues Al. They hate me. Everybody hates you, Stomach patiently explains—of course they won't let you in. That's why you need to sneak around in the dark, find out more about the secret ingredients in that pygmy chef's creation, and then hire somebody to recreate it, sell it, and make a fortune. A fortune, Al baby!

Which is how, some hours later, Al finds himself on his tiptoes, looking through the kitchen window of the ʻAi Kanaka Club, cold Nuʻuanu rain running down his back. Not that he planned anything, but he couldn't have picked a better night for his reconnaissance. Wind and rain have covered every footfall, every trip and fall, every curse he's uttered since he entered the grounds and began feeling his way toward the lights of the big building.

If only Al hadn't been in such a hurry and had remembered his cell phone. We could just have him point it at the window, go online, email it out, and it would appear on your screen, thereby avoiding the hassle of having to describe anything; however, before we kick ourselves (or Al) for this oversight, it should be noted that Al has never figured out any of these functions on his phone. He can barely make a call to see if his mistress is free for dinner.

The window is a little foggy, and even Al isn't dumb enough to wipe it so he can see better, but he recognizes the little chef right away. He's hard to miss, being so close to the ground and the hat and all. There seems to be a lot of people jammed into the brightly lit kitchen, moving quickly and in every direction, carrying what appear to be big pieces of meat, legs of lamb, sides of beef maybe, dropping them into big stainless steel pots sitting on a stove roughly the size of an aircraft carrier deck. The chef is orchestrating every move, directing the movement of meat coming from offstage right—probably a big walk-in cooler there, Al is thinking.

There is something odd about the people in the kitchen. Straining to see through the glass, it dawns on Al what it is. Though they have the expected aprons on, underneath the aprons they are all wearing bland aloha shirts and slacks. These guys aren't the normal Filipino kitchen help you expect to see. Leaning even closer to the glass, straining to get the last bit of altitude out of his toes, Al is suddenly looking into the face of Case Izumi. He ducks down, fast, like someone just took a shot at him. It's raining harder now. He's shivering; he's miserable; he should be at home drinking a beer, watching TV. Stomach tells him to quit complaining and get back up there: no way Izumi saw you with all that light in there and you out here in the frigging dark, dumbbell.

Slowly, with trepidation, he peeks over the windowsill—everything is as it was, nobody's noticed him, though there seem to be fewer people in there now. He doesn't see Izumi, but recognizes another 'Ai Kanaka member—he had lunch with the guy just a few days ago, owns a bunch of self-storage facilities here and on Maui. A real Class-A prick, if you ask Al. Speaking of which, what's the deal? Why would these high-powered types be working in the kitchen like a bunch of gofers?

Just as he's pondering this, he sees the midget chef push the self-storage guy away from a counter where he's been slamming away with a meat cleaver the size of one of those Viking battle-axes Al remembers from *Braveheart*, or maybe it wasn't *Braveheart*—jeez, the little chef is holding the cleaver up to the guy's throat and yelling so loud that Al can almost make out the words, despite the wind and rain. Now the midget is wheeling around the room, swinging the cleaver, while the men in aprons stand in a rough circle with their eyes downcast like a bunch of first-graders being read the riot act.

With a violent nod of his chipmunk head the chef yells at one of the guys. Fast as shit he whips a stool into position next to the counter. Still waving the giant-killer cleaver, the chef jumps up on the stool, looks around to make sure he has everyone's attention, then holds up the leg of lamb or whatever it is the storage guy was working on and proceeds to chop it into, like, a hundred little pieces in like three seconds with a vicious forehand that Al, a sometime tennis player, can only envy.

Holding the bloody cleaver at his side, a little winded, the chef lets the demonstration sink in for a minute or two, then jumps down from the stool. Pointing with the cleaver, barking another command, he waits impatiently in the middle of the kitchen while a couple of the guys leave and, a minute later, push a wheelchair into view from offstage left. Al immediately recognizes the young man in the wheelchair, but he can't say from where exactly—the standard, hapa good looks, athlete build: a model, an actor... Then something Case Izumi said makes him tumble to it. Something about a journalist snooping around the Club. Not that Al would ever call the pretty boy a journalist, but he knows now where he's seen him before. The evening news at six. Rod—what's his name? Rod Long, that's it. Live, local, fast-breaking. The news at six with Rod Long.

Rod has looked better. Tied to the chair with ropes that look like the ones used on King Kong, his hair is mussed in a million swirls like some sicko hairdresser's been having her way with him. He has dark circles under his eyes; he needs a shave. The chef approaches him with the cleaver held at a menacing forty-five-degree angle above his head. Rod, needless to say, recoils, squirming in the chair, trapped. Al can't believe it. Is he really watching this? He's forgotten about the rainwater running down his back, forgotten his soggy socks, forgotten, even, why he came.

The chef swings the cleaver around some more, just fucking with Rod Long, trying to scare him, and succeeding. Finally, he tosses the big blade up on the counter, turns his back for a second two, then spins around to face the terrified guy with a flourish. In his hand he is holding something he picked up from the counter. Straining to see through the glass, Al is having trouble making it out. It looks like a leg of lamb maybe, maybe, but whatthefuck is that on the end of the leg there? A hoof? It looks like a hoof. The insane chef is holding the leg up close to Rod's face—Rod's seen what it is but has closed his eyes tight, his face turned away. The chef pokes him, yells at him, and as Rod Long opens his eyes the chef turns the leg, the light hits it just right, and suddenly Al sees that the leg is leg all right, but that's no hoof on the end of it. His brain is lurching along behind his eyes, and in that instant it finally catches up, earning its keep, informing Al: Al, hooves do not have toes. Feet have toes. Not to mention toenails.

Let's stick the camera back on Al's forehead; let's turn it on. As the image comes into focus and we see details of the leg, the foot, that, given the context, we'd just as soon not see, Al cuts loose with what sounds to us like simultaneous exclamations.

"Jesuschrist!"

"Ho!"

The camera abruptly swings ninety degrees to our left and a terrified, wild-eyed, wild-haired visage fills the screen. Another person has been standing nearby all this time, looking into the same window as Al, witness to the same travesty. It's a person, just another human, and vice versa—but try to explain that to either of these guys at this moment in the darkness and rain. Again with the simultaneous audio.

"Ahhhhh!"

"Naaaah!"

Lacking steady-cam or a track to run the camera along, it's a bumpy ride from now on as Al turns and runs full tilt through the bushes, leaves in his face, rainwater all over the lens. He stumbles, he falls, gets up, pushes through more bushes, slips, falls again hard, and on the way down a branch strips the camera from his forehead. It falls to the ground. Lying at an angle, it captures the big ass of Al as he struggles to his feet and limps across the expanse of lawn; until the darkness and the trees swallow him up and all we hear is the sound of rain patting the earth and all we see is not too much.

All over the world tonight there are people tossing and turning in their beds, unable to get to sleep. They've seen too much, perhaps, or thought too much. It's inefficient, being human. We need sleep; every night we should just crap out and wake up refreshed, ready to go in the morning. But, odd to say, our brains don't really care about our bodies. Brains will demand drugs until we overdose, demand sex until our marriage is shattered by infidelity, etcetera.

Al, if he were smart or introspective enough, could have come up with some similar analysis of the human condition, but he can't because he isn't. All he knows is that he is being tortured, sweating in the dark, with the knowledge of the little chef's secret ingredient. He spent some time, when he first got home from his adventure in Nu'uanu, barfing into his low-flow toilet.

(Apparently, even Stomach—voracious, every-man-for-himself, I-don't-care-what-they-gotta-do-to-the-goose, just-spread-some-more-of-that-on-a-piece-of-bread-and-send-it-my-way Stomach—has been revolted by the revelation, leaving the door open for Freewill, who returns, dragging with him his usual baggage of guilt and recrimination.) What was Al thinking to let a cretin like Stomach take control? Stomach's not management material. And now see what he's done: he's turned you into a cannibal.

There it is; the word is out. Al sits up in bed. Cannibal. 'Ai Kanaka. Why couldn't the motherfuckers stick with dog-eat-dog? Well, they didn't, Al didn't, and now he's crossed a line he wasn't aware even existed. You thought anal sex was a big deal. Ha! Chump change.

He thinks about it some more, Freewill working him over. The consequences. His law practice, his political career. Freewill doubts that there are many cannibals among his constituents…

While he's thinking, Stomach sneaks up behind Freewill and begins strangling him with a handy length of small intestine. It takes a while; Freewill kicks desperately and tries to grab Stomach's hair, all the while shouting moral platitudes and aphorisms that might work on Al if Freewill had time to explain them, but he doesn't. His voice slowly fades to a squeak. Stomach stands above him, swelled with victory.

With Freewill out of the picture for good it doesn't take long for Al to forget it ever existed. What matters, Stomach whispers in his ear, is Flavor, Taste, Texture on the Tongue (one of Stomach's slaves). You might not remember much, Al, but I bet you remember how that 'Ai Kanaka specialty melted in your mouth, don't you? Yes. And I know you want to taste it again, don't you? Yes, yes. Too bad you can't order it in your favorite Chinese restaurant—bet you Chi Wai could do a bang-up job, if only he had the magic ingredient. Because that little 'Ai Kanaka chef is no culinary genius—no way. Anybody could do what he does, with access to the raw material.

Raw material. That would be … people. Al knows people. Sees them every day. Hundreds of them. He has just never considered them as a food source before, never thought of their thighs, arms, shoulders as different cuts of meat, but suddenly he sees that things have changed; he's a cannibal now and, goddamit, he better start thinking like a cannibal.

Inside the confines of his head, he runs through a visual listing of various people he might want to consume, but it's hard. He considers some of his relatives—people he's long hated anyway, why not kill two birds with one stone— but nah, they're all too old, probably tough as a rubber slipper. Nope, Stomach interjects, what you need is young and tender.

And then it comes to him: an image of a smooth, plump elbow, connected to a chubby body, an innocent face—no, make that two innocent faces, faces with names: Kai and Kawika, his secretary Kili's two kids. That time he volunteered to take the rug rats to the water park, give their mom a break for the day; Kili surprised and hesitant at first, the big surprise ultimately being that Al was great with kids—he appreciated that, in their utter ignorance, they liked him.

Yeah, Kai and Kawika, still with plenty of baby fat, little Michelin men in baggy swimsuits. Stomach takes the opportunity to jam another image into his mind's eye. It's the older kid, Kawika, turning slowly on a spit. It's a minute or two before Al notices that he's been drooling down his pajama front.

He paces his room for the next two hours, waiting for the sun to come up, impatient to the point of being driven insane with the slow rotation of the planet beneath his feet, until he can't stand it anymore and calls Kili at home, of course waking her up, shattering the Saturday morning snooze she's banked on all week, the receiver to her ear for half a minute before she figures out who is on the other end.

Well, no, she doesn't have anything planned for the boys today; yes, I guess it would be okay, and I'm sure the boys would love another day at the water park. Pick them up? Well, the park doesn't open till ten … What's that? You'll take them to breakfast. You'll be over in twenty minutes. Could you make that an hour? Everybody's still asleep over here.

There's a sound, like someone being strangled, on Al's end, and a loud noise that sounds to Kili like a chair being thrown through a sliding glass door.

Okay, Al finally bleats—one hour.

Chinatown opens early. Saturday, seven a.m., the place is jumping. Al gets caught in the middle of twenty old ladies who have just descended from a bus on Hotel Street. He tries pushing through them but they are a Chinese phalanx, hardened shock troops, and he a temporary conscript swept inexorably forward to the vegetable stands of Maunakea Marketplace when all he's really trying do is reach the cookware shop on King.

With some hard elbowing—boy, these broads are tough—he breaks free, turning briefly to watch the women descend on the first vegetables, seeing the looks of horror and brave resistance on the merchants' faces. He knows that today many fruits will lie bruised and battered in their wake.

In the shop, Al picks out two of the biggest and sharpest cleavers the guy has. They are not the finest quality, but what does Al care—they'll do the job. The guy wants to wrap up them up, but Al grabs them out of his hands and rushes out of the shop and onto the sidewalk, where he takes two days off the life of a bag lady pushing a shopping cart; this big, unshaven Hawaiian fucker in a bathing suit and rubber slippers all of a sudden in her face, flashing shiny steel blades like in that movie *Braveheart*, or maybe it wasn't *Braveheart*, nearer my God to thee this is how the world ends save me Jesus, Mohammed whatever I don't wanta die…

Back in the Hummer, driving ninety up the Pali, Al works hard to calm down enough to pass Kili's inspection. Looking into the rearview mirror he gasps—he looks like shit. There's a bottle of water on the passenger seat. He opens it, pours the contents over his head, screaming. A wet dog, he shakes his head back and forth for a while, runs a comb through his hair, slaps himself repeatedly. By the time he makes Kāneʻohe he can pass for a reasonable facsimile of Senator Al Alakawa.

Kili, amazingly adaptable and organized person that she is, has the boys ready and waiting when he pulls into the driveway. An ordinary, sane adult would see the two kids as almost painfully cute in their swimsuits and tank tops and cheap sunglasses, jumping up and down with anticipation. Oh boy, oh boy, oh boy. The water park! With Uncle Al. But of course Uncle Al is not really their uncle—even if he was, it wouldn't do them any good now. Because Al is no sane adult, no sirree.

And to Kili, the boss does look a little odd this morning. Maybe a hard night last night, maybe just stress. A day off will do him good. More importantly, a day off will do her good. With a kiss for both of them, Kili waves goodbye as Al carefully backs the behemoth into the street and drives away. Three minutes later she is back in bed, sound asleep.

An hour later—it feels like thirty seconds—Kili is jarred awake by a crash and a clang. In the kitchen, she finds her brother Lee, haggard, mud-splattered, shivering uncontrollably, attempting with little success to make some breakfast.

"Where have you been?"

He doesn't answer, just stares at her, past her.

"You're a mess. Are you okay?"

"Do I look okay?"

"It's … the drugs again, isn't it? Well, I'm just glad the boys aren't here to see their uncle…"

"The boys," he cuts her off, returning halfway to focus. "Where are the boys?"

"Al Alakawa took them…"

"Took them! Where?"

"Calm down, Lee. It's gonna be all right. We'll get you through this…"

Shouting now, shaking her: "WHERE DID HE TAKE THEM?"

"Just to the water park. But they don't open till later. He said he would have them over to the office for breakfast first."

"WHAT?"

He runs out the front door, Kili on his heels. He stops at the door of his sagging old pickup, parked next to Kili's Mazda.

"Your keys. Go get your keys!"

Five minutes later, with Lee a maniac behind the wheel, they are speeding up the Pali, driving hard toward downtown.

On the way to the office, Al stops at McDonald's and buys the boys Happy Meal breakfasts, just coffee for him. In the office, he turns on his wide-screen; the two of them sit in swivel chairs, watching Saturday cartoons and grinding away at the food. Meanwhile, Al is behind the shoji screen, picking up and putting down the cleavers and thinking complicated thoughts—at least for Al.

Looked at from a certain angle, becoming a cannibal has not been a big transition for Al. After all, a cannibal is a carnivore. So is Al. He has always hated vegetables. He thinks about what he's seen on TV about chicken factories or what they do to calves to make veal or about the time he ate whale on that junket to Japan.

Holding a cleaver in each hand, he considers the likelihood that if steak lovers had to witness the last minute of a cow's life, well, maybe there would be a lot less steak lovers out there. Then again, Stomach butts in, maybe not, as Al pushes aside the screen, raising the cleavers over the boys' head, closing his eyes, Stomach screaming: Now! Do it now!

There's a panicked fumbling of a key in the lock, the door bursts open, and it's Kili and this familiar-looking, crazy-ass guy standing there, and Al with the cleavers in midair, quickly lowering them, hiding them behind his back. Where has he seen this guy before? It comes to him.

"You."

"Drop 'em," Lee says.

Al drops them. The cleavers hit the hardwood with a clatter and a ring. As Lee moves toward the boys, Al steps to one side then runs like hell, out of the office, down the hall, and with a stroke of luck, into an open elevator.

Lee kneels next to his nephews. He runs a hand over their heads, presses their little shoulders, feeling the satisfying wholeness, the resiliency there, before leaping to his feet and tearing off after Al. Kili is left in the office, crying softly, holding her babies tight.

If this were a movie we could have one hell of a chase scene right here. It would end with Al dangling from the ledge of the office building at 1188 Bishop Street. Lee would have a hold of Al's arm in a last-ditch attempt to save him. A close-up of Lee's face would reveal determination, the will to do the right and noble thing despite the fact that Al is pond scum. Al's close-up would reveal simple terror. Maybe he would beg Lee not to let go.

Not that this is reality or anything, but it doesn't happen like that. Al takes the elevator to the lobby and runs onto the plaza in front of the Catholic cathedral. He knows he's in trouble now and should keep on running, but he doesn't. He is suddenly rudderless. Stomach hasn't been heard from since Kili and Lee broke through the door and caught Al in the act. What did Freewill say about Stomach—not management material? No shit. As for Freewill himself, he's in intensive care on life support and is not expected to recover. Al walks around in a vague circle, occasionally looking up at the cross atop the cathedral.

When Lee runs out of the office after Al, he doesn't even consider taking the elevator—this is time for action and he's an action kind of guy. He starts down the stairs at breakneck speed and almost does break his neck by tripping and falling on the seventh-floor landing. By the time he reaches the lobby, the night of no sleep and the morning of no breakfast and the simple circular nature of the descent have left him so dizzy that he exits the building onto the plaza stumbling in little curlicues that eventually bring him to the vicinity of Al.

"Hey!" he yells.

Al turns, snaps out of it, and takes off, running with surprising agility toward Bishop Street. Lee weaves after him. Saturday it may be, with downtown half-deserted, but Honolulu is in the midst of a construction boom, and across the street the men and women in hardhats are working overtime on a big parking structure.

Al runs blindly across four lanes of traffic, just misses being flattened by a bus. On the other side he encounters an eight-foot-high plywood barrier built right up to the sidewalk. Lee, regaining his equilibrium, is gaining on Al, his hand just inches from grabbing Al's voluminous tank top.

Al, no surprise, doesn't think first. What is surprising is that an overweight guy in his fifties can scale an eight-foot wall in what appears to Lee to be a single bound. One second he's there, sweating in the street, the next his feet are disappearing over the top, one of his size-twelve rubber slippers flying through the air and landing in the middle lane of Bishop Street.

With some difficulty, Lee lifts himself to the top of the wall. Immediately below is Al, his body facedown, spread-eagled in a bed of freshly poured concrete. To Lee's horror, Al slowly pushes himself up, out of the gluey gray mess, and has just stood up and is trying to say something, his arm extended for emphasis, when a bell goes off above him. Lee and Al automatically look up as a boom swings into position and unloads a stream of concrete directly on Al's head. Al is somehow able to remain standing for a second or two, captured forever in an oratorical pose, before the awful weight overwhelms him and he becomes part of the parking structure.

EPILOGUE ONE

Two evenings later, Lee and Kili are sitting in front of the TV watching the local news when Rod Long appears, standing in front of a familiar-looking building, smiling into the camera.

"I thought you said he was…" Kili starts in.

"What the…" Lee leans forward, not believing what he sees. Rod Long alive? And not just alive—isn't that the 'Ai Kanaka Club driveway in the background? What's going on?

"I'm up in Nu'uanu today, to continue our series *People Behind the Scenes.* These are the movers and shakers here in paradise, major players in our community who you've probably never heard about."

The scene shifts to the vast lanai of the building. Rod Long sits at a wicker table with … wait a minute, isn't that the murderous midget chef from

Friday night?

"I'm here with Kamea Ono, CEO of 'Ai Kanaka, Inc. Mr. Ono, thank you for letting us visit your beautiful headquarters up here in Nu'uanu. This is a great old building."

"Yes it is, Rod."

"Uh, I know there are many Hawaiian speakers among our audience who are wondering about your organization's name. Doesn't 'Ai Kanaka mean…'"

"Cannibal? Yes it does, Rod. And we enjoy having fun with it sometimes—like we did with you the other night when you unexpectedly dropped in."

Rod Long smiles thinly. Lee notices that the newscaster doesn't look as fresh-faced as he used to. And is that a shot of grey in his sideburn?

"Ha, ha, ha. That was a good one. But seriously, Mr. Ono, your group has some big plans in the works for our island, some of which have surfaced as rumors in the press. Any chance of you clearing the air a little for us today?"

"I'd be delighted, Rod. What we've done, working in conjunction with a group of international investors and, of course, Kamehameha Schools, is to design—and now begin to build—a world-class theme park, right here on the island of O'ahu. The investors have supplied much needed capital. Kamehameha Schools has generously agreed to sell us a hundred acres of underutilized land on the windward side. And now we're ready to break ground on O'ahu Nui."

"O'ahu Nui. Big O'ahu, right?"

"You know your Hawaiian, Rod."

"But, and excuse me for asking, if the park is only a hundred acres…'"

"Only a hundred acres, Rod? Do you have any idea how much Kam Schools stiffed us—how much a hundred acres of O'ahu is worth today?"

"Point taken, Mr. Ono. But still, why call it Big O'ahu, when it's obviously considerably smaller than this place we all call home?"

"Because O'ahu Nui will be a bigger, more fully realized concept than O'ahu the island. Everything that O'ahu has, O'ahu Nui will have, only better, and with ample parking. O'ahu has 'Iolani Palace. Smack-dab in the middle of O'ahu Nui will be a perfect replica of this wonderful landmark—only you won't have to wait half the morning for some senile docent to show up to tour the place, there won't be homeless asleep under the bandstand or a thousand radical Hawaiians occupying the grounds on the Fourth of July. Ever want to surf Banzai Pipeline, but you're too old or out of shape or you just don't want to break your neck when you wipe out? On O'ahu Nui's North Shore you'll be able to ride a wave machine that will recreate the Pipe exactly—and it will be completely safe (although you will be required to sign a waiver)."

"Fascinating."

"There's more, Rod. Much more. One of the problems with the real

O'ahu is time."

"Time?"

"Yes—as in 'time marches on' or 'time waits for no man'. Contrary to what most of the outside world thinks, the people of O'ahu no longer live in grass shacks—they live in Kapolei. Inside the walls of *O'ahu Nui*, we will be able to turn back the clock to an earlier time, when natives lived in harmony with nature. We'll have a real Hawaiian village with taro patches worked by real Hawaiians in authentic outfits."

"But weren't there taro lo'i on the property before you bulldozed them?"

"Yes, Rod, but they weren't in the right place. Chinatown goes there."

"Oh."

At which point, Lee shuts off the TV. He and Kili sit in silence for several minutes before Kili gets up and heads to the kitchen to prepare dinner.

Epilogue Two

Try GoogleEarth O'ahu Nui, a couple of years from now. Fly over the sea, over the mountains, zero in on an odd-looking conglomeration of structures sprouting out of the still green hills of the windward side. Go lower. There is a palace, a monorail. Go left, aim at the rectangular patches of green. Go lower. The resolution is blurring—we need a clearer focus than technology can deliver.

Abandon the computer. Come with me. We are descending from the sky. A figure comes into view, standing just there next to the taro patch. As he comes into focus we see that he is tall, deeply tanned and naked, save for a drape of cloth around his loins. He is holding a long wooden staff in his left hand. His right hand is extended upward toward the sky, toward us, as we descend, descend. His face is coming into view. It is Lee. And he is flipping us off. ✺

Beautiful Mahealani Moon

Ku'ualoha Ho'omanawanui

Inspired by the Legend of Hina, the Goddess of the Moon

Hina lived at Ka'uiki, Hāna, Maui. She was renowned as an intelligent, indus-
trious woman, with exceptional expertise in creating fine, soft kapa. She was
married to 'Aukele (alternately 'Aikanaka), who was considered lazy and shift-
less, and her sons followed in their father's footsteps. When Hina tired of their
laziness and ill treatment, she sought to escape to the sun via a rainbow arch,
but the sun was too hot; therefore, she decided instead to escape to the moon,
which was a much more suitable home. But when Hina was making her way up
to the moon, her husband saw her and ran to stop her. She was almost out of
reach, but he managed to catch one of her legs. She tried to shake him off, but
as he fell, her leg was broken off and fell to the earth with him. Hina chanted
to Pō, the night and female deity of creation, to assist her, and she was able to
escape her abusive husband and live peacefully on the moon. Hereafter she was
known as Lonomoku, or "crippled Lono."

     There are many Hina stories; however, this particular one detailing
Hina's relationship with 'Aukele is centered on what we today call domestic violence, a problem that persists within Hawaiian and all societies across the globe.
I began thinking about rewriting this mo'olelo and putting it in a contemporary
setting a few years ago when I was teaching a Hawaiian mythology course at the
Center for Hawaiian Studies, University of Hawai'i at Mānoa. One of my students at the time, an older woman, was working at the law school and putting
together a handbook for women who were victims of domestic violence.

     After we covered this story in class, she and I began discussing how tra-
ditional cultural stories provide lessons for contemporary society; thus, the idea
of rewriting this mo'olelo emerged. I wanted to write something powerful and
affirming to honor victims and their memories. If anyone can be touched by this
story and find the courage to get out of an abusive relationship, or is inspired to
help someone else, he or she can honor those who have lost their lives to violence
by refusing to be a victim anymore.

"THAT WAS A GREAT STORY, AUNTY MAHEA. TELL ANOTHER ONE,
PLEASE?" KAIMANA BEGGED.

"YEAH, AUNTY, KE'OLU'OLU?" KAHA'I CHIMED IN.

Mahealani looked at her two nieces and smiled. The radiant light of
the full moon bathed the Ka'a'awa coastline in shimmering blue light, which
bounced off the murmuring sea just beyond them. The little metal bells on
fishing poles stuck firmly in the coarse sand were mute, while the Coleman
lanterns, hanging on the aluminum poles with shiny gray tarps strung tautly
between them, emitted a whispered hiss.

"It's getting late. Time for bed," Kanoe called out from under the silver
tarp protecting their camping gear and securing everything for the night. "Your
aunty tired already."

"Aw, Mom. It's summer vacation, and we wanna stay up all night!" the
girls complained.

Mahealani laughed. "It's okay, Kanoe. We can tell stories all night under
the eye of the moon, or until we catch something." The girls laughed, too.
Mahealani looked at them and smiled. "So," she inquired, "what do you want to
hear next?"

The girls giggled and looked at each other. "We don't know, Aunty
Mahea," Kaimana said.

"You pick one," Kaha'i offered.

"Hmmm, let me think." Mahealani looked up at the moon, heavy and
full like a luminous wana, or urchin, gliding across the sky. Mahealani, the full
moon—her namesake. How could her parents have known how prophetic her
name would be? "Did I ever tell you," Mahealani began, "about the story of the
moon?"

"Oh, we know," Kaimana said. "The moon is made of cheese."

Mahealani laughed. "Oh no," she said. "That's a Western fairy tale meant
to tease children like you."

"I know," said Kaha'i. "There's a man that lives in the moon."

Mahealani laughed again. "Well, some people think that, but do you
know the real story, about Hina, the goddess of the moon?"

The girls looked at her with big brown eyes open in wonder, as round and
bright as the moon. "Oh no, Aunty," Kaha'i said reverently. "You never told us
about Hina and the moon."

"Oh, tell us, Aunty, tell us," said Kaimana, clapping her hands. "We want
to hear the story."

Across the campfire, Kanoe looked at Mahealani with a steady gaze and
slight frown. She could only imagine what memories this story would bring up
for her sister. But Mahealani stared back at Kanoe with a calm, even look. *The
girls need to know*, she said silently to her sister: *Not all men are bad, but not all*

men are what they appear, either.

Liko whined softly at Mahealani's feet, thumping her tail on the soft sand and licking Mahealani's toes.

"Liko wants to hear the story, too, Aunty!" the girls shouted, and then they all, even Kanoe, laughed.

"Okay then," Mahealani started. "There are many Hinas, and many stories about Hina. This is the story about Hinaʻaikamalama, the goddess of the moon, who was married to a charming, handsome man named ʻAukele…"

<hr />

The day I first met him, Mahealani remembered, I was floating in the water at the end of the day, relaxing on the tide, my mind drifting with the current, the emerald and jade Koʻolau mountains backlit with fiery gold from the setting sun. I heard a whistle and saw him emerging from the sea like a god— tall, muscular, shirtless, red swimming trunks dripping ocean water—calling to a brindle-colored pit bull bounding down the beach clenching a weathered stick of driftwood clenched in her powerful jaws. When she heard her master's whistle, she stopped dead in her tracks and then spun sharply on her muscled haunches and returned to him, dropping the stick obediently at his feet, wagging her tail.

Mahealani emerged from the water only to see the playful pit bull come toward her, ears and tongue flapping in the warm afternoon breeze. Most people would have been terrified, but Mahealani loved animals. She was the type to rescue strays and nurse them back to health. The pit must have sensed this, too.

"Liko! Liko! Get back hea, you kolohe buggah," the man yelled, now jogging in Mahealani's direction.

"Oh, your name is Liko? Hi, Liko! How are you Liko?" Mahealani leaned over to play with the dog, who dutifully rolled over on her back, paws dangling in full submission. Mahealani laughed and rubbed Liko's belly as she wriggled with delight in the wet sand.

"Oh, she like you!" the man said. "But sorry eh, I know some people stay scade."

"It's okay," Mahealani said, smiling and looking up at him. "I love dogs."

The man smiled back and introduced himself as Keone. He was from Kaimukī on the other side of the island and was out here on the windward side visiting friends for the weekend. They ended up talking until dark, the moon rising full and bright over Kailua, a golden orb in the darkening plum sky. It was the first of many evenings spent together, swimming at the beach, playing with the dog, laughing, joking, and eventually making love. It didn't take long before they became a couple.

Mahealani's family and friends had never seen her so happy. She spent her days creating her art, photographing Keone surfing, running with Liko on the beach, sleeping on the pūneʻe in the front room. She took a class in kapa-making at the university, painstakingly learning the intricate process, thrilled with her newfound skills.

Keone's family and friends said the same thing about him. He was home more often, laughed a lot, and seemed more at ease with himself. *Maybe she can change him,* they whispered. *Maybe she can save him,* they said, with hopeful tones. But no one told Mahealani he needed changing or saving. That, she would find out on her own.

The first time Keone yelled at Mahea, calling her a stupid wahine, she thought he was just tired from working too hard. She didn't understand why he seemed to have such a hard time finding and keeping a job.

"Stupid haoles no like hire me," he complained. "They scade I goin' take dea jobs."

The criticisms began slowly, so at first no one, not even Mahealani, really noticed. He would yell at her for being too slow in responding to his call. He would criticize her for not cooking rice, or mixing poi, or frying fish the way he liked it; for not buying the right beer; for spending too much money or too much time with her family and friends. "You're mine," he said. "Your place is home with me."

But then he started staying out of the house, disappearing with his friends, and leaving Mahealani to walk the beach and swim with Liko alone. Mahealani tried to talk to him about what was wrong, what she had done to make him so upset all the time, but all he said was: "Nothing. Leave me alone."

Kanoe had been the first to notice the bruise on Mahealani's thigh. It was deep blue-black-purple, the size of a fist. "What happened to you?" she asked with great concern.

Mahealani tried to laugh it off. "Oh, you know me," she said, "always bumping into things."

"What are you talking about?" Kanoe responded. "That's not like you at all."

It took months before Mahealani revealed to Kanoe what was really going on. That Keone's behavior had become increasingly violent, that she suspected he was doing drugs with friends he wouldn't introduce her to—friends who only pulled up in the driveway and waited for Keone, or hung up the phone when she answered. Mahea confronted Keone, but he got angry and smashed things, and threatened to kill her and her family if she tried to leave him. Mahealani cried and cried, not from the physical pain, but from humiliation and shame. Keone made her feel so bad about herself. She cried from fear, too—that he would make good on his promise to hurt her family if she tried to leave. She felt hopeless and full of despair. She had kept all of this from them, she told Kanoe, because she wanted to protect everyone from Keone's violence.

"I can help him get better," Mahea said. "He's had such a difficult life."

"Sister," Kanoe said. "We all love you. You are a kindhearted woman who sees only the best in the world, in other people. But some things are beyond your kindness. Keone may have had a tough life, but that's not your fault and it isn't your problem. He needs to want help himself, and he doesn't. You need to get out. You need to help yourself get better. And we are all here to help you."

Mahealani loved to travel, to experience new places and meet new people. Keone had been enthusiastic at first. The first time they had gone camping at Mālaekahana, he seemed to enjoy it well enough—swimming, taking charge of the barbecue, pitching the tent. But the time they hiked out to Kaʻena point so Mahea could photograph the sea birds nesting there, he complained about the heat, how her art was stupid, expensive, and a waste of time. The next time they went to Kalalau on Kauaʻi, he complained about the mosquitoes, picked a fight with some other campers in the valley, and flirted with a younger haole girl who liked to spend the day topless on the beach, collecting shells. Mahea was so embarrassed and angry. Through it all, he picked on her, blaming her for every insult, real and imagined, mocking her interests, criticizing things she loved that gave her peace and pleasure.

Soon, Keone was criticizing her in front of his family and friends, who seemed uncomfortable but did nothing. For them, it was a familiar pattern they didn't know how to break, one they had seen too many times before.

"Knock it off," his brother warned. "She's a good wahine, and good for you."

Keone snickered. "Brah, you don't even know," he retorted, and stomped off.

Then it started in front of her family. Kanoe was furious. "Why you put up with this, Mahea?" she demanded. "You don't deserve this crap, no one does! Get the hell away from him."

A family barbecue at the beach was the last straw. Mahea had wanted to surprise Keone for his birthday, so she called family and friends and arranged a potluck barbecue at Kualoa, the beach where they met. It would be a surprise. Keone's friends would pick him up to go surfing, and Mahea would set up everything. Everyone came to help pitch the tent and prep the barbecue. Cousin Rocky brought his reggae CDs, Aunty Momi made her famous mac salad, Keone's brother cooked the teriyaki and char siu chicken to perfection. Mahea was so excited just thinking how happy Keone would be.

But the guys had stopped off to buy beer on the drive back down the coast, ran into a few friends in Punaluʻu they hadn't seen for awhile, and with talking story and more beer, Keone's friends forgot about the surprise party. They arrived hours late, drunk, the food and most of the guests long gone. She and Keone argued in the parking lot, and Keone managed to make it her fault once again. Mahea was so angry that she turned her back on Keone and started to walk off; Keone was so mad that he threw his beer bottle at her, yelling, "Don't walk away from me, bitch!" The bottle hit her in the back of the head, nearly knocking her out and causing a small cut that wouldn't stop bleeding.

"What the hell you doing?" Keone's brother roared and tackled him to the ground, their mom screaming at them to stop, Kanoe whipping out her cell phone, dialing 911.

Keone was hauled off in a police car, and Kanoe drove Mahea to the ER. The next few days were a blur of people talking to her, at her, about her, in hospital triage rooms, pharmacies, doctors' offices, police stations, courtrooms, Legal Aid. There were counselor's appointments, TROs. Mom talking, sister talking, friends calling, Keone apologizing, then swearing, "I'll get you, bitch, just wait. I'll get you."

A week after Keone was released from prison, Mahea woke up to find a box of photos of her and Keone torn into thousands of bits of confetti littering the front porch. A knife was stuck in the kitchen door, the four tires of her rusty old Toyota were slashed, and her driver's side mirror was smashed to pieces. Mahealani immediately packed her things and moved to her mother's house.

Later, she, Kanoe, and their mom went to Kaua'i for her cousin Lani's baby's first lū'au. When they returned, the ti plants and red ginger in the front yard were hacked to pieces, the lock on the back door broken, and Mahea's room trashed. So then there was more: police, attorneys, paperwork, TROs, talking, and fear. *What would he do next?* they whispered. "Mahea, be careful," they warned.

Mahea was careful. She never left the house alone, she made sure someone knew where she was at all times, and Liko was an almost constant companion, Keone long ago having abandoned his dog, too. But Keone was clever. He knew Mahea's weaknesses: the ocean, her fondness for animals, and her attachment to Liko.

One afternoon after a long and trying day, Mahea took Liko to Kailua Beach, thinking maybe a swim out to Flat Island on the Lanikai side of the bay would be good for both of them. A pale crescent moon rose, smiling above the blue horizon. Keone had borrowed a friend's car, so Mahea never saw him as he parked near the bathroom, the car camouflaged among the light trucks and surf sedans owned by the afternoon joggers and swimmers and windsurfers who frequented the bay.

Mahea felt refreshed by the warm breeze that tasted of salt, Liko happily bouncing at her feet. She entered the warm water, paddling with even strokes toward the island. She didn't hear the long sharp whistle from the shore, only felt Liko's comforting presence drop farther behind her, replaced with a bigger, more menacing one she sensed more than felt. As she turned to look, Mahealani felt the steely grip of his hand grasp her right ankle and pull hard, stopping her motion in the water so suddenly that she choked on the salt water that bubbled up into her nose.

The shock and fear lasted a split second, and then Mahea felt anger and determination well up inside of her as she had never felt before. She struggled to free the leg imprisoned by Keone's grip, but he was much too strong. They struggled in the water, Keone trying to strengthen his grasp, Mahea fiercely writhing to break free.

Not like this, she thought. *It's not going to end like this.* There was no breath for words, no energy for screaming. *Help me*, Mahea prayed silently. *Please, God, anyone, help me.* She could feel Keone's grip get stronger as he used his weight to slowly pull her under, trying to drown her.

No, Mahea thought. *No, no, no, no, no.* Mahea's head surfaced for a second; as she took as deep a breath of air as she could muster, she spied an older Hawaiian man on a surfboard swiftly paddling toward them. *Oh please, help.* With her last bit of strength, Mahealani tried to visualize Keone's face behind her, cocked her free foot, and kicked with all the force she could, aiming for where she thought his face would be. Just as her left foot smashed him square in the nose, Liko's sharpened claws raked across Keone's back, her shark-like teeth piercing his side. Keone yelped in surprise, gagging on the salt water, and then the man Mahea had seen on the surfboard leapt on him, pinning his arms to his side.

Mahealani swam away as fast as she could, heart racing, adrenaline pumping, propelling her toward the shore where a handful of onlookers pointed and shouted. A woman gestured while talking into her cell phone, a lifeguard on a quad rolled up from the far side of the beach, and a police cruiser with blue lights flashing pulled up sideways on the boat ramp behind them. Somewhere behind her, the older Hawaiian man had subdued Keone and was paddling back to shore a short distance down the beach from her, intent on delivering him to the police officer. A few people met Mahea when she reached waist-deep water, pulling her to shore, asking, "Are you okay? He nearly killed you," while wrapping a towel around her bare wet shoulders, lifting her to safety. Liko stuck to her side like a shadow.

More hospital triage rooms, police officers, paperwork, Legal Aid, courtrooms, TROs, counselor's appointments. Mom talking, sister talking, friends calling, Keone apologizing, Keone behind bars, Keone silent. Mahea's things packed, a flight to Cousin Ikaika's house in South Kona, days spent sleeping on the pūne'e on the front porch, nights spent talking to the stars and the moon, days spent in the embrace of the sea at Keauhou, at Hōnaunau, at Miloli'i, Liko protectively at her side. Nights talking to aunties, cousins, friends in Honolulu on her new cell phone number, analyzing, reviewing, looking forward, letting go. Days spent hiking the hills of Kohala, the trail to Waipi'o, photographing sunrises, sunsets, cousins' children, tourists in Kailua town, lehua at the volcano, waves crashing in Puna, fishermen in Ka'ū. Nights spent sitting around a campfire with Ikaika and his friends, Liko securely at her side. Time spent grieving and healing, embracing life—her life—grateful for signs and blessings, the healing touch of the sea, 'iwa birds flying beneath rainbows, baptized in moonlight, her spirit renewed. Time to go home, all the time singing in her head:

Ha'ina 'ia mai ana ka puana	This is the story
O ka wahine Hina'aikamalama ē	Of the woman Hina'aikamalama
Ka mea i kūkū ai i ke kapa nani	The beater of beautiful kapa
Ka wahine maika'i a 'olu'olu ē	A good and generous woman.

"Wow, Aunty, that is an awesome story." Kaimana said. "Well, I mean, it was terrible that 'Aukele treated her bad. But Hina showed them—now everyone can appreciate and love her."

"Yeah, Aunty, that was the best story. I'm never gonna let anyone treat me like that! If they do, I'm going to find a rainbow ladder and escape to the moon, too, and if anyone tries to stop me, I'm going to karate kick them so they fall to earth," Kaha'i said.

Mahealani and Kanoe laughed. "That's what I like to hear," said Mahealani. "No one ever deserves to be treated that way." Mahealani pulled up her knees and rested her chin on them. Unconsciously, she dropped her right hand down to her right ankle, fingering the crescent-shaped scar Keone left there during their struggle in the water. Kaimana saw her and crawled into her lap.

"You too, Aunty," Kaimana said softly. "We're glad you're not with Uncle Keone anymore."

"Yeah, Aunty," Kaha'i said, leaning up close.

At their feet, Liko thumped her tail in the soft sand and licked their toes.

"Oh, gross!" Kaimana yelled, giggling.

"She's gonna eat sand!" Kaha'i cried.

"Sometimes," Kanoe said to the girls, "it isn't always easy for people to leave the one they love. They hope they'll change, that things will get better. Sometimes, they are just waiting to gather the courage, or they wait for a sign to guide them."

"Did Hina get a sign?" Kaha'i asked.

Directly above them, the moon glowed brighter and brighter. They all looked up, their faces bathed in resplendent white light that lit up the Ko'olau coast as bright as day.

"Oh, look," said Kaimana. "Hina is listening to our story. I think she just said yes, she saw a sign."

Mahealani laughed, too. "Yes, she did."

They all looked up into the aubergine sky. A few scattered clouds floated high in the darkness, pinpricks of blue and gold starlight dimmed by the pulsating, luminous moonlight. ✺

Rock of Ages
Christopher Kelsey

Inspired by the Legend of Taking Lava Rocks from the Volcano

Rock stories have always been with us. Although the exact origin of these tales is unknown, they are consistent with Hawaiians' strong geological and geographical identities. As the taro plant is the blood relative to the people, so is the land; the 'āina is a living sacred entity to be treated with respect. As children, we heard countless tales of people—and not always visitors—who took rocks as souvenirs from Big Island volcanoes and suffered a number of consequences, ranging from broken-down cars to physical ailments, until the rocks were returned.

That a visitor to our islands would do so out of ignorance is perhaps understandable, but I always wondered why a native would disrespect his 'āina and his culture. Reimagining this tale reaffirmed my awareness that, even if its intricacies are not always understood, Hawaiian culture is very much alive and needs to be honored and respected.

❀ ❀ ❀

The rock in his living room had kept him awake again. Darkness covered Eli's world and the light had yet to be divided from the darkness. He glanced at the alarm clock he hadn't set in months. Pajamas, a sweatsuit, and double wool socks couldn't prevent him from remaining chilled to the bone, cold-blooded as a mo'o, the four-legged cousin of the serpent. Was it a test from God or a curse from pagan Hawaiian spirits? Eli could no longer tell the difference.

His wife Myrna gurgled softly, undisturbed by the scissoring bamboo thicket outside their mauka window. Although it was only ten minutes to the southwest as the mynah bird flies, the bustle of downtown Honolulu seemed light-years away. He used to love looking out on that peaceful mountain view, through the lush rain forest up to the Tantalus ridgeline above Mānoa Valley. But he hadn't felt that peace in weeks.

He rolled to his left, swung his icy shins over the side of the mattress, and perched on the edge. Eli rubbed his numb legs as he might sticks of frozen firewood but failed to create a spark. He creaked to his feet and lurched out of the room, no longer needing to duck under the doorway that used to brush against his silver crew cut.

He hobbled into the black hallway and trekked across moldy floorboards,

the varnish as worn down as his sagging faith. He shuffled through the tattered
gray shag of the living room carpet until his kneecap nudged his La-Z-Boy's
cracked vinyl. He sagged down into the bosom of the familiar old chair, groped
in the elasticized pocket for the remote, and switched on CNN. Eli searched for
answers in the flickering gray images but found none.

The room was dominated by the rock. It lay there near the front door,
next to the dusty spinet, like a small meteor the size of a flattened softball.
Pāhoehoe, his grandson had called it in a language Eli had allowed to seep out
of his life like tiny fish escaping through an empty net.

Growing up around the eroding fishponds of Heʻeia on Oʻahu's windward
coast, ʻElika Kealahou Kealiʻi had enlisted in the army before the end of the
Korean War, determined to make a new life for himself and his pregnant bride,
Myrna. He'd returned to the Territory of Hawaiʻi with a new haircut, a new
name—his company chaplain had shortened it to Eli because it sounded "more
Christian"—and a brand-new Bible. He'd pledged to keep Jesus in the center of
his life and had become equally determined to abandon everything that inter-
fered, especially the beliefs of his ancestors and reverence for the culture of his
birth.

"Eli," his wife mumbled. "Come back to bed."

He'd heard this plea so often that its emotional value had shrunk to the
size of a mustard seed. He'd tried to be the kind of husband and father he knew
he should have been, but other priorities got in the way. He'd dedicated his life
to God, the fire department, and his family, in that order, but walking in the
light of the Lord and fighting fires took up most of his time. He was a pillar
of righteousness and service among the Baptist faithful. Before his retirement
last year, he'd risen to the rank of deputy chief and had served a ten-year stint
as head of the rescue squad. His four children had all grown in various directions and his wife had her own life, filled with shopping, luncheons, and weekly
appointments at the hairdresser.

And now he was left alone with that cursed stone. He strained toward
the malevolent lump in the predawn darkness. He squinted, struggling to pick
up an aura or glow. There was nothing he could see, but he felt it pulsing, ema-
nating some kind of ancient message he'd long ago refused to accept.

————————

Three months earlier it had lain along the pathway to Halemaʻumaʻu
Crater in Volcanoes National Park. On that balmy Saturday morning in Febru-
ary, Eli had served as the day's tour guide for a handful of out-of-state Baptists.
They'd enjoyed his stories of Hawaiian Christianity: Opukahaʻia's hunger for
the Word, Kaʻahumanu's denunciation of the kapu system, and the work of
Binamu, one of the first missionaries to come to the islands. He regaled them
with religious fervor and slight disdain for what he'd constantly referred to as

his ancestors' "pagan rites."

"Praise the Lord," exclaimed Mrs. Angela Goodhew, "for your godly example, Eli." She flipped up her hinged sunglasses and displayed a set of teeth capable of efficient grazing.

"Thank you, Ma'am," he said. He warmed to her praise and the touch of her pudgy white hand.

"One of our friends back at the office told us something about not removing any stones from the park." A sudden gust jerked up the brim of her chartreuse bonnet.

"Oh, you know how these folk tales are perpetuated by the pagan unchurched, Ma'am," Eli replied, silently thanking Jesus for providing him with another golden opportunity to be more vigilant in the eyes of God or, at the very least, to continue to impress Mrs. Goodhew. "I'm sure these silly superstitions have no effect on one who walks in the light of the Lord." He gave her a big ingratiating grin.

"Amen, brother." She patted the back of his hand, her carefully manicured fingernails lacquered a delicate shade of cherub pink.

"Unbelievers insist that it's a violation of cultural law, an offense to Pele, the goddess of the volcano. But as the Good Book says, 'Thou shalt have no other gods before me,' and I'll gladly prove my faith." He reached down and picked up a softball-sized stone and plopped it into his backpack. "I'm not afraid of any pagan idolatry."

Mrs. Goodhew beamed at him. Then she squealed as a brisk island breeze blew down off Mauna Loa and sent her floppy hat sailing. Before Eli could catch the bonnet it had blown back up the pathway and into the cauldron. His flood of apologies was politely accepted, but something in her mood had changed. The ill wind blew harder.

When the group returned to the rental car a few minutes later, they found the trunk jimmied and their belongings ripped off. No amount of fervent prayer could make them miraculously reappear. Mrs. Goodhew's shopping bags, filled with gifts for the folks back home, were among the missing items. Despite Eli's stumbling apologies, she didn't utter an encouraging word all the way back down the mountain. Halfway to the Hilo airport, the right rear tire picked up a kiawe thorn, and when Eli went to change it, he discovered the spare was as flat as Mrs. Goodhew's mood.

While they were waiting for the Avis airport shuttle, she waddled back and forth, jiggling in the rising heat. "Maybe you shouldn't have taken that goddam rock, Mr. Know-it-all," she snapped.

Eli couldn't think of a single scriptural response. He sagged against the side of the white Ford Taurus, his brown ears burning bright red.

He was saddened but relieved to finally get the group onto their Delta flight back at Honolulu International, secretly praying that nothing else would happen. But it did. In the Honolulu airport parking lot, his new Saturn four-door wouldn't start and he had to have it towed. When he finally got home, he found the fridge on the blink and a note from the repairman: *Compressor dead—better buy a new one.*

He took the rock out of his pack and put it down. It reminded him of both his pledge and his denial. He wasn't going to let a few random coincidences challenge his faith.

Then Myrna's Toyota had roared up the driveway and squealed to a stop on the smooth garage concrete. When the downstairs door opened, he retreated to the safety of the kitchen. Footsteps reached the top of the front steps and paused. He smelled her hairspray before he heard her question.

"What's that rock doing by our front door?"

"Uh, it's just a doorstop."

Myrna put down her shopping bags and straightened her mauve pantsuit. "A doorstop?" Her incredulous tone shredded his flimsy cover-up. "It looks like a lava rock to me. You didn't bring that back from the Big Island, did you?" Her hands had locked onto her hips.

He knew what was coming next and tried to get off the defensive. He stuck his head out of the kitchen and raised it defiantly. "I don't believe in that pagan mumbo-jumbo."

"I don't care what you believe, old man. You've been hanging around those dumb haoles too long. Nobody in their right mind takes a rock from the volcano. Nobody." She stomped down the hallway and yelled over her shoulder, "And you'd better do something about it!" She slammed the door behind her.

He knew he was in for the silent treatment. He'd weathered it before, but this time it took on a whole different dimension. The Shama thrush's tremolo lost its usual rapture. The gardenias bloomed but they might as well have been plastic. Poi and sardines became as tasteless as cold McDonald's fries. He wanted to feel the warmth of his wife's ʻūhā, the skin of her upper thigh, still soft and supple after forty-two years of marriage, but his fingertips only irritated her—or maybe she irritated him. He wanted to care about life around him but some part of him wouldn't cooperate. He lived in paradise, but it felt like purgatory.

It was hard for him to believe that a two-pound chunk of hardened basalt could disrupt his whole world. He cried out to the rock like Job, whom he'd known all of his adult life. He prayed louder and longer, calling out to his Blessed Redeemer to give him the strength to endure, rocking back and forth on ancient knees, wrapped in blankets that refused to give him warmth or comfort. He recited every psalm he knew, every prayer he remembered. He read from the Beatitudes, from Revelation—even the Old Testament, the Ten Commandments—but to no avail. Nobody answered.

But the rock wasn't finished yet. After all that had happened, the lava had suddenly picked up weight. He couldn't lift it, he couldn't even budge it. And he didn't tell anyone else about it. He knew this had become some kind of test from God. It had gone far beyond the outermost reaches of vanity, pride, and self-righteousness. He knew the Lord would deliver him from this affliction in His time and in His way.

"...in Jesus's blessed name, Amen." Eli took a deep breath and exhaled. He hoped the troubles in his life would be released along with it, but he knew it wasn't so. The black living room curtains had turned to charcoal, but his mood had failed to improve with the approaching day.

He rubbed his freezing arms and covered his sweatshirt with an old robe. A duet of ring-necked doves warbled from the Apple of Sodom bush, but their once melodious voices fell on his now numb auditory nerves. And the silence had a deadly hum of its own, like death.

It all emanated from the rock.

"God give me the strength to endure this," he muttered. Drawers slid open and shut in the back bedroom as his wife thumped and creaked around. He reached for the remote again and flipped through B movies, televangelists, '70s reruns, and analyses of the analysis of the news. He lulled himself into a trance again, only to be yanked out of it by the cutting edge of Myrna's scolding.

"Eli! Pay attention when I'm talking to you. I'm going out. There's leftover stew in the fridge and yesterday's rice on the stove. I won't be home till later." She clacked down the steps to the garage, opened the door, but stuck her head back through the opening. "Do you remember what day it is? Your grandson and his instructor should be here any minute." She pulled the door shut, got in her car, and roared off.

He struck his forehead with the butt of his hand. He'd completely forgotten that the boy and his kumu were coming to help with the rock. Eli didn't need any college professor butting in where he didn't belong. This was personal. He wished 'Ikaika hadn't worn him down when they'd argued about it last Thursday.

"Grandpa," 'Ikaika had said, "I'm really worried about you." His bear-like frame engulfed Eli's recliner. "You don't look so good. I don't think it's physical—I think we need something else."

"I have all the help I'll ever need." Eli patted the weathered black cover of his ancient King James version lying in his lap.

"I understand." 'Ikaika put his paw on Eli's shoulder, and his voice took on a quiet intensity. "But I think we need to take the next step."

"Eh? What's that?"

"I'm bringing my Hawaiian Studies kumu to help you with the stone."

"I won't have any pagan idolatry in my house!" He struggled to lurch upright out of the recliner, but his grandson blocked out the room. "Let me up!"

'Ikaika lowered his face next to Eli's. "Relax, Grandpa. Kumu Ho'omanawanui isn't some kind of evil sorcerer. There are many paths to the mountaintop. He's a spiritual man, more experienced in these matters than anyone I know." He lifted his thick koa-colored braid off of Eli's grey crew cut and flipped it back over his massive shoulders. "Besides, he's gonna visit his family in Pāhoa this weekend. The crater's less than a half hour's drive from their house." He sat back on his haunches like some gigantic Buddha. Eli snorted.

The boy gently massaged the old man's stubbled cheek. "Don't worry. I know how hard this is for you. It'll be okay—really."

Eli managed a weak smile. But how could even his beloved grandson really understand? "We'll see."

"We'll be along early. Kumu wants to take advantage of the first light." 'Ikaika kissed him on the forehead before rumbling down the steps and out the door.

Eli nodded after the fact. The boy's battered VW van sputtered away and silence crept back over Eli's world. He didn't know how he'd be able to tolerate any native ceremonies in his God-fearing home.

The top edge of the curtain rod had barely begun to lighten when a soft knock sounded at the front door. "Grandpa, come onto the porch."

"Eh?" Eli lurched to his feet. "But—"

"Hurry, Grandpa. We must begin before the sun rises."

"But I'm not dressed." He shuffled toward the door, trying to make sense out of the belt on his faded terry-cloth robe.

"Kumu says it doesn't matter, Grandpa. Please open the door."

It matters to me, Eli wanted to snap back. With shaking hands he reached for the worn brass knob and the new deadbolt, but he forgot to remove the chain. When he tried to swing the door inward it almost jerked the anchor bracket off the wall. He recovered and fumbled with the slot until the chain finally slipped free. He opened the door, embarrassed and more than a little afraid.

His grandson loomed in the doorway. Eli had never understood why the three-time, all-state offensive tackle had turned down those football scholarships—not only to the University of Hawai'i but to such powerhouse schools as Michigan State, Arizona, and Southern Cal. 'Ikaika had admitted that he missed it but that some things had become more important than football. He'd registered at UH, double-majoring in Hawaiian Studies and music. It still didn't make sense to Eli.

'Ikaika pulled open the screen door and held out his big mitt. Eli hesitated and then stepped out into the predawn shadows. The dark peaks at the back of the valley were edged diamond blue. His grandson turned to the rear of the small porch and ushered forward a short solemn Hawaiian with black shoulder-length hair.

"Grandpa, this is Kumu Hoʻomanawanui. Kumu, this is my grandpa, 'Elika Kealahou Kaliʻi."

The sound of his full Hawaiian name shocked him. It had been decades since he'd heard those letters run together so musically. But he couldn't remember when he'd ever told the boy his middle name. The teacher extended his hand and offered a deep soft greeting.

"Aloha."

He knew it had been overused, cheapened, diluted, and trivialized. But the way the kumu spoke it brought renewed meaning to the word. His warm, firm grasp added to Eli's surprise. He didn't know what to say. The proper response wouldn't come and he ended up simply nodding his head.

"Let's begin," said Kumu, "as the day begins." He reached into a white nylon duffel bag and removed a gallon-sized Ziploc that contained three maile lei. He draped one of the leafy strands around 'Ikaika's neck and kissed him lightly on the cheek. The boy returned the honor. Eli tensed up with the discomfort of being kissed by a man outside of his family, but the gesture, the ceremony, and the warmth that came from Kumu's touch left Eli surprisingly at ease.

"Join hands," said Kumu. "Let's have a quick pule to thank the Creator for this new day." They stood together on the concrete porch with heads bowed as Kumu intoned briefly in Hawaiian. Eli caught very little of it; the language of his birth was now as foreign to him as Aramaic.

When they released hands, the teacher reached into the bag again and retrieved two large green ti leaves the size of ceiling-fan blades. He held them by the stems and dipped the tips into a small koa bowl that 'Ikaika had filled with water. Eli would've backed off the edge of the porch if his grandson hadn't grabbed his shoulder.

"It's a blessing ceremony, Grandpa." Kumu began to chant, a rich melodious trumpeting full of swells, dips, and crests. "Open the door, Grandpa. It's time for Kumu to enter."

The teacher dipped the ti-leaf tips into the bowl and sprinkled water on the three of them, on the doorframe, and randomly throughout the room. The rich chanting continued, rolling like wind through ancient forests. But to Eli, it still looked like a pagan ceremony. He couldn't allow such blasphemy in his own home.

Just before Eli opened his mouth, 'Ikaika hugged him and whispered in his ear, "Please, Grandpa, I need your kōkua. It's not what you think. Kumu is here to help."

Eli's trust hung by a thread. He silently thanked God for his grandson's help and fought to keep his indignation under control.

"It's a welcoming chant, Grandpa. Kind of an introduction." He paused and closed his eyes as if searching for a better explanation. "It's a polite way to begin an event, honoring the sanctity of life, the participants, and the world around them."

Eli wasn't convinced. "He's not casting spells, is he?"

"Of course not. Hang in there, Grandpa." He gently wrapped his arm around Eli's shoulders and guided him into the house.

When Eli stepped across the threshold, the chanting stopped. Kumu stood motionless, staring at the stone in the half-light. He turned to face Eli.

"Please open the shades," Kumu said. "The pōhaku needs the blessing of the first rays."

But it's just a rock, Eli wanted to shout at the intense little man. 'Ikaika shot him a stern glance as if he could read his mind. Eli shuffled over to the windows. "Of course," he mumbled. He yanked on the drapery cords but the pulley wheels squealed in resistance. He didn't know how long it had been since he'd opened them. He turned sheepishly and began to offer an apology but the teacher held up his hand.

"Not to worry. Now is as good a time as any to let some of the outside in. 'Ikaika, can you please help your kupuna?"

Eli returned to tugging at the yellowed nylon cords, while his grandson reached above the rods and gently encouraged the binding plastic clips away from the center, and the two of them gradually opened the curtains. The first beams crept over the hemlock-green Mānoa peaks and entered the once tomb-like room. One of the beacons fell on the picture of Christ on the wall above the rock. Eli almost jumped in shock and fell back into his gloomy mindset. He couldn't take it anymore.

"Look, 'Ikaika, I know you folks are trying to—"

"'Elika Kealahou Keali'i, firstborn of Kainoa and Kawaiho'ano Keali'i of He'eia, please be still. There is still much to be done. We need your kōkua, not your doubts."

Once again, Eli was overwhelmed by the musicality of the syllables—but how did Kumu know those names and where he was from? Even 'Ikaika didn't know all of it.

In the meantime, Kumu had unrolled on the living room floor an intricately woven lau hala mat the size of his Lord's Supper tablecloth. He then spread out a layer of finely beaten kapa on top of it. He slipped his hands under both, lifted them, and turned to face the sun. He chanted while 'Ikaika whispered in Eli's ear.

"He's thanking the Creator for the beauty of this day ... praising His many names ... and giving thanks for the healing warmth of the rising sun. He offers the lau hala ... and the kapa ... as a suitable foundation ... for the transport of the stone back to its rightful home."

The sun's rays had crept down the wall beneath the picture of Christ and approached the blackness that enveloped the rock. Eli wondered if the light would be able to penetrate the darkness that had slithered into his life over the past few weeks.

The teacher had finished his chanting and turned again to Eli, who had slouched against the side of the door. "Now comes the most crucial time. I alone cannot complete this ceremony. I need your help, brother 'Elika."

"Eh? My help?" Eli shrank down against the doorframe. The sharp edge of the molding stabbed his chilled backbone. "I've been trying to do something about this—this—" He gestured toward the stone.

Kumu stepped toward him. "This part of the 'āina?"

He felt as if he was being challenged. "I see it more as a cold, dead piece of lava." Eli rose to his full height, less intimidated than he was just a few seconds before.

"On the contrary, friend," said Kumu. "The pōhaku is anything but cold and dead. It is a part of a living, breathing 'āina, connected to everything around it." Part of Kumu's face had yet to emerge from the shadows, but his dark eyes seemed depthless, like stars in polished obsidian. Eli felt like he would be sucked into them but he somehow wasn't afraid.

"Grandpa, some part of you knows this," 'Ikaika pleaded. "It's been inside of you for years. You've been able to deny it all your adult life, but you can't resist it forever. Please forgive me, Grandpa." He grasped Eli's hands. "I mean no disrespect—it's part of who you really are."

He loved his grandson dearly, but this sounded like liberal, New Age monkey business.

"'Elika," said Kumu, "I know this is hard to understand, but your parents knew this wisdom as did their kūpuna." The teacher and the student had gradually moved toward him until they were all grouped tightly by the front door. "We have allowed the new ways to wipe away what was once meaningful."

Eli reflexively shook his head in denial. The room smelled like limu. A part of him rushed back to a time over fifty years ago. He was waist-deep in a He'eia fishpond. His Grandpa Keali'i had been teaching him the proper way to throw a net over a lively school of mullet. The tall white-haired man had been patient and tender. "It's all about pono, keiki, the special balance that exists in your body, in your mind, and most importantly, in your spirit. The life and the land are one."

When he looked at the picture of Christ, Kumu and his grandson were
out of focus. When he shifted his concentration to 'Ikaika and the teacher, the
picture of Jesus blurred. At the base of the wall lay the thing that had blocked
out a big part of his life. If he could only somehow roll away the stone.

"I'm quite sure you're aware," said Kumu," that it's not the pōhaku that's
causing your troubles."

Eli felt the warmth and care of Kumu's grip around his left wrist. "What
do you mean?" He pulled his arm back, but Kumu wouldn't release his grip.
"Are you saying this is all my fault?" Adrenaline shot through his wiry sinews
and he pulled with all his might. The powerful jerk freed his wrist and sent
him stumbling back into the wall. His grandson's support prevented him from
collapsing, but the vibration had shaken the framing in the adjacent wall where
Christ's countenance had been hanging. Until now.

"The picture," he gasped. He staggered across the room, expecting to find
the glass-covered frame lying in pieces. It had fallen and struck the rock but to
Eli's amazement hadn't sustained any noticeable damage. He snatched it off the
surface of the lava and scrutinized it as closely as the early morning light would
allow, but he couldn't find a single scratch.

Eli hung it back on its hook and leaned against the wall. It had become a
giant jigsaw puzzle in his head. He hardly knew where to begin. He turned to
the other two in utter amazement. "I don't know what to say."

"I think it's time," said Kumu, "to allow this pōhaku to return home."

'Ikaika had opened a woven lau hala container about the size of an offering calabash. The inside was lined with fresh ti leaves. Kumu placed the mat and
kapa on the floor directly in front of the stone and stood next to Eli.

Kumu spoke softly from the shadow. "Say whatever is in your heart. I'll
translate it into Hawaiian."

Eli felt as if he stood on a stage in front of a million staring eyes. He
looked at Kumu and 'Ikaika but they only nodded in support. His tongue
was swollen and stuck to the back of his throat. He stuttered and stammered,
hemmed and hawed until the calming vision of his white-haired kupuna
appeared in his mind, holding that ancient throw-net. He closed his eyes. "Oh,
gracious Creator of the Universe, help me to appreciate all the beauty that is
around us. Help me to bring it all into balance, into the moment, and to appreciate that the life and the land are one. Help this part of the 'āina to be returned
safely home whence it came. 'Amene."

He opened his eyes to see his grandson gently placing the wrapped rock
into the lined lau hala box. The kumu tied it tightly with a stripped ti-leaf stem
and placed it gently into his bag.

"You did well, 'Elika Kealahou Keali'i," said Kumu. "Life and the land are one."

A ray of morning sun crept onto Eli's stockinged feet, comforting and warm. ✿

No Look Back
Timothy Dyke

Inspired by the Legend of Māui the Fisherman

Māui ventured out to sea with his brothers, who made fun of him for not catching as many fish as they did. Frustrated with her son's inability, Māui's mother, Hina, sends him to his father to receive a special hook to help him fish more effectively. His brothers eventually allow Māui to come along on their fishing adventures, and for a while, they are only moderately successful; but then Māui baits his magic hook with the 'alae, a bird sacred to their mother, casts his line into the sea, and almost immediately, the magic hook snags a great fish that pulls the boat past the waves and deep out to sea.

For two days, Māui and his brothers follow the hooked fish on their taut line. Eventually, as the fish tires the line slackens, and Māui yells for his brothers to help him reel it in. As they pull, land rises out of the water. His brothers watch in amazement, but Māui instructs them to pull with their eyes straight ahead, never looking behind at their snagged prey. One brother cannot resist, and when he looks back the line snaps. Māui had been on the verge of pulling up a new continent, but when his brother gazes back, the land lies beyond their reach, fragmented into islands.

In Māui stories there is a fine line between destruction and creation, between mischief and genius. I'll always be drawn to Māui, and while I would never be so arrogant as to compare myself to him, I will say that I know what it's like to be the troublemaking brother. I admire the way he turns awkward family interactions into opportunities for magic. Like many great legends, this particular tale satisfies a need to give mythic explanation to complicated scientific phenomena. How did the Hawaiian island chain emerge? This story provides a poetic and compelling answer, and in its warning not to look back, it also echoes some themes found in myths and legends from other cultures. Personally, his admonition resonates.

I'm trying to construct a tale about my friend, Logan Cabrera. It's difficult for me to look back at all the events that happened between us and find one clear instance of narrative-launch. I could begin on the day we met, or on the day I was born. I could focus on the way the trouble started. I could start with the morning I came out of the closet. I could begin today and move backward.

Back in the day, there was a high school teacher and a former student. Once upon a time, I drove the kid out to Sand Island when he was strung out on OxyContin. I could begin with the moment I picked up the telephone. I could describe the afternoon in Phoenix when I watched him snort heroin through the shaft of a ballpoint pen. Or I could start, as I often do, by wandering off on a tangent connected to some recent conversation from English class.

I teach an elective for high school seniors called "The Bible as Literature." Early last semester, I was talking to my students about the story from Genesis about Lot and his wife. I find that story hard to analyze, and I was asking the kids in my class to explain specific plot points. Some of them have it in their heads that God destroyed Sodom to purge his land of gay people, and while I wasn't necessarily trying to contradict their upbringings, I was attempting to steer them toward a more nuanced interpretation.

"Hey," I asked my class as we got to the part where Lot's wife turns to a pillar of salt. (She would have been fine if Lot had resisted the temptation to turn around and check on her.) "Doesn't this remind you of the Greek myth of Orpheus?" They looked at me with mild recognition. "In Greek myth, Orpheus goes down to the underworld to rescue his lover, Eurydice." I saw a kid move a thumb toward his iPhone, but I ignored him. "Do you all know this story?" Most did, but some didn't, so we etched out important details: Orpheus is allowed to take Eurydice from Hades, but he's told that when he exits the underworld, he's not to look back at her. He starts walking and, as he gets anxious, he turns around to gaze behind. Eurydice disappears, never to return again. Erica, the girl with the mushroom design on her hoodie, announced that a Māui story went the same way.

"Really?" I asked. "How does it go?"

"I'm not sure," she said. "We read it in fourth grade."

John Cho told us that Māui was a fisherman who tricked his brothers, and one time he started pulling up what seemed like the biggest fish in the sea. Māui was pulling up a continent. He warned his brother not to look behind the boat, but the brother was weak and looked back. The line snapped and the land broke up into islands. John Cho ended his recitation with a pronouncement: "That's how we got Hawai'i."

Caroline Wong seemed to think John had it wrong somehow. "You're mixing up a couple of stories. You told it more watered down."

Attempting to grab control of the discussion, I asked a question about human nature. "What does it tell us that three different cultures across time and space all tell sacred stories about the dangers of looking behind?" I glanced briefly at the clock and then at a girl playing with her earring. "Why would human beings keep reminding each other not to look back?"

Let's just say my Sand Island story begins when Logan called me at five o'clock in the afternoon. That day I stood in line for what seemed like hours at Satellite City Hall, and at seven I was due at HPU, on the other side of the island, for a theater audition. I'd known Logan since he was my creative writing student ten years before; we stayed in touch after graduation. For whatever reason, he turned to me when he dropped out of UH, after his parents kicked him out of their house in Waipahu. For whatever reason, I felt compelled to act as his savior. It's easiest, I suppose, to retreat to language of pop psychology and say finally that ours was a codependent relationship. I don't really like using such reductive description, but these words express certain truths: He was a drug addict; I was an emotionally needy gay man. In other ways, I'm sure it makes sense just to say we were friends.

An hour before I was to drive out to HPU for *The Cherry Orchard* callback, my phone rang. It was Logan, and as soon as I heard his voice I was overcome by simultaneous waves of worry and relief. The last time we'd talked he told me he was relapsing. He had been clean going on two and a half years. He had returned to school, restored his relationship with his parents, and devoted himself to recovery. Then he called me after Christmas and said flatly, "I'm using again." Now he was calling me from Chinatown, asking for my help. Something had happened to his car and he was stranded. He wanted me to pick him up in front of the rRed Elephant Café in thirty minutes. Remember that place? I kind of liked it, though at this point, it's difficult for me to associate it with anything other than spell-check and drug relapse.

I told him I had an audition for a play at HPU. "I have to be there in an hour…"

Even as I fought traffic on my way to Chinatown, I knew I shouldn't be picking him up. Logan has told me many times that if his addiction asks me to do something, I should tell it no. Still, I was just so glad to hear his voice. It seemed wrong not to pick him up.

I waited in front of the rRed Elephant for ten minutes, illegally parked, nervous about time. When he showed up—when he walked up to me with an ice-cream sandwich and asked if I wanted a bite—it was all I could do not to crumble. He looked nothing like himself; he looked like Addict Logan, puffy and red. After narrating a sad story about an ATM and a tow-truck guy, he asked me to drive him out to Sand Island to pick up his car.

Here's the thing. I don't need anyone to tell me it was wrong to take Addict Logan to Sand Island. He told me himself that he had just snorted Vicodin. "Dude," I asked lamely. "If I leave you at the towing place, are you going to be all right to drive?"

It's hard to remember stuff I'd rather forget. As we rode down Nimitz, I asked him if he wanted to tell me about his relapse, but he said only that it start-

ed three weeks before when his friend Micah found him at Zippy's "with a little
bit of everything in the bloodstream." We got to Chiyo's Towing and Logan
told me he only had fifty dollars. I gave him the four twenties in my wallet as
he climbed out of my car. His hand wiggled while he took my cash. "This is the
first time in two and a half years that I've taken money from you," he said.

Conclusions might be even harder than story beginnings. "Happily ever
after" is the default option, but not every tale lends itself to joyful closure. The
Lot story ends with municipal destruction. The Māui story ends with fissure
and emergence. The Bible ends in Revelation. I watched Logan stumble over to
the tow-lot man, a large guy with a cigarette and an unbuttoned shirt. Maybe he
was Chiyo. I waited until my friend turned around and threw me a wave. This
was my signal to leave, and even though I knew it was wrong to flee, I put the
car in reverse. I drove away because it was less painful than staying. I tuned to
KTUH on the radio and backed my Element off the lot. *The Cherry Orchard*
audition would begin in twenty minutes. On some level, I knew I wasn't going to
get the part I wanted, but I kept driving and compelled myself not to look back
in the rearview mirror.

That's probably where I should end, but there's this other detail that
keeps popping up on my memory screen. Symbols are important for distinctive
stories. Māui has his fishhook. Orpheus has, what?—a lute? A lyre? Margari-
taville has its lost shaker of salt. Me and Logan had this five-peso coin. A few
years ago, as he dropped me off at the airport, he reached into a cup holder and
grabbed a coin. "Have you ever seen a peso before?" I told him I had. I took the
coin—he seemed to be offering it as a kind of gift—and kept it in a drawer for a
while.

While Logan worked on his sobriety, the coin seemed like a good thing
for me to hold onto. I slid it in my wallet between my driver's license and my
credit card. It fell out a lot. That seemed to be one of the magical things about
this lucky charm. I would lose the coin for any number of days or weeks, but it
would always come back to me. I'd find it in the dryer. I'd find it in a pocket of
random pants. Then, six months ago, I lost it for good.

One morning I left Makiki and walked down to the Ala Moana Barnes
& Noble. It was around nine on Saturday morning and there was no one else on
the sidewalk except for homeless people. I walked past a shirtless, bearded man
on my way to the bookstore, and forty minutes later, I walked past him on my
way home. As I crossed his path that second time, swinging a Michael Pollan
book in a green plastic Barnes & Noble bag, I heard him say hello. I looked, just
for a moment. He didn't shake his plastic cup, but my eyes went there anyway. I
felt the weight of loose change in the pockets of my cargo pants. Scooping coins
into my palm, I said, "Here you go, man," then emptied my hand above his cup.
He thanked me and we separated.

As soon as I retreated, I knew I'd just given away my Mexican coin. I hadn't realized it was in my pocket, but I felt its weight lift, and I've never seen it since. The coin meant a lot to me, and it had no value to the homeless man. On the other hand, I like to imagine that peso gives him some kind of power—mana. I wonder if he carries it around with him, if it lightens his burdens. I'm idealizing all of this way too much, but I feel better when I imagine the peso traveling around the city—from Makiki to Ala Moana, from Chinatown to Sand Island.

Logan got home safe that day. I guess he had a couple of close calls, but when I spoke to him after the callback audition, he assured me he was okay. He sounded like he knew he was going to have to go back to Hina Mauka for treatment. I didn't get the part I wanted in *The Cherry Orchard*, but I did get cast as a minor character. It's almost too melodramatic to reveal that I was given the part of The Vagrant, but that's actually what happened. My character walks up and down the pre-Soviet countryside, drunk and begging for rubles.

Logan told me the other day that he was struggling to forgive himself for breaking two and a half years of sobriety. "Today," he said, "I've been clean for just over a month." We were standing in a parking lot outside a Pizza Hut.

"That's great," I told him, watching him light a cigarette.

He seemed to understand that counting days could be a trap. "One day at a time," he said to me. He reached into his pocket and pulled out his one-month sobriety coin.

"One day at a time," I repeated.

"One step forward," he chanted back. "That's the way I got to do it. One step forward. No look back." ✿

LOVE AND FAMILY

LANGUAGE OF THE GECKOS
Gary Pak

INSPIRED BY ʻAUMĀKUA TALES OF THE MOʻO

In the evenings, when I was small, I would look out the screened windows of our house at the geckos, their translucent undersides sometimes showing an egg or two. Geckos covered the outside of our house, scurrying this way and that, calling or challenging each other with staccato voices, and once in a while one would find its way inside. I never was able to see it inside; it was just too elusive, too fast, too deceptive. But once in a while, its call would give it away, or in the morning I'd notice droppings on the kitchen counter or along the inside of a window. Geckos were all around us all the time.

Back then, I never knew about their significance to the ʻāina, what they represented, their connection to Hawaiian mythology, or how some believe the moʻo to be their ancestor or ʻaumakua (guardian spirit). It was something I never thought about. Like the spirits and ghosts that freely meandered all over the land of my birth, I just lived with them. They were just a part of me, and perhaps I could say that I was a part of them. Only later, as an adult, did I learn that geckos, or perhaps only some of them, were considered moʻo and an important part of Hawaiian mythology and the Hawaiian ancestral belief system.

❁ ❁ ❁

THE GECKOS WERE ALL OVER GABRIEL HOʻOKANO'S HOUSE, BUT IT DIDN'T BOTHER HIM FOR THE SIMPLE REASON THAT THEY HAD ALWAYS BEEN THERE. GENERATIONS AND GENERATIONS OF GECKOS had populated the Hoʻokano property, even before the house (which Gabriel had built himself) existed. Gabriel knew the genealogy of the geckos, or the moʻo as he would correctly call them, since he regarded their lineage and his to be one and the same. He would call particular geckos Uncle or Aunty; and with the death of his wayward brother, the newest gecko to appear on Gabriel's nightly screen was given the name Kopa, Jacob's childhood nickname.

It was amazing that even with a failing memory Gabriel never forgot the names of the hundreds—perhaps thousands—of geckos that surrounded him. What was even more astonishing was his ability to communicate—rather, "talk story"—with the moʻo, with the exception of the new one, Kopa, who had never once kah-kah-kahed since his advent at the Hoʻokano house (though he had taken a royal share of termites, flies, mosquitoes and other resident arthropods).

Even if Kopa never talked to him, Gabriel made it a habit to talk with him anyway, for he knew Kopa was hiding in some nook of the porch and listening. In the early evenings, after finishing the supper that he now often cooked, and while Mary and Harriet were washing the dishes and talking stories (Harriet had taken up the habit, as requested adamantly by Mary and not so enthusiastically by Gabriel, of having her meals at the Hoʻokano residence; for the most part, she had moved in, taking quarters in the back bedroom of the house, which was ideal for her since the room gave her a near panoramic view of her pasture [with the old garage partially blocking the right side] and it was but a one-minute stroll to her beloved cows), Gabriel would talk stories to Kopa. He'd relate the day's events, and if he could not remember what had happened, then he would make them up. This was done with an understanding of his brother's situation: Kopa, frolicking in the spiritual world that made him know almost everything, would know how to interpret Gabriel's stories and turn them into truths.

Gabriel noticed how boisterous the geckos had become over the past few days (with the exception of Kopa, though Gabriel did note how he had become a bit edgy at times, skittering back and forth across the dusty screen faster than usual, as if anticipating a big storm), with the geckos on the mauka side of the house being contentious with the geckos of the front porch. They'd meet at the intersecting corner of the house, usually near the eaves, and have it out. Most times Gabriel heard them argue about how many more termites the other side was getting, though once there was a savage fight that involved two geckos locked in each other's jaws. Gabriel, who couldn't stand the sight of a family fighting (there had just been too much of that in his immediate, human family), shooed them off with a bulldog look and a loud kah-kaht! But the next evening, Gabriel heard more racket, this time coming from the makai Diamond Head corner of the house. And this continued for the next three days. (Or was it four?) Something was definitely bugging the moʻo, and Gabriel found no rest when the moʻo were in such a troubled state.

And then it rained hard for five days and nights, which gave some peace to the residents of the house. The heavy, wet air seemed to pacify the geckos and, correspondingly, Gabriel, too. The rain had come in from the ocean, and at first the showers were intermittent. When there was a break in the rain, Gabriel would look toward Waiola Valley (where his brother had lived), lost in low-lying clouds. "Kopa, I know you behind all of dis," Gabriel would say repeatedly in the day, but with a smile, since Gabriel knew that Jacob, even after years and years of indifference and downright mistrust, really had a soft spot in his soul. Once, after gazing toward the rainy clouds by Waiola and making his comment, Gabriel was sure that he heard a subdued kah-kahing somewhere above him.

But on the second day, the rain came down hard, and it got harder as the day progressed. By the third day, a small lake began forming in the front yard of the Hoʻokano house. Gabriel called John Kim, the newspaper district manager, to temporarily terminate delivery of the morning daily, and John apologetically agreed. Now Gabriel would look up at the always cloudy sky and the rain and begin cursing his brother: "And den! You going float my house away or what?"

Strange things began to float in the growing lake. At first, Gabriel took no notice until Mary peeled off a scrap of newspaper that had washed up on the second from the bottom porch step.

"Look, Gabe, how old dis newspaper is."

Gabriel continued rocking in his chair, wrapped in that moldy mood of his that was getting moldier by the moment.

"August 19, 1956," Mary announced, as if the date had a special significance.

It didn't, but the uttered month and last digit echoed through those mossy arches in Gabriel's mind. Funny that with all his forgetfulness he was able to remember the exact date of his induction into the United States armed services: August 6, 1944.

"Mo' bettah I should have quit when I was ahead," he said.

"What was dat?" inquired a half-listening Harriet, who was sitting on the other end of the patio.

Turning to his cousin, Gabriel repeated his comment and added, "Das what history is all about, I think, about having to do things not yo' own way but den you da one gotta face da truth or consequences."

And funny how Gabriel's words triggered a recurrence of bitter memory in Harriet, of the day when she received the telegram declaring her husband's death on the USS *Indianapolis*, one week after its sinking. Harriet didn't cry, but she had a sudden desire to visit her cows.

"I'm going," she said to no one and everyone.

"Where you going?" Mary asked with alarm, looking up from her self-appointed work of piecing together the soggy bits of the old newspaper. "How you going out of dis house wit' all of dis rain ... and dat?" She pointed to the lake. Though it had lightened up, the rain was still falling miserably. "And where you going?"

"I ... I have to go," was Harriet's answer. And then she rose from her seat and entered the house.

"Dis funny kine weather making everybody funny kine, everybody jumpy," Gabriel quipped. He sat pensively, his face as solemn as a doorknob of an old church. Nodding his head, he said, "Dat damn war ... if it wasn't fo' it, I would be da one making all dis rain instead of suffering from it."

The bit of old-time newspaper that Mary discovered washed upon her shore—if we may so describe it literarily—was the first of many. Other vintage newspapers appeared, all soggy and broken into constituent parts, though not dissociative enough to denote the date or style of a time gone by. Even newspapers printed in Hawaiian were discovered. The residents of the Hoʻokano house were alarmed at the ominous regularity of news from the past turning up, which they could not read well since the newspapers were in fragments or the ink had bled, now too weak to be discriminating. And they were also getting more and more isolated from everyone else since the lake was growing like an epidemic and was becoming more or less a lake of dislocation, cutting them off from the rest of Kānewai.

Come the fifth day and with the rains stopping, they began to resist the admonishing touches of despair; they became rejuvenated with the expectation that the lake would recede, and they rose with the hope that it would take but a short time before life would swing back to normal: driving casually down Kānewai's streets and shopping for specials at Leong's Market.

But the lake did not recede, and the objects they fished out of the lake were more old newspapers that were concocting a strange sense of time past and time lost. Their conversations were now tempered with nostalgia, at first reminiscing about happy times but moving invariably toward dark memories that Gabriel, Mary, and Harriet thought were vanquished by over-remembering. They also were running out of food, though the condition did not alarm them since, as they found, with the days moving lugubriously on, they were requiring less and less food. (A pot of rice, for example, would last them four to five days.)

But when Kopa began making his first, undecipherable sounds (like anyone introduced to a strange kind of existence, part of the new experience is to learn the requisite language, if applicable; in Kopa's case, facility in the moʻo language came quickly since he was a fast learner, though he needed practice [he had refused to talk to anyone or any of the other moʻo when he first arrived on the scene] to be able to manipulate this new means of communication), Gabriel was all ears. Gabriel and Kopa rekindled a relationship that was marked with the openness and aloha that had distinguished their uncompetitive, unjealous, uncontrived, and timeless boyhood years. In the span of one human day, they compressed the love and understanding that should have been theirs during that long period when both held animosity to one another. (Though Gabriel would deny that he had a feud with his brother, everyone, including Gabriel's inner soul, knew he was a damn liar.)

Gabriel and Kopa at long last were united in blood and soul; their hearts now understood how to weep and rejoice as one. Gabriel did not stop the relationship from spreading. In fact, he actively shared this new experience with Mary and Harriet, for he believed—and Kopa did, too—in the importance of sharing the love of loved ones with other loved ones.

Their isolation then became a blessing, since they were not distracted by diversions of the community. Even the cows were included. They'd eat their fill (the pasture was on higher ground and not affected by encroachment of the lake), then leave through the now unfastened gate and wade through the belly-deep water to the front of the house where they'd spend their time learning, too, this language of isolation. ❀

Places of Entry
Christine Thomas

Inspired by the Legend of Halemano

Halemano dreams of a woman named Kamalalawalu—the daughter of two high chiefs, raised under a strict kapu—but upon awakening can't remember her name. He falls so deeply in love that he won't eat or drink, becomes very ill, and finally dies. His sister, the sorceress Laenihi (who can transform into a fish), arrives at Halemano's bedside at their grandmother's house and brings him back to life. When Laenihi learns of the mysterious dream woman, she tells Halemano all about her, her favorite brother, and their beloved dogs.

After paddling a canoe to their enclave, clever Laenihi and Halemano draw the siblings to shore. Halemano recognizes Kamalalawalu from his dreams and she him, and they paddle together back to O'ahu and live as husband and wife. Soon, though, they must run from two powerful kings who had been courting Kamalalawalu; jealousy ensues, and a homesick Kamalalawalu eventually leaves Halemano for the king of the Big Island. Only when it's too late does she realize she really loves Halemano; she leaves the king and wanders lovesick throughout the Islands, while Halemano searches for her in the forest.

That's the story I discovered while doing research for my first novel at London's British Library, which has a surprisingly ample Hawaiiana collection. About three-quarters of the way through my draft, I came upon "The Legend of Halemano" and realized its strange echo of my story. I hadn't intended or ever thought of rewriting a myth, but there it was—an ancient tale to which my contemporary one was unintentionally connected. In retrospect, this discovery was the first seed of this collection, so I wanted to include a portion of the story to reveal how I unknowingly inverted the original myth.

PUA HAS LONG BEEN ACCUSTOMED TO HER BROTHER'S SHIFTING MOODS, PARTICULARLY JUST BEFORE HIS GIRLFRIEND RETURNS AND AFTER SHE LEAVES AGAIN, IN A PERILOUS CYCLE OF ELATION AND GRIEF. HIS USUAL response is isolation, playing 'ukulele alone in his room for hours, rarely eating or hanging out with friends. Yet, with a little prodding, after a day or so he is back to normal, paddling, surfing, and laughing while everyone pretends nothing ever happened.

But this time things are different. Eliza hasn't even gone back to the mainland yet and for a week Kai hasn't left the house. He won't eat, and when

Tutu tries to talk to him, on a chance meeting in the hall walking to or from the bathroom, he only nods, his face a moonless night, then returns to his room to sleep. Tutu finally calls Pua, and with steady worry in her voice asks her to come to the farm.

Tutu has always been economical with words, but hearing her voice empty of its usual music makes Pua pause. Phone still cradled in hand, she stares out the window at the treetops, at the sea's lonely blue spray, wishing she could jump into that blue somehow. She already has a long night ahead, working a banquet at the Convention Center, built for the exclusive use of mainland and foreign guests who book the required number of Waikīkī hotel rooms. She needs the money, and driving first to her grandmother's farm in Waimānalo risks arriving late, but her grandmother's words are beginning to haunt her. She needs to make certain for herself that Kai is all right.

On the way, she plays the stereo loud and sings along; soon she's feeling better and decides that Tutu is probably overreacting. Or, when the hand-painted sign for Jackson Chameleons has disappeared from her rearview mirror, she thinks that Tutu knows that if she comes over it will cure Kai of any funk he might be in—that way she won't have to live with him moping around the house all day. Tutu believes people belong outside, not in. *Get out of here*, she'd say when they were kids. *You acting like you a prisoner in this house or something.*

Pua turns mauka, still singing, any knots in her belly disappeared like a name drawn in sand washed clean by a smooth wave. But the notes die when she pulls up to the house and sees Tutu waiting outside, blue pāreu patterned with violent yellow maile vines ending in an infinity tie at her neck, kinky grey hair pulled into a careful knot. Pua has the same hair undulating down her back.

"He never eat or drink..." One tense hand cups the side of her neck as she states the facts. Then she pats Pua reassuringly on the back, except she doesn't stop.

———————————

Pua taps on the redwood door of Kai's room, and then shouts her brother's name loud as she walks in. The room is dark, the afternoon sun blocked by a coarse bamboo shade; when she rolls it up, Kai's deep voice cracks, asking her to close it again. She hears but acts like she doesn't, leaning over the bed to peer at his face, casting a new shadow over him. She keeps her voice crisp, not wanting to betray worry or acceptance of what could still just be elaborate self-pity.

"What you doing? I have for go school or work ev-ery frick-in day and you just lying in bed whenever you like. No fair."

"Go. Away."

"How 'bout I lie down and you go serve grumpy mainlanders at that dumbass Convention Center. 'Kay? Get up or you going be late."

The mattress dips as she squeezes in beside him and then shakes as she forces a laugh. But when humor provokes no movement or response, the knots return to Pua's stomach, tentacles tightening. Tutu leans her head in, then vanishes.

"You okay? Should I be worried?"

"It's nothing. Just go. Go to work."

"Tutu says you're not eating. And you sit in here all day, see nobody or even talk. I mean, alone time is one thing, but…"

Silence.

"You need to eat, Kai. Get fresh air."

She stares at the ti leaves outside the window, can almost feel the heat soaking into the soft fibers. She gets up and turns on some music. Still nothing.

She is definitely going to be late, and if it's even one minute they dock her pay. So she asks the inevitable question, utters the name she thinks will rouse her brother and allow her into his thoughts.

"Is it Eliza?"

No response—not even a shift in position or tensing of muscles. He remains stiff, cold, as though long soaked in water.

She looks again at her watch. "Hey, I've gotta go. I'm really gonna be late." She hesitates. "But I'll be back later, 'kay?"

Then she creeps into the hall, afraid of what might happen if she stays, of what will happen if she leaves.

On the way to the car, she and Tutu just look at each other. Sometimes it's difficult to speak the truth in words.

The next day, Pua drives through the carved wooden gates of the Rothwell Estate just as Eliza and her brother Ryan are returning from surfing. Their four poi dogs cavort in the grass, rolling in plumeria petals fallen from rows of trees lining the property, shining in oranges, yellows, and pinks. But Pua is watching Eliza's face as she catches sight of the car, watching so she can't try to hurry inside as if she hasn't seen her. But it's Ryan who calls out, carefree and in charge, and waves her on to park on the lawn. After all, he's expecting her.

As she climbs out of the car, the mountains rise up in the distance and Pua stares for a moment at the deep notches in the highest peak, shadowed in stories. It can be difficult to believe those tales when the sun is blazing and the reality of modern day glares the brightest of all. Pua doesn't want to be here, doesn't want to see Ryan any more than Eliza, but she has to find out what's going on. Even though Kai said nothing, she's sure only Eliza will have answers.

"Hey," says Pua, pushing up on her toes to kiss Ryan on the cheek.

"Where is it? You said you had a big ulua for us, yeah?"

"Uh…" She tucks her hair behind her ears and glances at Eliza. Maybe it wasn't the best plan to get them to see her, but so far it was working. "Shoots … I forgot it. Next time okay? I promise—the next fish my cousins catch is yours."

The three of them look at each other, the scene quickened and intense like a film fast-forwarded. The three of them are never together in the same place long.

"Well, I guess I'm gonna grab a shower," Ryan says, turning and running up the steps into the house.

Pua watches the red and white pattern of his boardshorts disappear and Eliza sink down on the steps and stare out at the yard. Now that her plan has worked and Pua is actually here, the words that have been circulating in her mind have vanished. She's surprised to feel a weighty sadness pressing on Eliza—for some reason Pua had expected her to be the happy, positive image of her brother. Instead, it feels as if she is now standing over Eliza just as she had hovered over Kai, willing her to explain.

"I need to understand what happened," Pua blurts. "Kai's doing really bad, and you're not looking great either."

Shaking her head slowly, Eliza fixes her eyes on a point much farther away. But when she finally looks up, Pua sees Kai's face emerge from hers like a figure appearing in a dream.

"Whatever it is, you can tell me. We used to talk, once. We used to be there for each other." Pua reaches out her hand, then drops her arm at her side. "I'm just saying, I can still be a friend, you know, even if things are different now."

Eliza stares at Pua as if she is going to break open, as if the truth is finally going to spill out. But all she says is: "What did Kai say?" Her face brightens strangely at his name, but retains its tight mask.

"He won't say anything. Just lies in his room, doesn't eat."

Pua's fists clench and unclench as she thinks of him. Of all the times Eliza does whatever she wants, no matter whom she hurts. She didn't have to put Kai in this position; she could have released him a long time ago.

"I can't believe this. You've always been like this, E, like you're above it all, above me. And now Kai? You have to have it all, don't you? Even when it hurts people."

Eliza's face contorts. "You haven't called me 'E' since high school," Eliza says, her voice surfacing, soft but flat. "Remember when we'd be out with everyone? Hanging out at the pumping station, and I'd always seem bored, or like I didn't want to be there? That wasn't it at all. I just didn't fit."

"I remember you used to be honest and tell me what you really thought. I know you're upset, but you owe me an explanation. And Kai, too. If you won't tell me here, come with me and tell us together."

"I've talked it over with Ryan, and I think he's right. I'm leaving tomorrow night. Back to the mainland. For good. Like you say, me being here does no one any good."

Pua fights the haze of this new information. For good? She can't pretend that surge of excitement doesn't flow through her at the thought. But it's there and then gone. "I thought you loved Kai. You said … you said he's the man of your dreams."

"I do!" says Eliza, too quickly and too loud, jerking to her feet. "Pua, talk to Kai about this, not me. It's not right. It's not my place."

Pua rises and looks toward the mountains. The clouds are thick and dark, moving swiftly into the valley like fallen warriors. "He won't talk to me, remember? Why else would I come here? You think I like that I need *your* help?"

"No," Eliza repeated. She looks as if she is about to cry, but then her body stiffens. "I've said too much. I'm sorry."

"You've said nothing!"

Eliza runs into the house and Pua senses that this encounter might have hurt more than helped. She calls out anyway, trying to keep her voice calm.

"Is this really the way you want to leave it with us?"

A few seconds later, Eliza comes from the house carrying a lei, and holds it out to Pua. "For Kai."

Pua takes it, and Eliza walks away, locking herself inside. And no one, especially not Pua, can enter.

Now it's up to her to help Kai, and as Pua drives away she reminds herself that there are many more places she can go that Eliza cannot.

When Pua enters Kai's room later that night, carrying everything she needs, the ceiling-fan chain is clinking against the glass lamp in time with the shade flopping against the louvers. Kai's lids are half-open, eyes rolled back and whites showing—the way he's slept since he was a child. Still, she looks hard for his rise of breath.

"Kai." She whispers at first, then louder. "Kai."

There isn't even an eyelid flutter. He's still here, though, just lost in dreams, in illness borne on bitter emotions. Tutu told her long ago that the entry spot for dreams is in the corner of the eye. Everyone has two spirits: one while awake, and one while asleep that takes on another form, carrying on a life of its own apart from the body. Pua stares there and struggles to focus: the past above, the present below, and the future in her hands.

Taking the pala fern, 'awapuhi, and maile she gathered in the mountains, Pua begins, first using fragrance to entice Kai's spirit, just as she has been taught. She drapes the plants around him, then speaks softly, using ancient words to call him back from where he is lost, calling on Uli to save this young fish. Massaging Kai, pushing upward on the bottom of his feet, her words become chant and soon she loses the meaning as the prayer pours from her, through her. Power focused toward restoration, calling on 'aumākua to watch over and enfold Kai until boundaries blur, divisions mend, and spirit joins with

earth. *Come back to life*, Pua prays. Eat, drink, and be of this world. *Come back.*
Finally, she places Eliza's lei around Kai's neck.

In the morning, the sound of her brother's voice rouses Pua from sleep.
At first it seems to come from somewhere deep and far, and she feels for a
moment as if she is floating on water. But when the voice comes again, she raises
her head and he smiles.

"I've been dreaming the most amazing dreams," Kai whispers. "I was in a
misty forest, moving through shadows. The air glowed with moonlight and fog,
sometimes disappearing around corners and following behind me like a guardian."

Pua moves from the chair where she awakened to his bed.

"I looked everywhere, but I couldn't find her. Sometimes I mistook the
curled bark of a tree for her hair, or a cushion of moss for the feel of her skin.
When the wind blew I turned in circles, thinking it would lead me to her voice.
At times it was so dark, I felt like I was walking in the middle of the earth."

Her brother's voice has softened so much that it sounds like the whisper
of the night sky.

"I looked so long that I got tired and sat on a rock at the top of a ridge.
Somehow I began to string lei—endless strands of maile, 'awapuhi, and 'ie'ie
appeared, and I just kept stringing. Until I woke up, just now."

Pua glances at the strands of maile and 'ie'ie she had picked, marker of
dreams and reality. One, split in two.

After they eat, Pua and Kai walk to the ocean and toss the leaves and lei
blossoms into the sea. They spread their arms out and float on the water, the sky
blooming with morning color and the long ridge of mountains glowing orange
and red, setting fire to the sea. Kai splashes the surface, arcing drops of water
onto their faces.

All has been restored. Kai is revived, again full of life.

For now. ❋

AHIWELA
Marion Lyman-Mersereau

INSPIRED BY THE LEGEND OF THE NAUPAKA

A jealous goddess, Pele, kills two lovers—one on the mountain and one on the beach. Other gods—some say Pele's sisters—take pity on the lovers and transform them into naupaka plants. Though the leaves are different, the mountain plant's half flower perfectly matches the half flower of the beach plant, together making a whole blossom.

I chose this legend because I'm fond of the hearty naupaka kahakai found near the beach, and I've always been intrigued by its half flower, whose story I first heard as a child. I didn't see my first naupaka kahakai in the mountains until I was an adult, and I liked how the half flower indeed matched the other perfectly, yet the leaves were so different.

❋ ❋ ❋

THEY WERE TWO HALVES OF A WHOLE; WHEN TOGETHER THEY FELT COMPLETE. EACH HAD A DISTINCT WAY OF BEING, AND THEIR OWN WAHI PANA—THEIR OWN SACRED PLACE THAT MADE THEM FEEL akin to their surroundings.

Kanani attended a school on a mountain that was founded by a princess for children of Hawaiian heritage. She lived up to her name and was a natural beauty. She had a boyish, athletic figure with strong, broad shoulders, slender hips, and slim, toned legs. Her wavy, dark brown hair was usually wrapped around itself and fashioned into a topknot, out of her way. It was a nuisance, but her hula teacher insisted that it remain uncut. In rare moments when she let her hair down, to dance or just for a few moments to refasten the topknot, one could see blonde highlights like burnished gold weaving through the rich grain of varnished koa.

Her boyfriend, Kainalu, attended school in a valley that was founded for children of missionaries. He was a ruggedly handsome young man—a tall, muscled athlete with a physique reminiscent of those Michelangelo chiseled out of marble. He had a noble presence that conjured images of ancient Hawaiian aliʻi or the powerful demigod, Māui. Kainalu was most content in and near the ocean, but this was no surprise since his name meant "ocean wave." He spent as much time in the water as he could, happy when swimming, canoe paddling, body boarding, snorkeling, or just walking a beach, but happiest when surfing. Kainalu revealed incredible grace and agility as he walked toward the nose of his longboard to increase the board's speed along the face of a wave.

From the time Kanani was a keiki, her parents took her and her brothers on hikes into the kuahiwi. The mountains were her place of relaxation, where she felt most secure and at peace, and she knew the Kapālama loop like she knew the features of her lovely face. She knew where to find the precious lehua 'āhihi on the Kamanaiki trail, and knew the song "Pua 'Āhihi," about a rare lehua flower, which her mother, who was her kumu hula, had taught her. One morning, as Kanani hiked the misty trail toward Lanihuli, the highest peak above her school with breathtaking views of Nuʻuanu and Kalihi valleys, she spotted the lehua blossom and quietly sang the love song's five short, sensual verses in her warm alto. She recalled the legend of the lehua, about two lovers transformed into a tree and a flower, and when the blossom was separated from the tree, the gods wept and it rained. She thought of her boyfriend, Kainalu, who had gone for a "dawn patrol" surf session. She was also on a dawn patrol, but hers was a hike in the forest mist, well before it became too hot to labor up the steep trail.

Kanani wondered if she and Kainalu would ever grow to enjoy each other's favorite activities. Whenever she went to the beach with him, she found herself looking mauka, longing to be in the lush green coolness of the Koʻolau rainforest behind Honolulu or, when Kainalu chose to surf at Mākaha or Mokulēʻia, in the dryland Waiʻanae forest. Whenever the surf wasn't very good and Kainalu went hiking with Kanani, he would spend much of the hike at various viewpoints admiring the blue hues of the sea, which was where, he confessed, he'd rather be.

Despite their preference for different environments, they both understood the other's devotion to their special places because they were both outdoor people. They'd also been devoted to each other since their first meeting at a mutual family friend's baby lūʻau in Hilo. That day, a strangely beautiful Hawaiian woman sat across from Kainalu and Kanani at one of the long tables. She appeared to be alone and listened quietly to the two youths, who had just been introduced, noticing their attraction. The woman eventually engaged them in conversation and asked who their 'ohana was, where they lived and attended school. In turn, she explained she was from the Big Island and was aunty to the honored baby's father.

As the woman spoke—explaining that she always liked attending this family's celebrations even though they were in Hilo, but she didn't like the long drive at night from the volcano—Kainalu noticed she surreptitiously pulled a flask from her bag and regularly filled her paper cup. At one point she even asked him if he would like to "fortify" his fruit punch with some gin; he declined.

Kanani, on the other hand, noticed that the woman blatantly flirted with

Kainalu. The word "cougar" came unbidden to her mind—an older woman who was attracted to and sought out men at least ten years her junior. She listened as the woman explained how much she liked ʻōhelo berry jam, nodding to the many jars that lined the center of the table beside half pineapples filled with pieces of haupia. And as she left the lūʻau, Kanani noticed she put several jars into her bag.

———————

Kainalu had just finished a surf session at Bowls and was paddling across the Ala Wai Harbor channel to Magic Island when he heard the greeting, "Huuuui!" He was delighted, thinking it was Kanani, but then saw a woman sitting comfortably on the black lava boulders and waving to him. She wore a red and black aloha print pāreu around her hips and a matching bathing suit top. Her waist-long hair was black and shiny, like the wet rocks she sat on. As he paddled closer he realized it was the same woman who was at the baby lūʻau in Hilo.

"I remembered you told me you liked to surf at Bowls," she said as he paddled toward the small beach, where she greeted him with a kiss on the cheek as though they were old friends. Her hands felt hot on his cool skin.

"Oh, yeah," he replied absently. He was disappointed that Kanani wasn't there and was trying to figure out why this woman would be here, apparently waiting for him. Remembering his manners, he asked: "How are you, Aunty? What brings you to Honolulu?"

She looked troubled by his response. "Please, call me Ahiwela," she said. "I'm in Honolulu on personal business for a few days and I often swim here at Magic Island when I'm in town. When I remembered this is where you like to surf, I hoped you might be here so I could ask you to join me for dinner tonight."

"I'm already going out tonight," Kainalu said. There was something about this woman that made him feel very uncomfortable, so he started walking toward the showers.

"Then maybe lunch or dinner tomorrow?" she said, walking beside him.

"My surf club is meeting tomorrow and I have lots of homework," he said hoping to dismiss her.

She removed her pāreu, revealing a bikini of the same red and black aloha print fabric. As she stood beside him at the outdoor shower and rinsed the salt water off her body, he noticed that despite being at least a decade older than him she was quite fit, her sinewy muscles and strong back and shoulders similar to Kanani's.

She followed Kainalu back to his car, telling him how impressed she had been when they first met in Hilo at the lūʻau. She said she had hardly been able to think of anything else since meeting him.

Kainalu was silent. He did not want to be disrespectful but did not want to encourage this woman; her obvious intense interest in him made him feel awkward and, strangely, in danger. It was unusual for him to feel threatened by anyone, being the strong fellow he was; the only thing he'd ever feared was when the surf was a little bigger than he could handle. Even then, he fed on the challenge.

After loading his board into the truck, he said a quick goodbye, yet she still managed to give him a hug and kiss before he closed the door. There was a unique scent about this woman, he thought as he drove home. It reminded him of the smell of smoke and wet ashes after fire has been doused with water.

A few nights later, Kainalu and Kanani had a pleasant evening together with Kanani's family eating Chinese takeout and watching *Whale Rider* at her home in ʻĀlewa Heights. He told her how much the young actress in the film reminded him of her—strong, determined, and beautiful. She teasingly replied that he was like the grandfather—grumpy and stubborn. The family laughed but agreed that there was some truth to her point. Kainalu could be grumpy and he was definitely stubborn. Kanani reminded him that the positive side of being stubborn was being persistent, and they excused themselves from the family and sat out on the lānai in the cool night air.

"I heard a wahine at Magic Island yell, 'Huuuui' as I paddled across the channel after surfing at Bowls today. I thought it was you," said Kainalu.

"You forgot I was hiking?"

"No, it just sounded just like you."

"Who was it?" she asked.

"It was strange. It was that lady we met at the baby lūʻau in Hilo— remember? She kissed me when I got out of the water like we were old friends. She said her name was Ahiwela and asked me to go to dinner with her." Kainalu was obviously embarrassed by the entire encounter.

"I remember how she kept looking at you. She made me feel really uncomfortable that night. There's something kind of scary about her," said Kanani.

Kainalu felt better after he told her and the two moved on to discuss mutual friends, their clubs and classes, and all that interested the friendly couple. Kanani felt complete and comfortable sitting close to Kainalu, looking up at the mountain where she had spent the morning hiking. As she lay her head on his shoulder, she told him about seeing the pua ʻāhihi and about her search for the elusive naupaka kuahiwi. She wanted to find a cutting to plant next to the naupaka kahakai she had in her yard.

"Remember the legend of the two lovers who were killed by a jealous god- dess, one on the mountain and one on the beach? They were transformed into naupaka plants, and the half flower of the mountain plant perfectly matches the half flower of the beach plant to make a whole blossom, even though the leaves are completely different."

Kanani explained that she thought these two plants symbolized her and Kainalu. "You're like that naupaka kahakai, since you love the beach and ocean." She pointed to the bush that grew beside the lānai. Kainalu agreed and pointed out that the rounded leaf was shaped just like his favorite pintail, nose-riding surfboard.

"I'm like the naupaka kuahiwi, since the pointed, jagged leaves are like the peaks of the Koʻolau range, my wahi pana. And the mountain flower has a fragrance the beach flower doesn't, and I smell better than you," she teased.

Kainalu chuckled. "Yes, you do," he said, wrapping her in a warm embrace.

Kanani then thought that if she could grow the two plants side by side, their relationship would be cherished forever.

————

Kainalu had just finished a grueling Saturday morning water polo practice and was not sure if he'd have the energy to do some big-wave surfing, as he'd planned. But his uncle had told him the surf was "epic" at Mokulēʻia, so Kainalu decided he would recover after lots of water and the long drive out to the country. Besides, Kanani was going to hike the glider crash trail right above where he'd be surfing, and they'd planned to meet for lunch at his uncle's house afterward.

Later, as he knee-paddled his longboard out through the small channel, Kainalu watched the set line up with perfect glassy peaks. He paddled to the outside lineup where he could rest for a minute and enjoy the view of the Waiʻanae mountains where Kanani was hiking, so much more relaxing than staring back at Waikīkī hotels. Then he remembered the mysterious Ahiwela, and how she seemed to show up in the most surprising places, and looked around as if she would suddenly appear.

After all, she'd been in the bleachers at several water polo practices and had greeted him after practice, always with a kiss, which made him feel very awkward. His teammates teased him relentlessly about the "cougar" who'd obviously set her sights on her handsome prey. He'd always ask her why she was still in Honolulu, and each time she replied that she was on personal business and would say no more, yet she'd persist in invitations to join her for coffee, breakfast, lunch, dinner, or even a picnic after surfing. He now understood what it meant to be stalked. Even though he declined every invitation, she still appeared, always wearing a black and red outfit, until he grew angry and finally told her as politely as possible that she needed to stop showing up wherever he was, that he wanted nothing to do with her and hoped she would respect his wishes and leave him alone.

"I know you think you're in love with that Kanani girl, but she's not the one for you." Ahiwela smiled. "And you'll discover this soon enough."

Shaking her from his mind, Kainalu picked his waves carefully, and when he had good rides he hoped Kanani was watching from someplace on the mountain. He wiped out a few times and was rolled and jerked around underwater like a rag doll, but he made himself catch one more wave—his superstition was that his last wave always had to be a good one—and finished the long left with a graceful cutback before allowing the whitewater to push him to the beach.

Kainalu spent the rest of the morning visiting with his cousins and waiting for Kanani, who, they'd agreed, would meet him at his aunt and uncle's house at noon. At one o'clock she hadn't appeared and he became worried. His cousin tried to reassure him. She could only get lost if she left the trail, which she was smart enough not to do, he said. But he also mentioned there were pig hunters with vicious dogs that hiked the area where she had gone.

As she hiked, Kanani enjoyed the strength of her legs working uphill, the rhythm of her breath matching her stride. She felt she was a symphony in motion and the mountain world a great symphony of beauty. The flora and fauna, the varied hues of green, the different smells on different trails during different seasons had always fascinated her. As she walked, she looked out for the mountain half flower shrub, entwined in her mind with Kainalu. She thought of how honest and loyal he was, and how, besides being a good-looking guy, he was respectful.

Just then she heard a twig crack behind her, and her entire body went into a state of alarm. She stopped. She listened. She heard nothing but a few birds chattering and so, after a few moments, continued walking. After awhile her breath resumed its rhythm with her stride, and she rationalized that what she had heard was probably just a mongoose rustling in the underbrush. She hoped it wasn't a wild boar, which she knew could be ferocious when confronted.

As she walked along the narrow ridge, she looked down each steep slope for the plant she sought. After about a half mile of intense searching, she decided it was time to abandon her quest and start back down the trail if she was to join Kainalu for lunch. Just as she was about to turn around, a small clump of the white half flowers caught her eye twenty yards down the makai slope of the trail—the jagged, pointed leaves confirmation that she was looking at a naupaka kuahiwi sapling.

She made her way slowly down the slope, grabbing hold of whatever plants she could to slow her descent, bracing with her feet. Then she heard the angry growl of a dog on the trail behind her, and looked back to see a large white dog snarling and barking. It must be a pig hunter's dog, Kanani thought, and she began scrambling more quickly toward her goal. When she reached it, she quickly asked permission, broke off a small branch, and said mahalo to the shrub just as she'd been taught. All the while, the vicious dog continued to snarl and bark from above, and Kanani's growing fear knocked her off balance. She tumbled backward and began to roll down the slope, grasping at whatever she could to stop herself. She thought she heard a woman's laugh as she tumbled down.

Finally, she reached the bottom, stunned and bruised but still holding the precious branch. As she struggled to stand, Kanani heard laughter again and saw an old woman dressed in black with a red sash around her hips. She was holding a large black rock in one gnarled hand.

The bright, sunny morning had become an overcast afternoon and a light rain had begun to fall. By two o'clock, Kainalu was so concerned that he and his cousin decided to drive to the trail where Kanani had said she was going to start her hike. The two young men saw Kanani's car and parked next to it, then went to the trailhead, where Kainalu began to run. His cousin shouted that it was a long hike, but Kainalu neither turned back nor slackened his speed.

Kainalu ran as far as he could until he was out of breath and had to walk, but as soon as he recovered his breath he ran again. He kept up this walk-run pace for many miles up the switchback trail, reassuring himself that Kanani was an experienced hiker. When the rain became heavier, Kainalu felt a presence that alarmed him. He stopped and squinted into the clouded trail ahead of him but saw nothing. He looked over his shoulder and into the deep forest on either side of his path and again saw nothing. Still, he sensed he was not alone and continued his pace with intensified awareness.

After an hour of picking his way carefully on the muddy ridge, he came to a place where it looked as though someone had slipped. A few plants had been pulled from their place and the root holes were now filled with rainwater. He thought he heard a woman laugh as he carefully lowered himself down the steep slope, but he figured it was a combination of the wind in the trees, the pouring rain, and his exhausted state of mind. But Kainalu became more and more alarmed as he continued down the path, straining to see the bottom through rain and clouds. Finally, he made out a slender body lying face down in the greenery.

"Kanani!" he screamed, sliding toward the bottom of the ravine where she lay. Kainalu rolled Kanani over, shook her, and shouted. He listened for her breath, and then began to go through the lifesaving steps he had learned in lifeguard class. After several minutes, he heard his cousin's voice and shouted for him to call for help. His cousin soon joined him in the ravine and said a rescue helicopter was on the way.

Together, they continued efforts to resuscitate Kanani. As he rested between the breaths he forced into her lifeless mouth, Kainalu noticed that Kanani's hand grasped a naupaka kuahiwi branch. He also saw a lava rock the size of a large mango next to Kanani's fair head. The bruise and light bleeding from her temple told him it was this rock that had killed her. Kainalu took the branch with its small white flowers from her hand and wrapped the lava rock in his wet shirt. After answering the firefighter's questions, Kainalu and his cousin slid back down the muddy trail in silence.

After dropping off his cousin at his house, Kainalu went to the beach. Alone, he could let the hot tears stream down his face. When he had recovered, he carefully wrapped the precious naupaka branch and took out the lava rock. He would throw the murderous rock as far out to sea as he possibly could. He wanted to be rid of it, sink it, and keep it from defiling the earth. He staggered to the beach, and then he saw her.

She stood with her back to him, her black, wavy hair cascading down her back, wearing the same red and black pāreu and bathing suit she'd worn the day he'd seen her at Magic Island. She turned toward him and smiled seductively.

"I told you she was not the one for you," she said, chuckling.

He dropped the rock. Then he stormed toward her.

"I told you to get out of my life! Get out of here—stay away from me!" Kainalu shouted and pushed her to the sand. Then he ran into the water with his board and paddled through the shore break.

"I will get out of your life. I will get out of here and I will stay away from you," she muttered in the voice of an angry old woman as she stood and brushed herself off. She bent down to pick up the rock he had dropped beside her.

Later that evening Kainalu's aunt and uncle went for a sunset walk on the beach with their dogs. They saw Kainalu's white truck and scanned the surf spot, but they saw no one surfing and grew concerned. Kainalu's aunt pointed to a group of dogs digging in the sand farther down the beach. When they got closer they saw that the dogs had uncovered a shallow grave beneath a thick clump of naupaka kahakai, and they wailed when they saw the handsome, death-gray face of their beloved nephew, Kainalu.

The only apparent sign of injury was a bruise to his temple. On the other side of the naupaka bush, a black lava rock the size of a large mango sat in the middle of Kainalu's longboard.

Days later, Kainalu's cousin threw the rock out into the depths of the Mokulēʻia sea with all his might. He found Kanani's naupaka kuahiwi branch in Kainalu's truck and took another branch from the bush where Kainalu's body had been found on the beach. He planted them both outside the family home, which rests between the beach and the mountains.

The two naupaka plants eventually became thick shrubs that grew tightly entangled together, each with its own character, its own unique way of being. ✹

STRANGE SIGHTINGS
Maxine Hong Kingston

INSPIRED BY HAWAI'I'S EVERYDAY SPIRITS AND LEGENDS

A supernatural presence must be real if you saw it before you'd ever heard of it. Children describe coming across little glowing people, and we categorize and name their sighting: "That was a Menehune. You saw a Menehune." I have heard the explanation that Puerto Ricans were the original Menehune.

We see rows of people carrying torches, walking across the night waters, and we say to ourselves, "Those must be the Night Marchers." One explanation for Night Marchers is that they're the ghosts of King Kamehameha's warriors. Seeing a phenomenon and *then* hearing the myth is evidence that the magical and the mystical are true.

I originally wrote this piece as one of a series of columns about Hawai'i for *The New York Times*. It was very strange trying to get the far end of the Mainland to understand us here in Hawai'i.

※ ※ ※

ACCORDING TO MYSTICAL PEOPLE, SPIRITUAL FORCES CONVERGE AT HAWAI'I, AS DO OCEAN CURRENTS AND WINDS. KĀHUNA, KEEPERS AND TEACHERS OF THE OLD RELIGION AND ARTS (SUCH AS SONGWRITING, the hula, navigation, taro growing) still work here. The Islands attract refugee lamas from Tibet, and the Dalai Lama and the Black Hat Lama have visited them. Some kāhuna say they see tree spirits fly from branch to branch; the various winds and rains are spirits, too; sharks and rocks have spirits. If ancestors and immortals travel on supernatural errands between China and the Americas, they must rest here in transit, with nothing but ocean for thousands of miles around. They landed more often in the old days, before the sandalwood trees were cut down.

Whether it was because I listened to too many ghost stories or was born sensitive to presences, I spent about three years of childhood in helpless fear of the supernatural. I saw a whirling witch in the intersection by our house. She had one red cheek and one black cheek. Surrounded by a screaming, pointing crowd, she turned and turned on her broom. Maybe she was only somebody in a Hallowe'en costume when I didn't know about Hallowe'en, but she put me into torment for years. I was afraid of cat eyes at night. Wide-eyed with insomnia, I listened in the dark to voices whispering, chains dragging and dragging, footsteps coming my way.

At about the same kidtime, Earll saw a little witch dancing on his dresser. Hoping to help our son become a fearless down-to-earth person, we have raised Joseph secularly. We explain things to him logically.

Joseph had already gotten through his babyhood when we came to Hawai'i; he would seem no longer in danger of succumbing to the fear of ghosts. But Hawai'i, new land that has recently risen out of the water, has overwhelming animism; that is, it seems more alive than cities that have been paved over for hundreds of years. Or, Joseph developed his sixth sense at a later age than we did, and, and, person and place coming together, he started to see things.

Even our friends with Ph.D.s see things in Hawai'i. Our friend from Minnesota kept telling us about the row of fishermen walking into the ocean with torches at night. "They're chanting to attract the fish," he said. Later, he learned he was describing the march of the dead warriors. Another sensible friend tells us how he ran from block to block to dodge the nightwalkers. "I would've died if they crossed my path," he said. The most unimaginative people hear the hoofbeats of the princess's horse and lock their doors. They wrestle with invisible foes at ceremonial grounds, see—and photograph—the face of the goddess Pele in the volcano fire, and offer the old woman—Pele in disguise—water when she comes asking for it, floating on smoking feet.

We were driving one day when I caught a sign that Joseph was not the simple little boy I had hoped for. He held his head, shaking it, and crying out, "I can't stand it. The thoughts are moving so fast in there." I didn't like that; he felt his thoughts apart from himself; the very process of thinking hurt him. With my hands on the wheel, I gave inadequate comfort.

One night I heard him walking about, and in the morning he said he had seen a light come over the top of the wall. (The wall of his room didn't join the ceiling.) He had gotten up to shut off the light. What he saw in the living room was one window lit up and a man standing in it. The glow was coming from the man. We lived on the second floor.

When he was about twelve, and should have been old enough to outgrow his fancifulness, he came home early in the morning and jumped shaking into bed. He and his friends had been playing at a construction site before the workers came. Hiding from his friends, he had lost them and was running home when he saw a Menehune, one of the little people of Hawai'i, standing on a lava rock fence. "It had a shiny crown on its head," he said, "and its mouth opened and opened until there was nothing but this big hollow in its face. Its head moved like this, following me." He tells about this laughing Menehune as factually as he tells a math problem, without self-dramatization or doubt.

Months afterward, he wasn't sleeping well; he kept groaning and tossing. "You know the voices calling your name before you go to sleep?" he said. "I usually like listening to them. But lately they've been very loud, and I don't like their sound." I was alarmed that he thought that everyone has voices, though pleasant ones, calling them. "The voices are coming out of the closet." And I noticed that the closet door kept opening. I would shut it myself when he went to bed, and when I checked on him, I'd find it open.

Without mentioning it, he bought five pounds of rock salt with his own money and sprinkled it all over the house; Hawaiians do that to stop hauntings.

I remembered Chinese stories about voices calling, and the lesson would be that you mustn't answer when you hear your own name. You mustn't follow the voices. I recalled Goethe's poem about the Erl-king's daughter. To find guidance, you have to use the lore that science scoffs at. If Joseph had started being afraid of bats, we would have hung garlic around his neck and around the house.

I pulled his ears while calling his name and address the way my mother did for us after nightmares. He helped me seal the closet door with good Chinese words on red paper. We found a cross that had been part of a theatrical costume, also an ankh and a scarab, replicas from the Metropolitan Museum of Art, and hung them from the doorknob. We picked ti leaves and strewed his room with them.

Joseph had a few quiet nights, and we thought the strangeness was over. But then I found him standing in the hallway shivering in the hot afternoon. He said that something had come out of the closet and was in the hallway. "The cold spot is here," he said. "I'm standing in the middle of it. I'm fighting it." That spot did not feel odd to me.

We asked our friend from Thailand what to do, and she gave us a medallion of a saint for him to wear around his neck, and also a little stone Buddha that Thais wear, stored in a gold box. She said he should put the Buddha by his head when he went to bed. It had been handed down in her family, who have been rulers and rebels in Thailand. Joseph has had no more supernatural disturbances.

In a way it's a shame to have him put his powers away and fold his wings, but those abilities are not needed in America in the 20th century.

The writers' conference I went to ended with a kahuna who helped us perform hoʻoponopono; all animosities would be resolved. Fewer people stayed for that event than any other. Maybe in ancient Hawaiʻi a kahuna like this one would have trained Joseph, whose tendencies would have become useful. She asked us to shut our eyes and hold hands in a circle; she talked to us calmly, saying that a column of light was entering the circle. I opened my eyes to peek, to check out the reality of that column. There was indeed a column of light, but also a skylight in the roof that let it in. The way the world works now, Joseph needs to learn to see the skylight, too. ❊

HEROES AND VILLAINS

Ao 'Aumākua
Victoria Nalani Kneubuhl

INSPIRED BY THE LEGEND OF HIKU AND KAWELU

In the traditional story, Hiku and Kawelu meet, fall in love, and live together for a time. Then, Hiku decides to leave Kawelu, who in turn pursues him but is repelled by forces of nature that he calls up against her. Mad with grief, Kawelu hangs herself and her spirit flies to the underworld of Milu. A remorseful Hiku goes to Milu to rescue Kawelu and restores her spirit to her body.

Is there anything more compelling than a story about visiting the underworld? The tale of Hiku and Kawelu is a particularly rich one with its images of the underworld as a kind of twisted Las Vegas and the repeated motif of the sinuous koali vine, whose flowers are, in real life, quite beautiful. I have always wanted to work with this particular story as it continues to hold a numinous attraction for me.

❈ ❈ ❈

LET ME TELL YOU, BEING BROUGHT BACK TO LIFE IS NOT THE WAY IT SOUNDS IN STORIES. I DON'T RECOMMEND IT TO ANYONE. IF YOU DIE, YOU SHOULD PRAY THAT YOU STAY THAT WAY. NOTHING WILL BE THE same once you have had a glimpse of the bright worlds of the ao 'aumākua. After that sight, this world becomes a shadow land, its own dull and dank Milu. Your body never recovers, either. You have no appetite, and even though you are as thin as a sliver of bamboo, your flesh always feels like a load of boulders that you have to drag around. Your skin becomes translucent and your eyes look hollow and haunted. You emit an unpleasant odor, like decaying leaves, and your presence makes everyone uneasy.

Alone each night, I called out to my 'aumākua to release me from the miserable prison of mortal life. My mind screamed for escape—from the tricks of Hina, from chants and prayers and magic arrows, from Hiku. Knowing my hopeless state, Maka, the old healer who was in charge of me, did his best to cheer me up. I think he was the only one who felt sorry and more than a little guilty about my wretched half-life. One morning he unwittingly pointed out that koali vines were flowering on the little hillside right near my shabby mountain hut. Who knows? Maybe he was really hinting that I should give suicide another go and was not just trying to get me to appreciate the flora. It is ironic; I have always loved the koali vine. My mother used to tell us a story she made up about their green leaves becoming butterflies at night while we slept. She said the butterflies watched over us as we dreamt and knew all of our wishes.

I had only one wish in that miserable place. I wanted a real death that no one could undo.

Now Hiku knows, but no one else ever guessed that I had loved Kaleimanu from the time I was a child. Like his father before him, Kaleimanu was the konohiki of my father's lands, and it was due to the wisdom of this family that the land prospered and the people remained loyal and productive. My father may not be able to see *some* things for what they really are, but he knew that through Kaleimanu his little court would keep its reputation for providing the very best—and my father prides himself on being surrounded with refinement and pleasing luxury. Because Kaleimanu's rank was so far below mine, my father would never have considered him a match for me; so my long-term plan was to mate with whomever my father chose, produce a few genealogically appropriate offspring, and then, after I had done my family duty, take Kaleimanu as my chosen lover. Other chiefly women had arranged their lives this way, I reasoned, so why couldn't I?

I had never been a great attraction in my father's effete little group. His main aim in life was to surround himself with stylish hula aficionados. I am not a graceful dancer. I have no real wit for poetry, stories, or riddles, whereas he and my sisters and their fellow devotees can stay up for hours discussing the meaning and variations of a dance, or the true origins of a particular hula, or how so-and-so was straying too far from tradition in his or her movements. Once, they spent weeks trying to outdo each other by recalling all the mist references in various chants. But when the kukui lamps burned and the chanting began, when the dancers' shadows swayed over the pili-grass walls and their feet swept softly over the mats, I could always be counted on to fall asleep.

I like more practical things—things that have substance, things you can hold. I like to make things with my hands—kapa and lei hulu are my specialties. My father wore my lei hulu, slept under my superb kapa, and even bragged about my skills, but he didn't really like to have me around. He thought of me as his clever little drudge, so I was always left to my work, and after my mother died, no one paid much attention to me. No one ever noticed how I spent so much time with Kaleimanu. No one noticed how over the years we grew to love each other. No one noticed how happy I was with my little life.

I am not unpleasant to look at, but I am not as pretty as my younger sisters Pīlali and Ki'ilei, and certainly not beautiful like Lahilahi, who has everyone's attention as soon as she appears. She is not of our rank either, but my father brought her into our household because of her thick, rich hair, her flashing eyes, her graceful dancing, her quick wit, and her willingness above all to please him. My father, for all his strength and wealth, can be a foolish man. He is easily swayed by the charm of pretty things, and is always courting chiefs of higher rank and trying to impress them with the new and unusual. Lahilahi fit perfectly into his schemes. She was a lovely young plaything for him to show off, and he took pleasure in having her dance and prance around at his gatherings. It flattered his overblown vanity to think that she was in love with him, even though it's my opinion that my father actually prefers men as lovers. Perhaps, for a time, she did love him. He plucked her from nowhere and made her something far more important than she thought she would ever become, and anyone could see she was always hungry for more. I used to make fun of her sickening devotion that seemed to have no end, but everything changed on that one day—the day she first saw Hiku.

They were all planning a journey to the uplands. I was interested in gathering plants for my dyes and seeing the birds whose feathers I was so fond of fashioning into lei hulu, so I decided to join them. We walked a long way on the first day, and when the path became steep my sisters began complaining and had to be carried. Irritated by their complaints, my father sent attendants ahead to find a comfortable place to pass the night. We settled that afternoon, exhausted, on mats laid over soft grasses in a lovely grove of ʻōhiʻa trees.

The night passed, and we woke to morning light shining through a canopy of branches and the scent of cool mountain air. With red lehua blossoms swaying above us, and forest birds gliding through the trees, I felt as though I had awakened inside a mele whose poetry I could finally appreciate.

Lahilahi was leaning against the trunk of an ʻōhiʻa tree at the edge of a small clearing, fussing over Pīlali's hair while Kiʻilei was chattering away. The three of them sat just where a shaft of sunlight fell. They looked so sweet and tender, as if they had never done any of the mean things they always do, when suddenly an arrow flew through the air and struck the tree just above Lahilahi's head. She jumped to her feet and pulled the arrow out of the tree, and when she turned in a temper to face its owner, she saw Hiku standing on the hill above our glade.

The morning sun shone behind him, outlining his tall, perfect figure. His hair fell in spiraling curls around his face, and the tip of each curl was carefully bleached with lime so that it looked as though his dark eyes and high cheeks were perfectly framed with glistening leaves or delicate flowers. When he smiled directly at Lahilahi, it was as if he entirely expected the complete adoration that surged out of her. From behind Hiku stepped his mother, the luminous Hina. With hair like silver moonbeams and tinkling laughter, she welcomed us into her forest realm. My father came forward to answer her greeting, and for the days that followed we lived on the mountain under the hospitality of Hina and Hiku.

Lahilahi took great pains to hide her craving for Hiku. I know they met in secret, because I am quick to recognize the ways of secrecy, having practiced them for so long. But Lahilahi burned so hot that she and Hiku became reckless, and it was only through luck that they were not discovered. She'd come back from her "solitary" walks, lips still swollen with desire, eyes glazed over, and body still trembling with love. I've never seen anyone so completely obsessed, and I'm sure it was in her desperation to keep Hiku that she devised "The Plan."

For several days in a row, Hiku offered to take me to gather plants, or to show me where different birds nested. Once, he shot an arrow at an 'ō'ō bird. The arrow flew, and the cord, slender as a shadow, wrapped around the bird so it fell, tied but not hit, and he removed some of its precious feathers for me before letting it go. Of course, my sisters and Lahilahi always came with us, but on these excursions, Hiku directed his conversation to me. I didn't think much of it and assumed his attention was a courtesy. There was certainly no romance or courting in his behavior. He gave me information about the habits of birds and the places where certain plants could be found. He also shot arrows for our entertainment, and his skill was unmatched. He told us that Hina made him these arrows and spoke charms into them.

I was shocked when my father came one day to inform me that Hiku wished to take me for a wife and would come and live with us at our home near the sea. Of course, my father never asked or cared how I felt about it. I could see that he was thinking only of the prestigious alliance he could make with the exalted family of Hina. What could I do? Formal connections matter in this world. And I'm sure in their scheme it was Lahilahi, not Hiku, who targeted me as the intended one. No doubt she saw me as no competition, the least likely to arouse any passion in him.

On our journey back home, as we left the mountain, Hiku came to walk beside me. His little bow and his arrows were slung in a basket on his back. He asked me if I was happy with our match.

"I am happy for you, happy that you will be getting what it is you wish for," I answered.

"And what is it you wish for, Kawelu?" he asked.

I tried my best to disguise my contempt. "I am doing as my father wishes, for that is my duty, but we have just met and I hardly know you. Telling you what I wish for is not a duty, and reserved for those I know to be trustworthy."

He was stung by my reply but pretended to be amused. "And how do you know who is trustworthy?"

"I listen to what people say, and then I watch what they do."

He looked confused and hung back to walk with my father and Lahilahi.

My father had a showy ritual to celebrate our union. I can't remember what it was like. I did put up a dignified face, but all I could think of was Kaleimanu. A hale was prepared for our first night, and Lahilahi had designated herself my companion. When it was time to retire, she came into the hale under the pretense of attending to my needs. Hiku followed us a few minutes later, and when he arrived I said that there need be no games between the three of us and that if they left me alone, I wouldn't tell on them. Hiku frowned and looked a little surprised, but nothing could have pleased Lahilahi more. I slipped out and left them to their lust. I went straight to Kaleimanu, and for the first time we slept the night together as husband and wife. I sneaked back in the dark of morning before anyone was awake. And so it went for several days, until Hiku got a little bored and Lahilahi became jealous.

Lahilahi had decided that Hiku and I should spend some time together each day so that everything would look normal and my father would suspect nothing. She, of course, being my dear companion, would always be present. We walked, we went to the beach to play in the surf, and sometimes we swam in a nearby waterfall.

One day, I sat to work on a lei hulu using some of the feathers I had gathered in the mountains. Hiku watched and asked me questions about my methods, admiring the pretty thing I was making. The next day, he took a great interest in my kapa and questioned me about the designs, the colors, and the fineness of the kapa moe I was printing. At first, Lahilahi was only uncomfortable with these small attentions, but as the days passed, she grew jealous and resentful when Hiku tried to engage me in any kind of thoughtful conversation. I tried to be casual and aloof about it, but between his curiosity and her cloying need for attention a wave of trouble was rising.

I can't say for sure if Hiku caused what happened next, although at the time I was sure he did. And I thought he did it because what he saw and what he said were so close to the event that they all seemed connnected.

It began with such a simple thing. I was walking with an armful of wauke stalks to the place by the stream where I like to strip the bark. As I walked along the path, I saw Kaleimanu talking to some of the mahiʻai. When I passed near him, I tripped over a stone and fell; the wauke sticks flew in all directions. Kaleimanu rushed to my side, held me up, and soothed my hair because I was a little dazed. He asked me if I was all right. Then Hiku appeared from nowhere. He stared at us and in an instant seemed to plainly understand what we had been able to hide from others for so long.

"I'll take care of her," Hiku said with a sharp edge in his voice.

"I'm fine," I said. "I don't need taking care of."

"Are you sure?" Kaleimanu asked, ignoring Hiku.

"I'm sure," I said. "Just help me gather up the stalks."

Near the stream, as I peeled the bark away, Hiku asked me about Kaleimanu.

"I've known him since I was a child," I said in a matter-of-fact way. "He's like a brother to me."

"No," Hiku said as he turned his head away from me. "That is not how a brother and sister look at each other."

The very next day, my Kaleimanu was found dead. He had gone up mauka with some men to check on a stream above the lo'i that wasn't flowing properly. The men said they found a place where the water was stopped up by a fallen tree and began to clean it out, but Kaleimanu left them to look at another part of the stream that in the past had also collected debris. It was higher and required a climb up a steep cliff. They said Kaleimanu didn't return, and they found his body at the base of the cliff as if he had fallen and hit his head.

I won't recount the succession of terrible feelings that passed through me. I pretended to be sick and asked to be left alone. I curled up and cried for hours. I lost track of time. I don't even know when Lahilahi came to the hale all silent and sullen, and later Hiku, in a peevish and restless mood. It's a great confusion in my mind, all the things that happened afterward.

I remember Hiku and Lahilahi arguing and yelling. I tried to cover my ears. I know it was raining hard. I remember that Hiku ran out in a rage with Lahilahi chasing after him. But I cannot recall how all the koali vines came into the hale, woven like a rope, or how they ended up tied around my neck. I can't remember if Lahilahi did it to me or helped me do it to myself, or whether, as they say, I did it all on my own without help from anyone.

I don't really know how I came to be dangling from the ridgepole with the life squeezed out of me. I do remember my spirit floating up to the corner and watching as Lahilahi stood below and called for the others until my father and my sisters and everyone crowded beneath me. I do remember how just before I flew away I heard Lahilahi say that Hiku and I had quarreled, that he had left me, and that in my sorrow I must have taken my life.

———————————

Don't believe what they say about Milu. The land of shadows is only a resting place. The ones they talk about living there are the ones who in life fed on meanness, fear, pride, jealousy, and hatred. They gamble and occupy their time with idle talk and a filthy kind of hula that mocks all the beauty of the dance my father loves so well. The beings there eat moths and lizards, drink dirty water, and think themselves feasting on fine food. They are stuck in this pit because none of their 'aumākua will come for them. Being despised in life, they are alone in death. But for everyone else, it is only a place we pass through.

Beyond are many bright realms and many layers of heavens in the ao 'aumākua. I had come to the place of shadows and, as many others before me, had at first received the taunts and jeers of those unhappy souls in Milo who can't move on. I admit I was afraid and cold, and I did tremble with fear to think

I might be there for all eternity, but a feeling of peace spread through me a little at a time. The thick, chill mist that surrounded me began to part, and I saw a soft glowing light that grew brighter and warmer, although it was not so much a feeling of heat as it was an increase of hope.

Slowly a passage opened, and as it did my spirit seemed to burst free from within as every sorrow, trouble, and fear melted away. At my feet was a path leading into a beautiful world where everything was vivid and alive with the kind of joy that makes you want to laugh and weep at the same time. And down the path, walking slowly toward me, was my Kaleimanu, holding before him lei fashioned from delicate flowers and ferns whose scent floated and encircled me with the familiar love we had always shared.

As we moved together in this ritual of welcome, I was drawn away from the realm of death. I felt I was on a voyage, like the ones my ancestors had taken, sailing into the unknown and seeing a new island of life, a new home rising up before me, when suddenly a barbed arrow pierced the center of my back. Its silver cord whirled around me and in an instant I was pulled back into the thick mist of Milu, my spirit bound tighter and tighter by the cord and arrow.

I saw Hiku reeling me in. Then I felt myself rising fast, up and up, and the next thing I saw was my old body lying stretched out in the hale. I heard the sound of Hina's chanting. It was the sound of her voice that sucked me up and forced me to become smaller and smaller. It pushed me inside the body where the weight of flesh came crashing upon me like a mountain, suffocating and crushing me until I thought I could never breathe again. I was gasping and coughing as my eyes flew open. When I saw they had brought me back, separated me again from what I loved most, I screamed as I never had before and then fell back into blackness.

Of course, Hiku was a great hero. They immediately began to tell stories and make up chants about it all: how he grew tired of me and left; how I chased after him into the stormy night; how I was repelled by plants and other ridiculous things; how, mad with grief, I hung myself; how remorseful and brave Hiku made his miraculous journey to the underworld in search of my spirit. One of them even added a romantic touch by saying that we were in a game, swinging together on koali vines, which I think is a perverted artistic twist. But as usual, the stories are all about the winner. No one wants to know about the defeated: how the sun felt after being choked by Māui's rope, how Lono-makua felt when Pele betrayed him by stealing his fire sticks, how all of those moʻo suffered when Hiʻiaka clobbered them. Well, we all know how it is—a clever storyteller rarely goes hungry.

Shortly after my so-called rescue, Hiku got fed up with my father's court and decided to return to his home. As a polite excuse, he told my father that I needed the care of his mother and the fresh mountain air, and of course my father was only too glad to be relieved of me. After all, I looked like a ghost, could hardly walk for lack of life, and was perpetually cranky. Of course, Hiku also requested that Lahilahi should come to look after me and make me feel at home, and though my father was loath to let his darling prize go, with a little coaxing from Hina he relented. Once I arrived in the upland forest, I was quickly banished to a hut—I won't say hale—far away from the others and placed under the watchfulness of Maka and his motley troop of helpers. Maka is an expert healer, but he knew from the beginning that I was a lost cause. He's simply decided to keep me quiet and comfortable.

After several weeks, Hiku began coming to my hut at night. At first he sat in the dark just outside, beside the door. Then, after a few silent nights, he started to ask questions. He had nothing to say about himself, only questions for me to answer. He asked me the most mundane things about my childhood. What games did I like to play? Whom did I play with? What did I like to eat? At first I was irritated. Then, over the course of a few nights, I began to detect anxiety in his voice, as if there was something he desperately wanted to find out.

Eventually, his questions grew more personal. He asked about my mother, my father, and soon he worked his way around to Kaleimanu. He asked me everything about him. He spent hours and hours asking about the details of his life. I gloated over descriptions of Kaleimanu's character, which was in every way superior to Hiku's. I told him everything and, to my satisfaction, it only seemed to make him more disturbed—not angry, but agitated and uncomfortable. The more uncomfortable he became, the more I wanted to tell him; and the more I told, the less I felt attached to my body.

Finally, one evening after a feverish narrative about everything I loved and admired about Kaleimanu, I found myself completely detached from my body, my spirit hovering just over my emaciated shell, connected only through my voice but still unable to leave. Hiku had just asked me the one question he had been afraid to ask all these evenings: Did I think he had killed Kaleimanu?

I sat there over my body watching him in silence. It was only then that I saw what poor Hiku couldn't find, what all of them—my father, Lahilahi, my sisters, even Hina herself—were missing, because layer after layer of privilege, vanity, and self-indulgence had erased or obscured any recognition of others as real human beings. He had no connection to a common humanity.

Selfish people deserve each other. That's what I thought, just before I flew away.

It took some time for Hiku to realize I wasn't there anymore, so I got a head start. In no time, I was back in Milu. In no time, I was passing through that dull, dank place. Again, I found myself on the bright path to the realm of my ancestors. Before me, I saw Kaleimanu with his lei of ferns. Behind me, I saw Hiku poised with his bow, ready to fire his little arrow. I became confused and couldn't tell what was really happening. Was it only a dream I had about Hiku taking me back? Or was it all really just about to happen? Or was he going to make me live through it all again a second time? I turned back and faced him. I looked directly at him and as our eyes met, I suddenly felt genuinely sorry for him, the way you feel sorry for a little boy who has carelessly broken something beautiful and longs to undo what can't be undone—a little boy learning a painful lesson.

And when he saw that I knew and understood all these things, Hiku lowered his bow and vanished. ✸

THE LEGEND OF BLUE FACE BU

Robert Barclay

INSPIRED BY A MYTH OF MY OWN CREATION

I've always been fascinated with myths, and sometimes I wonder how they get started. I think it has something to do with our desire to gaze at all things larger than life, characters that transcend the limits of us mere mortals. At their core, myths are really just about telling stories, something that all people everywhere and for all time simply love to do. And we love to pass them along, adding things here and there, making them more magnificent, more meaningful, and sometimes more outrageous.

Maybe the printing press has taken this aspect of storytelling away from us, the way it fixes a story as if in cement. I think it was this organic quality of a myth I was trying to capture with Blue Face Bu, the story a patchwork of different perspectives getting handed along until what really matters is not what is grounded in verifiable truth, but the story itself and the value of being able to make it fly (or surf) as freely as the imagination can power it.

S OME SAY THE WAVES AT SANDY'S WERE A SPECTACULAR NINE FEET THAT MORNING, OTHERS SAY THEY WERE ABOUT TWO TO THREE, BUT MOST AGREE IT WAS THE FIRST TIME ANYONE EVER SAW THE SURFING bird, Blue Face Bu. He was a blue-faced booby, technically speaking, or more properly a masked booby or *Sula dactylatra*, or a spirit bird—and that depends on whether or not you were listening to an average Joe, an ornithologist, or Ben "Uncle Walt" Frietas.

Uncle Walt says he was the first to have seen Bu that morning, and many agree, but his Bu story lost some credibility years later when he served a short sentence for falsely claiming to be one of the heirs to Campbell Estate. The way he tells his Bu story, it was a perfect morning with a Kona wind blowing strong out of the Ko'olau, and it shaped the waves in long hollow barrels, further aided by a high, new-moon tide. It was a thirty-year high tide, he later claimed, but after his ancestry came into question, tidal charts were consulted, along with a weather report for that morning, and the facts indicated a low tide and light rain accompanied by a gusty, wave-mushing west wind.

His claim against Campbell Estate was finally disproved in court via a mandatory and indisputable blood test. Uncle Walt defended himself by saying that he was simply the innocent victim of misinformation. He was deceived

by his late grandfather, the original Uncle Walt, he told the judge, and upon
further reflection, this grandfather was probably a victim himself—of *maybe
alcoholic poisoning*, he said, when at a New Year's party in Kokokahi the senior
Uncle Walt stood on a chair and claimed to be the only son and secret love child
of patriarch James Campbell. Who was Uncle Walt to call his own grandfather
a liar? *And you know, Ms. Your Honor, Ma'am, if you no can trust ya own granpa,
ya own blood, how you going trus' dis blood test? Sometimes you jus' gotta go wit ya
heart feeling, yah? I not asking for much.* And that was when the judge, the honorable Lillian Howell-Lee, turned an angry shade of red and had Uncle Walt
taken straight off to OCCC. It was just a tragic misunderstanding, Uncle Walt
will say if you ask him about it, and he leaves it at that. But as for the weather
that morning he first saw Blue Face Bu, he still sticks to his story.

Some purists would stand on the beach and argue that Bu wasn't really
surfing, but if they said this in the wrong company they ended up being dragged
through the sand. Because as far as most were concerned, Bu was a surfer
through and through. He'd drop into a wave just as a surfer would, carving the
wave's face with the black tip of his great white wing as he zoomed low and fast
along the angle of the break. Then he'd pull out and up into the sky just before
the crashing wave buried him within a storm of tumbling foam. In the sky he'd
circle and wait, surely able to see the best sets coming before any of the other
surfers, and then he'd dive with perfect speed and timing straight into the curling belly of another wave. Like any surfer, he'd wipe out from time to time, get
tossed and tumbled by a sloppy breaking wave, but he'd right himself and with
great webbed feet race across the backwash of the wave and be airborne before
the next one could swamp him.

You had to go early to see him, usually before nine, because after that the
water began to get crowded and Bu liked to have his space. Before he'd leave
for the day he'd sometimes dive-bomb the other surfers if they got in his way,
striking with a sharp claw to the head to take them off the wave so he could
have it for himself. It became a mark of pride to have that scar on the top of your
head—the mark that proved you had been touched by Blue Face Bu. Pretty
soon there formed a sizable clique of those who had been touched, and you
knew them by the shaved circles on their heads where they proudly displayed
their scars. Then you began to see people with three or four shaved circles on
their heads, but after several people admitted to cutting their own heads, many
of them not even surfers, the style fell out of fashion.

Bu was there at Sandy's almost every morning that summer, drawing
larger and larger crowds, and he even made the local evening news, but then
one day he just stopped coming. Of course there were unconfirmed sightings
in the months that followed his disappearance, some coming from as far away

as Playa Kandahar in Mexico and the point break at Te Awanga in Aotearoa. One reported sighting even came in from a glider pilot over the coast of Kokopo in Papua New Guinea. Then one day a fuzzy photograph made the papers, claimed to have been taken at Cloud Break in Tavarua. It showed what looked like a bird in front of a wave. The photographer, a surfer who said he had seen Bu several times at Sandy's, swore that the bird in his picture was Bu. They ran the photo on the news that night, asking, *Could this be Bu?* But the next night the picture was discredited when an ornithologist from the University of Hawai'i came on and authoritatively identified the bird as *Fregetta grallaria grallaria*, a white-bellied storm petrel. Later, this ornithologist was embarrassed when an amateur birdwatcher, a Mrs. Emily Birch from Upper Makiki, conclusively proved on another station that the photographed bird was in fact *Oceanodroma castro*, a band-rumped storm petrel. The shamed photographer still claimed the bird could surf.

Uncle Walt also dismissed the various sightings, claiming that Bu remained on O'ahu and had moved to a remote, isolated break. He refused to reveal the location, and when asked why he still surfed at Sandy's instead of with Bu, he'd say he was being followed by government vivisectionists who wanted to capture Bu for military purposes.

Then one day in winter the call went out that the Eddie Aikau big-wave contest was on. For several years the contest window had come and gone, and this year both sponsors and surfers were desperate for action. The waves came to Waimea Bay before sunrise, beautiful twenty-five-footers, and reports from open ocean buoys warned of much bigger sets. By the time the surfers arrived, the waves had risen to thirty, some at thirty-five, and swollen purple storm clouds were slugging their way over the island. The rain came as the surfers paddled out, a drizzle at first that became a stinging torrent when the wind came in a blast over the mountains and churned the water into a treacherous, boiling mass. Uncle Walt was there, one of the judges, and when many of the other judges wanted to call off the contest right then—*too rough, too dangerous*—that was when they say Uncle Walt stood up in the rattling, windblown grandstand, silenced the naysayers with one scolding glance, and then with both arms extended toward the sea he said, *No. Eddie would go.* And so the contest went on.

The waves were close to forty feet when the first surfer dropped in, but the drop was too steep and his wipeout too gnarly to believe he could survive; but he did, and when the ambulance took him away three more ambulances arrived. One by one the surfers braved the waves and were defeated, and some did not try, calling for a jet ski to rescue them, until there was only one man left.

He was Eugene Brodhaus, a thirty-eight-year-old telemarketer from Yorba Linda, California, and he had not even been invited to compete. Many years earlier, when he was a teenager on vacation with his parents in Hawai'i, he had been duct-taped to a palm tree by a group of local surfers after he followed them to the remote V-lands break on the North Shore. After that, he took to lifting weights and became very large and rude, and he obsessively dedicated himself to surfing, believing that one day he would prove himself to be the best in the world. He never was, though, partly because he became too top-heavy, but mostly because his talent never caught up to the size of his ego. He did compete, though never once winning, and most surfers hated his cocky presence on the tour, which was why he was never chosen to compete at any of the invitationals. They say he came to Waimea that morning because he was getting older, seeing it as one last chance to prove something to the world, mostly to Hawai'i surfers, even if he had no chance of winning because of not being invited.

He waved off all attempts at rescue, angrily cursing at the lifeguards, and those that stayed to watch were mostly hoping they'd later be telling the story of how they witnessed the day he died. But Eugene Brodhaus would not surf. He remained out past the break, clutching his board, some saying he was waiting for a perfect wave, many others saying he was paralyzed with fright.

Then, some say by godly intervention, the wind died and the rain fell no more and the waves kept rolling in larger and larger, and just as a break in the clouds let through a beam of light that turned the water from gray to brilliant blue only over Waimea Bay, there came down from the sky a familiar bird. All along the beach you could hear the people, their voices just above a whisper, all saying, *Blue Face Bu.* He swooped low once over Eugene Brodhaus, then returned to the sky, circling, and those who knew him knew just what he planned to do.

Suddenly, looming up from the horizon a thousand miles away came what became known in Bu lore as *The Wave.* The wave first bulged on the surface of the sea like a titanic muscle, rising, still rising, from some perspectives seeming to rise as high as the underside of the sky. There are those who'll tell you that the wave was near a hundred feet, but more reliable estimates put it closer to sixty; at any rate, it was large enough that people on the beach began backing up, some of them turning to run, others never moving, never taking their eyes off Eugene Brodhaus and Blue Face Bu.

Brodhaus hesitated at first, and then mustered what courage he could and began to paddle. But just as the wave caught up to him and he seemed destined to ride, down came Bu, his wings half back, tearing down from the sky at a superluminous speed, his feet extended so that just as Eugene Brodhaus stood on his board and crouched for the drop, his head was savagely clawed, and some say Bu even got away with a clump of hair. Into the sea went Eugene Brodhaus and into the great wave went Bu, his wings outstretched as he raced down the face, low and speedily gliding, with the mountainous blue wall of water curling over him. *Pull out, Bu!* they shouted, but Bu only flapped his powerful wings and darted into the forming barrel and out of sight, the thunderous crashing water that followed him seeming to be the death of him. Then out of the narrow, almost nonexistent hole at the end of the wave, amid a deafening cannon blast of spray, shot Blue Face Bu with his wings drawn back to shape him like a bullet, and many more than Uncle Walt would say there was a small silver fish dangling in his beak. His wings snapped outward to catch the wind and he rose over the violent water to become a distant point in the sky, then back he came, most thinking he would go for another wave, but as if Bu knew there was no topping what he had done, he strafed the grandstand, and on his third screeching pass his great webbed feet snatched the great shining trophy that sat right in front of Uncle Walt Freitas. Then off he went, leaving behind a single white feather that drifted down to the beach.

Uncle Walt will tell you that he leaped straight from the grandstand in pursuit of the feather, while others claim that it was simply his big ʻōpū that carried him over in a fall as he reached for it, but there is no disputing that, after surviving the fall with only a broken hip, he did get his fist around the feather first, just ahead of a sprawling tourist from Hobart, Tasmania. Eugene Brodhaus survived that day, too, but for the rest of his life he limped, he was cross-eyed, and his head bobbed up and down with an awful twitch.

Bu was not seen again, by any reliable reports, until the following summer, when he returned from time to time to Sandy's. And it was there, early one morning, that a shot rang out, fired at dawn from a beach chair occupied by Eugene Brodhaus. Scattered reports say Bu was dead before he hit the water, others say he simply vanished—Brodhaus being no credible shot with those eyes and that twitch. What can be confirmed, because it was captured on video and shown nationally on reality TV, is that Eugene Brodhaus was caught and beaten unconscious by a band of elderly walkers after a slow-speed chase down the beach. It was later that morning, claims one resident, when Bu's lifeless and soggy body washed ashore. Her black Lab Maxie Boy grabbed him, she says, and ran off into the bushes with the great bird in his jaws. If you can believe her, that was the last anyone ever saw of Blue Face Bu.

Nowadays, people hardly ever speak of Bu, but if you stop by Uncle Walt's place in Oneawa Hills, you'll find him to be a most gracious host, and if you ask, and display the proper reverence, he'll bring out a little glass case and show you the feather he dove for from the grandstand on the day of *The Wave*. He'll tell you the whole story, too, the best version, really, that anyone ever tells about Blue Face Bu. ✹

No Dancing by the Light of the Moon

J. Arthur Rath III

Inspired by the Legend of Why Menehune Left Mānoa

Stories are ambivalent about why and how Menehune were chased from Mānoa. Did Oʻahu's Owl King terrorize them? Did King Kualiʻi's army overcome them? Did both kings collaborate? In *Voices on the Wind: Polynesian Myths and Chants* (Bishop Museum Press, 1986), folklorist Katharine Luomala writes that "bands of Menehune" once lived in Punchbowl, Mānoa, and Nuʻuanu Valley foothills, and different bands struggled over "unusually desirable rocks." Luomala asserts that Mānoa Valley Menehune were "the most courageous and energetic" and, after resisting eviction in A.D. 1700, were driven from their fort and heiau to an unknown location. Only Kualiʻi, storytellers held, "had enough mana to dispossess the little Menehunes."

In *Hawaiian Mythology* (Yale University Press, 1940), famed anthropologist Martha Beckwith suggested first that "[t]he Menehune have a heiau at Kukaoo. The 'owl god' at Puʻu-pueo (Owl Hill) summons the owls of Kauai and drives the Menehune out of the valley," and second that "Kualiʻi the great chief of Oʻahu is their persecutor." Other legends claim that Kualiʻi sent huge hordes of owls from Kauaʻi to attack Menehune happily ensconced in Mānoa, and thus the little folk were never heard from again.

Descriptions of the war against Menehune as "Kualiʻi's most famous victory" are apocryphal. I don't think my ancestor, Kualiʻi, battled these tiny, defenseless boyhood buddies. His famous code of conduct protected the helpless from aggression, and Menehune were stoneworkers, waterworks creators, and farmers—not fighters. They came out only at night, whereas Hawaiians battled during the day. This story, as told by others, doesn't fit with what I know, and bringing King Kualiʻi into the act is, I believe, a bad rap. So I decided to do something about it. While at their old haunt, I learned why these mythical beings left beautiful Mānoa Valley and have told my interpretation of the tale anew here.

A FEW DAYS EARLIER, I'D ARRANGED A VISITOR'S RESERVATION FOR ONE PERSON AT THE MĀNOA HERITAGE CENTER. A SWEETLY MODULATED, HAWAIIAN-STYLE FEMALE VOICE ON THE PHONE TOLD ME THAT THE Center, founded in 1996 by descendants of missionaries Amos Starr Cooke and his wife Juliette Montague Cooke, is set back from a long, ancient Hawaiian stone wall on Mānoa Road, where a flowering hedge, more than six feet tall, grows.

"Its blooms are very white native Hawaiian white hibiscus with a red center called koki'o ke'oke'o," she told me. "It is unlike any other hibiscus in the world because it has a fragrance."

I repeated the hibiscus's melodic Hawaiian name: "Kokee-oh kay-oh-kay-oh." Did I say it properly?

"You'll see a metal gate marker reading Kuali'i and National Register of Historic Places."

Hearing unexpectedly that my ancestor's name was posted on the gate made me gasp. Later, I learned that the historic site consists of the Kūka'ō'ō heiau and a native Hawaiian garden behind Kuali'i, the name of the private and closed-to-visitors home where the Cookes reside.

"Just follow the driveway to the mansion. Your tour reservation is ten o'clock a.m. and we'll be watching for you. Aloha!"

Three days later I climbed into one of Charley's Taxis at Waikīkī's Hyatt Regency Hotel and headed to Mānoa. The driver thought I was the only passenger, but I knew I was accompanied by two other friendly souls—a Menehune and a leprechaun. The secret of communicating with such faerie beings is not speaking out loud; instead, I use mental telepathy. Other humans neither see nor hear my companions, and I don't appear to be talking to myself or to be deranged. People such as the taxi driver remain unaware as my little pals and I chatter away. I avoid hand gestures or facial tics, and superficially I appear more blasé than someone who is Twittering intensely on a mobile phone.

One soul is stolid and bossy Kahu, almost four feet tall—large for a Menehune—who began mentoring me when I was just nine years old. *Being small, we've had no respect at all,* he has said to me. This trip was Kahu's idea—a way to clarify happenings that took place three hundred years ago in the valley and heiau where I—where we—are now headed. Seated on my left in the backseat, Kahu says: *The heiau was seminal in little folks' history and is part of the explanation of why Menehune left O'ahu.*

Kahu takes me into the past to broaden my perspective. Similar to many Hawai'i old-timers, he's mellow and understates things—except when instructing me on how to write. See, Kahu wants me to be a Menehune ghostwriter, to interpret what he says in my "modern way" with insight, deep feeling, and levity. *Smiles extend good moments' brevity. Keep facts concise. Make them dance with words so nice.* Except for this poetic way of speaking, Kahu sounds like the assignment editor for *Front Page Drama,* a weekly radio show that ran from 1930 to 1950, when I was a boy.

My other companion, a leprechaun named Miki who is seated to my right, has his own assignment to add, in his customary verse:

Write not a legend, we'll call it faction,
Literary genre with real action.
Making fictional dramatization
Our author's realization.

When very young, I learned not to be euphoric or giggly in response to Miki's amusing quips. It might cause others to think I was laughing at them. Imagine doing *that* in front of a tougher, older-than-me Hawaiian boy? It'd be broke face time!

It was a ten-minute drive from Waikīkī. Approaching the valley, I opened the window to breathe in Mānoa's cool and invigorating air; from the cab, I felt refreshing hints of misty rains wisping in the breeze.

It was easy to spot the stone wall and marker, and the tall green kokiʻo keʻokeʻo hedge laden with white blooms. Miki asked me to tell the driver to stop so he could sniff the fragrance, but I told him no—or, rather, I thought it: "We'll do that after our visit while waiting for the taxi to pick us up here." I know Dale Evans, the owner of Charley's Taxi, and I didn't want the driver telling her: "He acted strange—maybe we'll be taking him to Kāneʻohe soon." Otherwise, I'd have to pretend to be studying the hedge while Miki bounced around excitedly, sniffing ancient scents. Leprechauns are renowned for nosiness. Kahu, on the other hand, sat back quietly in typical old-time Hawaiian fashion, taking everything in. No idle chitchat. He was instead thinking deeply about what to explain to me at the heiau.

We entered the driveway and hopped out of the taxi. Huge rain trees, known also as monkeypods, with broad, spreading crowns provided wonderful canopy and partially concealed the massive, almost hundred-year-old Tudor-style building. As the driver pulled away, we three strolled and studied this gorgeous mansion—slanting gabled roof, high-timbered stucco walls and turrets, and little windowpanes leaded in a diamond pattern.

Once Miki saw it, his joyful shout made my ears ring: *A surprise—we're here in Shakespeare Country!* The Cookes' home reminded him of Elizabethan England, where Miki had shadowed Will Shakespeare around London's Globe Theatre. He claims to be the model for Puck of *A Midsummer Night's Dream*: *I am that merry wanderer of the night,* he says. Miki speaks mainly in iambic pentameter, his Shakespearean affectation.

Do you wonder how a leprechaun became associated with Hawaiian Menehune? I'd better explain, or he'll wiggle into ghostwriting himself. After Miki's hero, Will, died, the Black Plague raged. Miki hopped on a British pirate ship (Queen Elizabeth had no compunctions about stealing from Spaniards, and England's pirate culture was thriving) to escape England's misery, but daunting Spaniards sank the Brits' boat. Miki climbed aboard their sailing ship instead and stowed away until it anchored in the Marquesas Islands. From there, Miki hopped on a sailing canoe with local Menehune setting out to visit relatives in Hawai'i, Kahu among them. An amusing part of Kahu's gang for five centuries, Miki also happened to be at this Mānoa heiau when the Menehune were ousted.

―――――――――

"The house, with its 16th-century European medieval flavor, was constructed in 1911 for Charles Montague Cooke, Jr. and his wife Lila Lefferts Cooke," our knowledgeable guide explained. "Builders used lava stone quarried on site."

As we were guided to an exquisite garden of plants from ancient Hawaiian culture, the setting and gorgeous vistas unfurled before us—oh *my!* We felt quietness and serenity. There, another rare native hibiscus, koki'o 'ula'ula, bloomed. Pointing to its crimson petals, the guide explained: "Many old-time Hawaiian flowers were petite like this small, bright red flower."

"Petite" because we Menehune planted them to please our little selves. Tiny is prettiest, Kahu muttered. *We were Hawai'i's original gardeners.*

Kahu sounded irritated, likely edgy from reexperiencing events here. Not Miki though—*carpe diem*—who stood close to a beautifully groomed statuesque beauty. Instead of putting his nostrils next to ancient blooms to savor possible scents, his eyes had rolled to the top of his head, enthralled by the wafting aroma of this young woman's perfume. He crooned:

Verbena: fresh and crisp, yet it's piquant;
Bears lingering essence of patchouli,
Brings to mind the loving 1960s.

Kahu had urged me to visit this heiau so he could point out things and help me understand what things were like in the 1700s. Miki's mischievousness was an interlude before serious business, but Kahu explained he was integral to the outcome.

We approached the Kūka'ō'ō heiau—36 by 37 feet, the guide said, twice the size of an average contemporary living room. The three-foot-thick walls stand about five feet tall. Estimated to be almost one thousand years old, the Kūka'ō'ō heiau is tiny compared to huge heiau on the Big Island built by Tahitian later-comers who then became known as Hawaiians. Some celebrated war there and humans were sacrificed on them. The Mo'okini heiau, for example, is 280 feet long by 140 feet wide, with walls rising to nineteen feet.

Menehune built heiau in honor of plants grown as food for life. I remembered Kahu's earlier comment: *Tiny is prettiest.* From even a cursory look, I knew this ancient little stone heiau was a precious gemstone. The red-dirt floor was bare except for the oval offering platform. From the top of the heiau, we saw all the way to Kōnāhuanui, high point of the Koʻolau mountain range. Kahu explained that *Menehune built this agricultural heiau, the last remnant of fourteen once in the Mānoa area. Our stream work on the plain covered by Honolulu and Waikīkī created irrigation complexes and fishponds. Heiau were places to extend thanks for such bounty.*

Our tour group moved to gaze at valleys from another hillside level. I asked our guide if I might stay to meditate. She nodded understandingly. "Many visitors become spiritually moved." I lay down a packet of ti leaves containing kūlolo—baked grated taro and coconut cream pudding—a food offering made of products Menehune once grew here. Kahu had stage fright; he was agitated and stomped around, sneering: *Stories about us are apocryphal! What is described as a "fort" is where the elderly slept. Kualiʻi and his warriors didn't fight us.*

Miki piped up with glee:

What fools these mortals be!
From India, "gooses" bring mongooses
To kill and maim rats chewing sugarcane.
Mongooses active during days—diurnal!
Rats feast on sugar at night—nocturnal!

Giggling, he refocused animalism symbolism to today's discussion:

Fight Kualiʻi? What a big hee-hee,
Warriors battle when sun is shining,
(That's the time mongooses look for their dining).
Menehune do just as rats at night:
They come out when others are not in sight!

And then … daylight transitioned into moonlight, tiny puffs of yellow, green, and pale red materializing just above ground level and darting about as fireflies do—enlarging, blossoming, bursting. Menehune crowded together, dressed for a party, wearing every imaginable color combination. Men and women with maile lei and wreaths of flowers around their necks. Older men putting something in their mouths and chewing. *ʻAwa,* Kahu explained. *They'll soon be euphoric.*

I asked Kahu what year we were in. He replied: *About 1710.*

The crowd grew to about two hundred Menehune scattered on the hillside. Muscular young males wearing loincloths and carrying torches marched into the heiau followed by younger youths waving ti-leaf bunches. They formed a semicircle. A dignified elder waving a wand strode center stage.

That kupuna, our history teller, always orates before we celebrate. Watch him use that wand—the koʻo with feathers attached to it—for emphasis, said Kahu.

The kupuna recounted Menehune history in Hawaiʻi, explaining their origins from the Marquesas, describing life on Kauaʻi where they built walls, waterways, fishponds, and heiau, and made taro fields. He reminded all that more than one million Menehune were on Kauaʻi when this band canoed to Oʻahu, and how fortunate all were to enjoy privacy and freedom. He went on, summarizing Menehune contributions on Oʻahu: waterways that made plains fertile—even barren areas all the way to Waikīkī—and planting and nurturing that sponsored Mānoa's verdure. He spoke of Menehune ethos, belief in equality, respect for women, helpfulness for the weak, courtesy for all, and being honorable.

"Isn't he laying it on a little heavy?" I asked Kahu. "This is Stone-Age Hawaiʻi, not King Arthur's Court."

He is being inspirational so everyone will feel good before we celebrate, Kahu replied.

When the orator finished, a male and female band—comprised of a ravishing young woman holding a nose flute, an older fellow setting up two sizes of sharkskin drums, four little bare-breasted beauties holding ʻūkēkē stringed instruments over you-know-where, and six youths carrying ti-leaf trumpets—walked to stage center. A rotund Menehune came stage front.

He's the lead singer, Kahu explained. *A tenor.*

I was about to learn how Menehune Rock-Age bands performed. The music began—unlike anything the big Hawaiians of that era would have heard—and my interlocutor Kahu quietly interacted. I overheard him:

> *Cadenced refrains from voices pours*
> *Background thud-a-thud from beaten gourds.*
> *Gesturing hands, swift fingers bent in flight,*
> *Dark tropic eyes, deep sky-black pools of night,*
> *Young body melting in slow fluid curves,*
> *Swaying, brain-draining, awakening urges.*

I didn't realize my mentor had this verse within him, but I was distracted by Miki, who murmured as he looked at a phenomenon appearing in the sky:

> *Magical arch curving on misty air*
> *A lunar rainbow is shimmering there.*

Suddenly—in a blink—these exotic scenes disappeared, and Kahu, Miki, and I stood alone on the hilltop in present-day Mānoa.

———————

"Menehune just broke every major 18th-century Hawaiian kapu," I told Kahu. "Men and women eating and dancing together? New tonalities? Uninhibited Rock-Age music? No wonder Hawaiians wanted you gone."

We're nighttime people. They wouldn't have seen what we did. We were out of sight. They didn't know we practiced equality. Our good-times sounds were what bothered those below.

Now we got to the heart of Kahu's story:

"High-ranking chiefs who'd set up housekeeping down there went directly to Kuali'i at his Kailua home to complain. We considered Kuali'i a friend we'd known as a boy. Hunting rats together at twilight, we scurried through bushes and scared rats into the open so Kuali'i would have a clear shot using bow and arrow. He relocated to O'ahu, and that's why we felt safe settling here.

"He didn't send his army after us. Any references to our having a fort are bogus. All we had were a heiau and a sleeping shed that kept rain off the elderly. The rest of us snoozed under shady bushes during the day and worked or played at night. I'll show you exactly what happened. My magical powers can concoct a replay if you wish."

I wished.

Miki fidgeted nervously, tugged at Kahu's loincloth, and shook his head. Kahu caught on. "No replay," Kahu said. "Owls would peck your eyes with their beaks and shred your skin with their talons. Forget about experiencing that nightmare, I'll describe it from the beginning.

"An imperious owl watched us work. He sat in a tree, looked down, and made 'Who' sounds as if asking for our identification cards. When he was too insistent, we'd throw a pebble to shoo him away. He lived on a hill higher up the valley called Pu'u Pueo, or Owl Peak. Malihini moving in called him The Owl King because at twilight he sat and preened in a tree. They thought he was pretty.

"Humans asked the owl to shoo us away—that was a laugh, as he was inept and nearsighted! He asked other O'ahu owls to help him, but our band played and scared them away. O'ahu birds are chicken, not owl. Some of the upper crust went to Kailua to talk to Kuali'i. A Menehune working in fishponds listened in and told us what they said: 'As King of the Island you should aid our Mānoa gentrification efforts and force all noisemakers to leave.'

"Our Kailua Menehune spy agreed that if Kuali'i had been younger, no one would get away with telling him what to do. At that time he was more than 150 years old—he only had 25 more years to go—and had by then probably forgotten his fierce boyhood. Our spy said that Kauali'i told the Malihini, 'Leave it to me,' instead of whacking each complainer on his head with a war club as he had been wont to do. One of the king's men chanted this warning in the valley to echo and edify us: 'Menehune must leave right away or Kuali'i will reinforce O'ahu owls and drive you away.'

"'Hell no, we won't go,' was our slogan. 'We've invested hundreds of years here and deserve to enjoy the fruits, fish, and vegetables of our labor.' I don't know what message Kuali'i sent to Kaua'i owls. There'd been so many of us there and those birds knew our tricks. Anyway, they flew to O'ahu, hitched up with pussycat O'ahu Owl and his cohorts, and—"

Miki interrupted:

> That night we were dancin' with our darlin's
> To strains of a beautiful Spanish waltz…
> Then beating of wings, horrible screeches,
> Won't say what that fright did to my breeches.

I put up my hands, warding him off the memory of his breeches. Words such as "then beating of wings" brought to mind the flying monkeys of *The Wizard of Oz*. I turned to Kahu and asked, "What did the Menehune do?"

"We were helpless. Owls swooped down, tore at our eyes and faces, and befouled us. Miki rallied us and said: 'Shakespeare had the solution. We'll fight as Titus Andronicus did against the Goths.' He instructed larger Menehune men and women to grab digging tools and form a Roman-type phalanx, organizing us into a square. We were packed together with sticks upheld to spear and bat at owls dropping from the sky. We shuffled children into the center and told them to crouch. Owls flew to trees to regroup and Miki encouraged us by saying we'd reenact a scene from *Macbeth*: 'Just hold out until daylight; when the owls go to sleep as they should, we'll do as Macduff did and move the woods.'

"We remained fixed in our phalanx until dawn, when owls left in a swarm. After visiting the storage area to gather cutting stones, we went into the forest and cut twelve-foot-high banana tree stalks. After we ate some bananas, Miki told all two hundred of us to drink heartily from the stream and rest under the stalks until evening.

"'I'm leaving to do some errands and will be back before daylight,' he explained. 'A sleepy owl seeing me will be baffled because of my white complexion. Although small, I don't fit Menehune description at all.' Miki acted lighthearted to keep us from being downhearted. He returned just before twilight and, all business, he told us to hold up the stalks of banana leaves that were three to four times our size and formed us into an orchard.

"'I'm the red banana plant, because it matches my hair,' Miki said. 'Those in the first row do exactly as I do and move at my pace. Those behind, imitate what the banana tree in front of you does. We'll stay together and go from bat cave to bat cave. I've told them you're coming.'

"Miki had visited bats in the area while we rested. Hating owls and loving Miki, they were delighted to help put something over on The Big Hooters. 'Creepy, crawly,' he told us. We moved forward, I next to him, and he said owls might now be thinking something like the verse Shakespeare wrote for *Macbeth*: *I looked and methought the wood began to move.* He had abridged Shakespeare, summarizing our achievement: '*A moving grove and thus the Menehune were all gone.*'"

Kahu continued recounting Miki's crisis management: "Bats and Menehune had always been cordial to each other; because Mānoa's weather is lovely, we had for centuries chosen to sleep outdoors instead of moving into caves that bats might like to use. Groves of bamboo, bananas, small bushes, and curves in the valleys had all been safe and secluded for daytime sleeping. But bats now welcomed us to be their cave-mates until we decided what to do.

"Owls kept looking for us. We'd placed banana fronds over cave mouths to prevent owls from barging in and allowed only a tiny bat-sized opening so the parents could fly after bugs for their babies. Should owls peer in, bunches of bats attacked their huge eyes. Mother bats screeched, *Stay away from my babies!*"

The usually calm Kahu demonstrated how a mother bat shrieked at an owl. Once he believed my ears were no longer ringing, he quietly and amusingly added: "Menehune began referring to each other as 'Baby Bats.' Discouraged Kauaʻi owls returned home. Frustrated Oʻahu owls became meaner. We'd have to move away to find peace. One evening, shortly after Kauaʻi's owls left, a gentle-looking young Hawaiian man appeared at our heiau with three attendants carrying baskets of food. Two elders and I watched from behind those bushes." Kahu pointed to a rise by the heiau.

"The man called out: 'E nei … Menehune e … Komo mai e ʻai.' He invited us to enjoy the food, and so we did. Then a strange thing happened—he assumed Menehune form. Only Kualiʻi had ever done that before us.

"'I am one of Kualiʻi's sons, but not one of his warrior children,' the man explained. 'I am a spiritual guide. Call me Moki.'

"Moki was the man the king chose to let the Menehune go, and he was to give them freedom from fear."

I had a late friend whose Christian name was Moses; he was known in Hawaiian as Moki.

"'My father does not want you hiding in caves,' said Moki. 'He will help you find another promised land, away from those who hate you. He will send canoes for transportation and supply enough food and supplies for you to relocate. I will return two evenings from now.'

"We spread news of a relocation and met the next night at this Mānoa heiau. By now, we had armed ourselves with digging sticks. No one wanted to remain on O'ahu; most wanted to return to Kaua'i. I said I would go to Kona with a small group, and some of the strongest men and women wanted to be in Tuomotu to build canoes and sail with Rata. That huge and irascible god loved Menehune because we knew what trees made the best canoes, worked hard and well, and were jolly companions during ocean explorations, for which he had become famous.

"We threw our digging sticks in the center of the heiau, now defiled after being used as weapons. We weren't going to make war any more. We hugged each other, realizing this large group's unity was pau.

"Two evenings later, Moki arrived on schedule, and I explained our wishes. He said we'd leave after two more days. We would have to trek to Waikīkī and bring just one change of clothes because everything else would be supplied. He explained: 'You can come during daylight, and Kuali'i won't allow any Hawaiians out of their homes. Enough canoes, supplies, and experienced seamen for your destinations will be waiting for you seaside at Waikīkī.' Then he said aloha and left us to make the arrangements. And after that, all proceeded as he described.

"Now you know the entire story of why Menehune left Mānoa."

We'd left our time warp, daylight had reappeared. "I think I should check with the Heritage Center docent," I said, looking at my watch. Just fifteen minutes had elapsed since I'd asked for the chance to meditate. I would have doubted this if my watch wasn't precise as a goose-step.

Miki tugged on my sleeve, his eyes watery. He had his own final reflections to share, what I now think of as "Miki's Lament."

"Tell me, Miki."

Clasping hands together, bowing his head, wistfully he said:

Seeing Mānoa's open valley view,
Mountain range at head, hills each side of you,
Summits hid in clouds gathering moisture,
Supplying streams for the valley's verdure.

On the rugged slopes, endless shades of greens
While silver torrents lighten black rock seams,
Cloud shadows go chasing rifts of sunshine—
What happens next becomes truly sublime:

Drifting down one mountain, mists become rain,

While the other mountain remains the same—
Just basking in the sun, nothing undone,
Throws off a rainbow, radiantly begun,

Then doubles or triples its reflection:
Magenta, gold, blue, green, and vermillion.
Freshness of invigorating zephyr,
Salubrious and beneficial air.

Hidden recesses with fronds of bamboo,
Lush beds of ferns, 'ōhi'a groves to view.
This was a place we grew to love a lot,
Just briefly: Menehune Camelot.

It was now understandable—nostalgia is why Menehune stayed away.

———————————

I expressed thanks to the staff at the Heritage Center, stood under the monkeypod tree, and used my cell phone to call Charley's Taxi. The dispatcher said a cab would arrive in ten minutes.

"We'll be at the front gate," I told her. Miki would be able to sniff the koki'o ke'oke'o while we waited, if he wasn't too teary and stuffed up.

On the way back in the cab, Kahu seemed talked out. Miki wistfully said the Cookes' old English-style home had made him wistful. He was thinking of paying a visit back to "the old sod" and confided: *I have my most fun in an Irish pub.*

I offered a quick suggestion: "We've two on Nu'uanu Avenue, Guinness and other good beer near the pier. I'll tell the cab driver to take us."

This perked him up, he asked: *Do they have redheaded lassies in there?*

"Not often, but sometimes occasionally."

Miki shook his head and explained: *Has to be often for a leprechaun, who'll lift a glass to any Irish lass.*

Imagine sitting in Riley's or Murphy's, one beer in front of me, one at my left, another on my right. I'd be hogging three seats—the ones on each side might appear empty, but the glasses in front of them would be levitating, becoming emptier and emptier. Anyone watching might think they were experiencing the DTs or had finally had too much to drink. And instead of focusing on conversation with me, Miki's head would be pivoting to the front door every time it opened—asking himself, *Does the entering lass have red hair?* I'm all too glad to be skipping an Irish pub visit after today's emotional experience.

Instead, I told the driver: "Take us to the airport, Hawaiian Airlines terminal. We're going to Kaua'i."

If there aren't extra empty seats on the plane, these two can crowd on my lap. Kahu has already dozed off, and Miki's head will soon be full of dreams. This trip to Kaua'i would be easier if contemporary Kaua'i folks hadn't squeezed away the Superferry from serving "their island."

Long ago, "their island" referred to Menehune, residents who did a lot of lasting good there. ⚙

KALEIMANU'S REQUEST

W. S. Merwin

INSPIRED BY THE LEGEND OF THE BIRD MAN OF WAINIHA

The Kaua'i version of the legend of Lahi, the boy who ate birds, is centered on Wainiha Valley where Lahi and his uncle Kanealohi live. One day they go to Kilohana to catch, for food, 'uwa'u birds that live in a deep burrow in the cliffs and are difficult to catch. They face many challenges and enemies. The first is a giant, whom Lahi and his uncle trick into a hole and kill. Next is the local chief, who doesn't approve of killing birds and attacks with four hundred soldiers; Lahi and Kanealohi are alerted to their arrival by ripples in spring water and are able to hide and cause all the men to fall off the cliff. The last to arrive is the chief, Lahi's father, who invites Lahi to the village as a trap. Wise Lahi escapes, kills his father, and becomes chief. Many versions of this myth can be found in the chapter "Mu and Menehune People" in Martha Beckwith's *Hawaiian Mythology*.

In Merwin's epic poem *The Folding Cliffs*, the character Kaleimanu is a storyteller who loves to hear stories, especially about birds since his name means "the wreath of birds." This retelling is situated in the beginning of the book, as Ko'olau, suffering from the early signs of Hansen's disease, is forced to hide from those who would take him to Kalaupapa. He hides with his wife, Pi'ilani, and son, Kaleimanu, deep in the folds of Kalalau Valley on Kaua'i. Their friend, Kua, tells Kaleimanu the story of Lahi just as they are about to head into the valley. This section can be read alone as a retelling of "The Bird Man of Wainiha," and interpreted as a foreshadowing of what happens to the trio throughout the book during their years in the valley, as they, too, are alerted to foes by rippling spring water and must repel enemies on steep cliffs. Merwin's *The Folding Cliffs* could itself be interpreted as an expanded retelling and reimagining of "The Bird Man of Wainiha," connected also with the real story of "Ko'olau the Leper" from the 1890s.

She came to hills of bright cloud rolling up out of the valley
        and before noon she had arrived at Kilohana
where they had all dismounted that first time and had stood
        in silence looking around them at the stream slipping
toward the edge and at the falling away and away of the cliffs
        fin after fin drifting among clouds the great bay in the air
as deep as the mountain the valley of Kalalau
        its measureless hollow Kalalau The Straying
they could see through the white clouds threads of surf unrolling
        slowly into shadow the cliffs hung steep as blankets
on a fence she could see that Kepola her mother
        was frightened looking over past the edge and Kua
said he would say good-bye now and Kaleimanu
        went to him and embraced him laying his head against
Kua's stomach and then asked him if this was the stream now
        where it happened—Where what happened—Kua asked him
—Where they met the soldiers—Kaleimanu said—This is
        the stream—Kua told him—but this is not the place—
Kaleimanu said—Will you tell me the story once more
        right here—and they stood in a ring in the wind listening
to Kua tell of Lahi the boy who ate birds
        and his uncle who was Kanealohi Slow Man

He said—After they came up here to eat the ʻuwaʻu
        that live in the cliffs first there was the giant who tried
to kill them and Kanealohi told Lahi When the giant
        comes you hold out a bird to him but when he reaches
to take it you back up into the tunnel and he will
        follow you and since you are smaller than he is
he will get stuck in the rocks and then I will kill him
        so they did it that way and then the great chief heard about them
up here eating birds and he said Those birds are mine
        and he called together four hundred of his soldiers
to come up here and kill Lahi and Kanealohi
        but those two moved up this stream to a smaller one
that runs into it and if anybody steps
        in the stream anywhere along it even far below here
the surface away up there begins to ripple and they would know
        there was somebody coming and one day it began
to ripple so they came out and could see the whole army
        climbing up to kill them and Kanealohi was frightened

but Lahi went to where the rocks almost come together
      with the top of the trail between them and there only
one man could climb through at a time and he killed them as they came
      one by one and they fell all the way down from the cliff
and the last one was the chief himself and they say that
      he recognized that Lahi was his own son and he said so
and asked Lahi to spare him and the boy let him pass
      and it was Lahi who became chief later in the story

It was then that Kua had led Kaleimanu
      to the edge of the cliff where the light rose from the valley
and had showed him those two rocks that were the children
      of Naiwi and said to him—That is where the right trail
goes down—and he pointed to a thread like a goat track
      following the knife edge of one of the fins out in the clouds
—That is the one that goes all the way—he said—The others
      end in nothing—And he hugged the child and told him
—But it is not good to look back—Then he went to help them
      load themselves with the few things they would be carrying
Pi'ilani stood looking down at the clear water
      gliding in front of her toward the fall its surface
not appearing to move she knelt in the wet moss
      to put her mouth to the cold pane and drink from it
with her eyes open at first and then she closed them
      and plunged her head and hands into the unseen current
for a long breath overhearing the voices in the water
      talking and then she sat up and ate a few pieces
of taro and drank again and lifted her head to stare
      at the face below her in the stream with the sky
under it and the eyes burning from their dark places
      she looked at it feeling that she knew nothing about it
and then stood up in the day and walked to where the right trail
      disappeared over the edge into Kalalau ❀

ABOUT THE AUTHORS

A. A. ATTANASIO, born at the exact midpoint of the 20th century and terrorized from childhood by the threat of thermonuclear apocalypse, grew up convinced he would never grow up. Liberated from any hope of a future, he pursued a passion for creative writing—and ultimate questions. Twenty-two published novels and two short story collections later, this eclectic author is giddy to find that the world is still here, his two daughters have grown and left home to pursue their dreams, his wife still laughs at his jokes, and hiding from death in books actually turned out to be a life.

ROBERT BARCLAY grew up in the Marshall Islands and has lived in Hawai'i since the late 1990s. He has published several short stories and one novel, *Melal*, which is being made into a film. He recently finished a second novel, started working on a third, and can be found teaching English at Windward Community College or enjoying life all over the windward side of O'ahu with his wife, Stacy, and their two children, Ava and Nikko. At odd hours he finds some time to write.

ALAN BRENNERT, author of the bestselling historical novels *Moloka'i* and *Honolulu*, has long had an interest in multicultural and heroic mythologies. He has written short stories based in Hawaiian folklore, Greek mythology, pre-Aztec mysticism, and even a Vietnamese ghost story ("Ma Qui," which won a Nebula Award in 1992). Nor is he embarrassed to note that two of his comic book stories appear in DC Comics' anthology *The Greatest Batman Stories Ever Told*.

TIMOTHY DYKE moved from Texas to Hawai'i in 1992 and has lived and worked on O'ahu ever since. A writer and a teacher, he has published art reviews and feature articles in *The Honolulu Advertiser* and short stories in the *Santa Monica Review* and the *Honolulu Weekly*, for whom he has also written music reviews and cover stories. He is currently on leave from teaching English and working in the chapel at Punahou School and is pursuing an MFA in creative writing at the University of Arizona.

Kevin O'Leary, who writes fiction under the name **J. FREEN,** has lived in the Islands since 1970. During the 1970s and '80s he had several plays produced by Kumu Kahua Theatre. As a freelance journalist, he has written feature articles for the *Honolulu Weekly* and has published numerous short stories in *Bamboo Ridge*, including "The Copper Thief," published in late 2009. He lives in Kalihi.

Darien Gee is a national bestselling author of several novels written under the name Mia King. Her books have been selections of the Doubleday, Literary Guild, and Book of the Month Club book clubs. Her second novel, *Sweet Life*, was nominated for a *Ka Palapala Poʻokela* award for excellence in Hawaiʻi books. She lives with her family in upcountry Waimea on the island of Hawaiʻi.

Kuʻualoha Hoʻomanawanui, Ph.D., was born in the seaside town of Kailua, Oʻahu, and raised in the uplands of Wailua, Kauaʻi. A kanaka maoli (Native Hawaiian) scholar, poet, and artist with a love of diverse genres of art and music, Kuʻualoha is also the chief editor of *ʻŌiwi: A Native Hawaiian Journal*, the first contemporary journal featuring Native Hawaiian writers and artists. She teaches a variety of courses at different levels, focusing on Native Hawaiian folklore and mythology, contemporary Pacific literature, and indigenous perspectives on literacy. She is currently an assistant professor of English at the University of Hawaiʻi at Mānoa.

Christopher Kelsey, a lifelong Hawaiʻi resident, remembers when Aloha Tower was the tallest building in the Islands. Returning to UH in 1996 after a twenty-three-year absence, he completed undergraduate and master's degrees in English and is currently finishing his doctorate in creative writing. He has been fortunate to study with such esteemed writers as Phil Damon, Steve Goldsberry, Craig Howes, Rodney Morales and Ian MacMillan. He currently teaches in the English department at UH Mānoa, and his work has appeared in the anthology *Undrawn Lines* and in *Hawaiʻi Review*.

Maxine Hong Kingston has written the prize-winning books *The Woman Warrior: Memoirs of a Girlhood Among Ghosts, China Men, Tripmaster Monkey: His Fake Book,* and *The Fifth Book of Peace.* She is a Living Treasure of Hawaiʻi and is also the author of *Hawaiʻi One Summer.* In *To Be a Poet*, she tells of preparations for the writing of poems. Her long poem, *I Love a Broad Margin to My Life*, was released in spring 2011. She has edited the anthologies *The Literature of California: Native American Beginnings to 1945* and *Veterans of War, Veterans of Peace.*

Victoria Nalani Kneubuhl is a Honolulu playwright and author. She holds a master's degree in drama and theatre from the University of Hawaiʻi. Her many plays have been performed in Hawaiʻi and the continental United States and have toured Britain, Asia, and the Pacific. An anthology of her work, *Hawaiʻi Nei: Island Plays*, is available from University of Hawaiʻi Press, which recently published her first mystery novel, *Murder Casts a Shadow.* She is currently writer and co-producer for the television series *Biography Hawaiʻi.* In

1994, she was the recipient of the prestigious Hawai'i Award for Literature and, in 2006, the Eliot Cades Award for Literature.

Born and raised on O'ahu, **MARION LYMAN-MERSEREAU** is a teacher and paddling coach. She co-authored a four-volume book entitled *Character Education* (Incentive Publications, 2000). Her book, *Eddie Wen' Go: The Story of the Upside Down Canoe* (Watermark, 2008) has been adapted to the stage. She also published a slam poem, which was included in Fat Ulu's *The Statehood Project* and performed by Kumu Kahua Theatre. Her favorite place to be is in the ocean or on a beach with her family.

A Hawai'i resident from 1966 until his death in 2008, **IAN MACMILLAN** authored eight novels and five short story collections, one of which won the Associated Writing Programs Award for Short Fiction. His work appeared more than 100 times in literary and commercial magazines including *Yankee, The Sun, Paris Review,* and *Iowa Review,* and his work has been reprinted in *Best American Short Stories, Pushcart Prize,* and *O. Henry Award* volumes, among other "best" anthologies. Winner of the 1992 Hawai'i Award for Literature and the 2007 Eliot Cades Award for Literature, he taught fiction writing at the University of Hawai'i until his passing. A new novel, *In the Time Before Light,* is to be posthumously published by Lō'ihi Press.

W. S. MERWIN's poetry career spans more than five decades, from his first book, *A Mask for Janus*—chosen by W.H. Auden in 1952 for the Yale Younger Poets series—to his most recent, *The Shadow of Sirius* (Copper Canyon, 2009), which was awarded the Pulitzer Prize (his second), and including the book in which his anthology selection first appeared, *The Folding Cliffs* (Knopf, 2000). In 2010, Merwin was appointed the Library of Congress' seventeenth Poet Laureate Consultant in Poetry. He currently lives and works on Maui, where he has spent the last thirty years creating a sustainable forest called the Merwin Conservancy.

WAYNE MONIZ was born and raised on Maui. He received a double B.A. in English and communications from the University of Dayton in Ohio. In 1980, he obtained his M.A. in Theater Arts-Film from UCLA. He has been a writing and speech lecturer at Maui Community College since 1982. In 2005 he received the prestigious Eliot Cades Award for Literature. Dubbed "The Dean of Maui Playwrights" by *The Maui News,* Wayne has written fourteen plays, eight short stories, several film scripts, numerous poems, and song lyrics that deal with the people, events, and issues of Hawai'i.

Dr. M. Puakea Nogelmeier has taught Hawaiian language at the University of Hawaiʻi at Mānoa for more than twenty-five years. With a background in traditional dance, chant, and literature, he works extensively with the archival repositories of Hawaiian knowledge. As a teacher, translator, composer, and writer, he bridges those resources into modern use, empowering revitalization and renewal while fostering creative potential.

Gary Pak is a third-generation Korean American whose grandparents, fleeing an occupied Korea, arrived in Hawaiʻi in 1905. Published in numerous anthologies, magazines, and literary journals, he also authored *The Watcher of Waipuna and Other Stories* (Bamboo Ridge, 1992), *A Ricepaper Airplane* (UH Press, 1998), *Children of a Fireland* (UH Press, 2004), and *Language of the Geckos and Other Stories* (University of Washington, 2005). His children's play, *Beyond the Falls*, was produced by the Honolulu Theatre for Youth in 2001. He holds numerous awards and fellowships, including the Elliot Cades Award for Literature and the Council for International Exchange of Scholars (Fulbright). He is a professor of English at the University of Hawaiʻi at Mānoa.

J. Arthur Rath III, a descendant of pioneering Hawaiʻi institution founders David and Sarah Lyman (Hilo Boarding School) and James and Ragna Rath (Palama Settlement), began his national writing career at age fifteen while a student at Kamehameha Schools. He has authored more than a dozen books. His most recent include *Lost Generations: A Boy, a School, a Princess* and *Thy Boys: Hamilton College Stories*. His historical works cover the Civil War, World War II in the Pacific, and Death Valley days. His business books focus on photography, business systems, cable TV, economic development, and banking. His latest project, *Being Menehune*, provides creative perspectives on Hawaiʻi from antiquity to the present.

Christine Thomas was raised in Kailua and born in Honolulu, where she again resides, after earning a B.A. in English from the University of California at Berkeley and a master's in creative writing from the University of East Anglia in England, as well as other stints living and working across the U.S. She has worked for more than fifteen years as a freelance features and travel writer and book critic and has taught creative writing and literature at Punahou School and to undergraduates across the country. Her short fiction has been published in anthologies and literary magazines in the U.S. and in the United Kingdom, and her current work-in-progress, *To Lose is to Win*, features inter-generational short stories spanning the globe. ✸